ANNA SPARROWS

Where There's A Will

An MM Age Gap Romance

Cover Design by: Joe Satoria

Cover Model: Kevin R Davis

Cover Photography by: Golden Czermak/FuriousFotog

First edition

This book was professionally typeset on Reedsy.
Find out more at reedsy.com

For you, even if we've never met.
You're important. You're special.
You matter.
(And you're reading my book, so that makes you even more
awesome. Just saying.)

Contents

Preface iii

Acknowledgement v

Prologue – Connor 1

Chapter One – Connor 7

Chapter Two – Will 20

Chapter Three – Connor 33

Chapter Four – Will 44

Chapter Five – Connor 61

Chapter Six – Will 73

Chapter Seven – Connor 83

Chapter Eight – Will 96

Chapter Nine – Connor 109

Chapter Ten – Will 122

Chapter Eleven – Connor 128

Chapter Twelve – Will 137

Chapter Thirteen – Connor 150

Chapter Fourteen – Will 160

Chapter Fifteen – Connor 171

Chapter Sixteen – Will 186

Chapter Seventeen – Connor 200

Chapter Eighteen – Will 212

Chapter Nineteen – Connor 224

Chapter Twenty – Will 229

Chapter Twenty-One – Connor 236

Chapter Twenty-Two – Will   246
Chapter Twenty-Three - Connor   254
Chapter Twenty-Four - Will   263
Epilogue – Connor   273
Sneak Peek: You Don't Know Jack   281
About the Author   286
Also by Anna Sparrows   288

Preface

Dear reader, please be aware that this is a book set in Australia with predominantly Australian characters. As such, it is written in Australian English, with Australian spelling, not the American you are most likely used to reading from me. Yes, this is a bit of a mindfuck when half the book is from an American character's POV. (I never said I was clever.) I'm sorry in advance for the extra 'u's, and the 's's instead of 'z's. Don't even get me started on the word 'storey' in terms of building structure. I hope you still enjoy it anyway!

I would also like to take this opportunity to advise you that, despite the bulk of the romance being tooth-rottingly sweet, this book does touch on some **potentially triggering topics**. These include: death of close family members (both through terminal illness and also sudden means), traffic accidents, fire trauma, homelessness, mild homophobia, and the stress/-trauma of raising children, including sleep deprivation, self-doubt/anxiety, and the fear of losing one's child. It's **definitely got a lot more angst than my previous books**. But this story does *not* include any miscommunication between MCs or cheating, so there's that.

Finally, consider this fair warning: my extent of family law in Australia is limited to what I learned in Grade 11 and 12 Legal Studies, and my knowledge of actual firefighting procedures is even less impressive. This is a work of fiction and, while I have attempted to research for believability's sake, please blame any big inaccuracies on my love on melodrama and pop culture leading me astray.

Acknowledgement

Firstly, I want to officially thank Kevin R Davis for being my Will. I've been a fan for a while now, and it has long been a goal of mine to be able to purchase an exclusive Kevin Cover for myself. Whether you read this or not, Kevin, I want to thank you for being so supportive and so lovely to talk to on this crazy journey of mine. ~~Stalking~~ Following you on social media is always so uplifting and inspiring, and you have a lifelong fan in me. I don't think this will be my last Kevin Cover at all. Again I ask: why didn't I write Will as a twin?

Also, the cover wouldn't have been possible if Golden Czermak/FuriousFotog hadn't taken the stunning photo to begin with. From the moment I saw it, I knew I had to have it. Not creepy of me. Nope. Not at all.

Similarly, I want to thank Joe Satoria, whose books I've been devouring for a couple of years now, and who I never imagined would even know my name, let alone would design a cover for me. (Shhh, I won't tell anyone you're magic!) You took my frazzled, barely coherent ramblings and created a cover I cannot stop looking at. Thank you doesn't quite cut it, but it's all I've got. And your accent is still one of my absolute favourite things to listen to, so keep the voice messages coming, haha. (Oh dear, I fear I've made things weird again...)

Then there's Ky. You have been here from the very beginning of this project. You put up with my freakouts, my impostor syndrome, and my concerns that this book is so different from my usual fare, and you didn't run away screaming. You were the first person to read this and you gave me the confidence to push on with it and to send it out into the world. Thank you for being an amazing friend. One day, I'll hug you in person.

Similarly, Megan, your reader reactions give me life. You're not afraid to give honest critique, and that helped me to smooth this out into the best story it could be. I can't thank you enough.

Finally, Myf and Cindy, I was genuinely concerned about putting out something different, and your reassurance eased away the niggling doubts that I'm a one trick pony. I'll be forever grateful for that.

Prologue – Connor

Of course she's late, I think to myself as I glance at my watch for the fifth time in as many minutes. My twenty-two-year-old sister is nothing if not consistently tardy. One of the three servers on staff catches my eye and offers me a sympathetic smile, silently consoling me for being stood up.

I don't know whether to find it comforting or offensive.

Still, the bistro where we've arranged to meet is one of my favourites. It's got that hole-in-the-wall eatery kind of vibe: a narrow space, with the kitchen running down one half, separated from the dining space by a thick glass window. The dining space itself is warm and welcoming. The walls are a pleasant off white, the décor modern and sleek. The tablecloths are pristine white linen, and the overhead lighting is flattering and soft. The menu itself is described as 'modern Italian-Australian fusion' (whatever the fuck that means) and the whole place smells like fresh, warm bread and pizza.

Mmm, pizza.

I glance at my left wrist again and drum my fingers on the tabletop absently. After another look from the same server, I decide that when Daisy does arrive, I'm going to cheerfully strangle her.

"Sorry!" Daisy herself apologises emphatically as she drops heavily into the chair opposite mine. "I'm so sorry. Parking was shit. Had to circle the block twice and then *just* managed to snag a spot before some little old lady whacked on her indicator." She leans forward and plucks one of the warm bread rolls from the basket between us. "You snooze you lose, right?"

I roll my eyes and shake my head. "You're going straight to hell, Daze."

"Yeah, well, all the best people are. Or so I'm told." Her blue eyes sparkle with mischief when she grins back at me.

There was a time I was jealous of those eyes. I inherited my mother's hazel pair, while Daisy got Dad's baby blues. She was also blessed with Dad's dark hair and olive complexion, where I'm pale skinned, freckled, and my hair's a flat mousy brown, once again just like my mum. But then, I guess I resented Daisy for a lot of things when she came hurtling into my life.

I was ten when she was born, and to say she was a surprise for our family is an understatement. She was a particularly big surprise for Mum, considering Mum hadn't known Dad was stepping out on her until Dad's mistress turned up on our doorstep with Daisy in one hand and the DNA test results in another.

Needless to say, the day I met Daisy was also the day my life as I'd known it changed significantly. And, as a hormonal pre-teen who was also struggling with the realisation that he didn't like girls anywhere near as much as the other boys

2

seemed to, I didn't cope very well with the additional changes at the time, and I *might* have blamed the wrong person for coming along and ruining everything.

Twenty-two years later, things have drastically improved between me and my sister. We actually have a pretty good relationship despite our age gap. Once I got used to the idea of having a baby sister, I came to find she was actually kind of cute. A bit of a cock-block at times, but fun to have around, nonetheless.

Her teen years were rough, and it was equal parts surprising and sweet that she sought out my shoulder to cry on more than Dad's. Then, after he died three years ago, I was the only family she had left, her mother having shot through when she was barely a year old.

Which is why we make an effort to meet for dinner once a week. Neither of us likes to cook, though, so we always meet out.

"How's uni?" I ask her just before the sympathetic server appears by our table, his notepad in hand.

The guy looks between us and then looks me over, eyebrows raised. He's probably in his mid-twenties, with artfully styled hair and jeans that look painted on. If I didn't have a hot boyfriend, I might consider trying for his number. But, as it happens, I do have a hot boyfriend, and I'm not loving the judgemental vibes rolling off him, either.

I want to roll my own eyes right back at him. Whether he's judging me because my 'date' is a woman, or because she's clearly much younger than me, he can fuck off.

"Can I get you anything to drink?" he asks. "Do you need more time with the wine list?"

"A bottle of pinot grigio, please," I tell him, handing him the wine list, but Daisy places her hand over it and shakes her head.

"I'm not drinking," she tells me. "So, unless you're planning on drinking the whole bottle yourself…"

Mildly surprised, I shake my head. We *always* share a bottle of pinot. Flustered, I tell the waiter I'll just have a glass, then.

"And have you decided on your meals, or would you like me to come back?" he asks.

"Are you still eating pizza?" I tease my sister, and she rolls her eyes.

"I will *always* eat pizza," she huffs. "That is a genetic trait you and I are both stuck with: an addiction to carbs and cheese."

"Well, that's what the gym is for," I respond, my tone dismissive. "We'll have a large *Godfather* to share, please."

Our server, having realized that she's obviously related to me, shifts from snooty to friendly in the blink of an eye. He smiles easily, this time eyeing me appreciatively, and winks. "One *Godfather* coming up."

"Just hold the olives." Daisy interjects.

"Okay, seriously, what the fuck?" I ask her, throwing my hands in the air. "First the wine, now the olives? Who even are you anymore?"

Not wanting to get in the middle of a family spat, our server vanishes as quickly as he appeared.

Daisy worries her bottom lip between her teeth, fiddling with the edges of the linen napkin which is still folded neatly on top of the plate in front of her. She looks down towards her lap, then back up at me through her thick, falsely extended lashes. "Don't be mad, Con."

Her voice is uncharacteristically small. Nervous. I don't like it.

"Daze, what's going on?"

I really dislike the fact that her hands start to shake. I watch as she swallows, visibly steels herself, and then looks me in the eye. Then she says two words that take me completely by surprise.

"I'm pregnant."

Before I can breathe, before I can say anything, she keeps talking.

"Obviously, it wasn't planned. The…" she swallows, her voice trembling, "the father doesn't want anything to do with it, but I'm keeping it."

Rage bubbles up in me at the thought of some guy having his fun and running away to leave Daisy -my baby sister- to deal with it. But, more than that, I'm seeing her with fresh eyes. She's not the pain in the arse baby or toddler of my memories, she's not the hypersensitive teenager desperate for independence and adulthood. She's a grown woman with a future ahead of her: a future that now apparently includes a small human of her own making.

Slumping back in my chair, I'm aware that I'm gaping at her. "Holy shit," I murmur, immediately regretting it as her eyes fill with tears. Practically lunging across the table, I reach for her hand, squeezing it. "No, no; this is good news. I'm not mad. You're an adult. I just…*whoa*, Daisy. A *baby*."

"Yeah," she gives me a watery chuckle accompanied by a tremulous smile. "I'm fucking terrified, Connor."

I'll bet. She's only twenty-two. Hell, I'm thirty-two and the thought of parenthood freaks me out…even though it probably wouldn't be unexpected in my case. It would instead involve months -even years- of paperwork and planning. Surrogates or adoption agencies. And that's only if my partner was even interested in kids, which I know is not the case. Ant made that very clear when we got serious, and I've always been on the fence about it, so I didn't argue.

I give her hand yet another squeeze. "You're going to be an awesome mum," I tell her. "And you're not doing this alone. I've got your back, and I'll be there with you every step of the way."

Some of the fear and doubt recedes from her pretty blue eyes. "Thanks, Con," she says, then her lips quirk upwards. "Or should that be 'Uncle Con' now?"

"Oh. *Wow.*" I can feel the stupid smile spread over my face. "I guess it will be." As excitement at the prospect starts to fill me, I tease, "So, when's the due date? Do you think your kid will inherit your abysmal sense of timing?"

Daisy laughs, pinches some bread out of the roll in front of her and throws it at me, just as our server arrives with my wine.

Chapter One – Connor

"I still don't know why you didn't stick with law," my best friend, Henry, laments as he helps me put the finishing touches on the nappy cake I've built for Daisy's surprise baby shower. "Isn't party planning a cliché for a gay man?"

"Fuck you," is my witty retort, followed by, "and I'm an events coordinator, not a party planner, thank you very much."

"It's the same God damned thing," he counters, shaking his head. "Don't argue semantics with me."

Arching an eyebrow at him, I fold my arms across my chest. I've known Henry since we were five years old, starting grade one together. We look like chalk and cheese: he's got flawless dark skin and even darker hair, where I was the pasty-faced, freckled kid, but we bonded over a mutual love of *Goosebumps* books and have been inseparable ever since.

"How on earth does Sarah put up with you?" I ask him, letting my gaze drift over to where his wife is fiddling with the hessian bunting I bought for the party. Sarah's practically glowing, only a handful of weeks behind Daisy in her own pregnancy, with effortlessly curled blonde hair and wearing a flowing sundress that emphasises her cute baby bump. "Also, you should stop her from climbing onto that dining chair."

Henry spins to face his wife, aghast, and rushes across the room, telling her to sit her arse down and let him do the manual labour. I have to hide my smirk when her raised voice informs him that she's not some trained pet that he can just command.

"That was cruel," Ant tells me, and I look up to catch him leaning against the doorway that leads into the kitchen of our apartment.

Things between us have been stilted in recent months. Ever since I came home buzzing with the excitement of Daisy's unexpected announcement, it has felt like he's been pulling away.

I know he dislikes kids, but I would have thought he'd be happy for me -us?- to have a niece or nephew.

Instead, he's bemoaned every mention of the baby. He's huffed and complained when I've accompanied Daisy to her ultrasound and hospital appointments, and he was utterly horrified when Daisy informed us that she'd named me as guardian to her kid in her will should anything happen to her.

We actually fought over that one.

Ant isn't a bad guy. He's recently turned forty and is incredibly attractive; tall, lean and dark haired. Like Henry, he's a lawyer, only he practices criminal law where my bestie specialises in family practice. Anthony is somewhat anal retentive and is rather hedonistic: personality traits that, until recently, suited my lifestyle perfectly.

Taking the olive branch I've been offered, though, I shoot my lover a cheeky grin. "He was nagging me again."

"Yes, well, you're a lawyer, Connor. You've got the degree. You were admitted to the Roll of Lawyers. You *practiced for years-*"

"And I hated it," I scowl at him. "You know that."

Ant rolls his brown eyes and it makes a spark of something unpleasant simmer in my belly. "You were a good lawyer who got a run of shitty cases-"

"Drop it." I need to step away. It's one thing for my best friend to give me shit over my choice to change careers, another entirely for the man who is supposed to love and support me to do so. His snobbier side has shown itself more and more frequently lately, and it's starting to bother me. "I'm not doing this now."

A lot of things about Ant are starting to bother me.

But today is supposed to be a joyful one. I'm not going to let my boyfriend get under my skin and ruin the fun I've arranged for my sister. Yes, I know baby showers are usually an all-woman affair. However, Daisy is not the traditional type, and there was no way I was missing out on celebrating her and my unborn niece or nephew. Not to mention, there's also no way I'd let anyone else organise the party, either. Even if I wasn't an expert at event planning, nobody else knows Daisy quite as well as I do.

In reaction to my words, Ant throws his hands in the air, his impatience and irritation palpable. "Right. Well, I'm going to make myself scarce."

I'm frowning at him before I can school my features. "You're not staying?"

Anthony's handsome face screws up in disgust. "What, and hang out with people who want to talk about babies for hours on end? I'd rather get a root canal."

9

"Oh, fuck off, then," I huff, pointing wildly towards the door. "Thanks for supporting me and the people I love, arsehole."

Instead of biting back, he smirks at me and pushes off the wall as though he hasn't got a care in the world. "I'll be back when you're less bitchy."

I hold my tongue, the instinct to tell him not to bother coming home at all taking me by surprise. I mean, yeah, things haven't been great between us, but I still want to be with him. All relationships go through rocky patches. This one is ours.

Right?

Ugh. I'm sure the little voice in my head telling me I don't need him and I'd be better off without him is just being reactionary at this point. We're good together. Well, we can be. We have been. We will be again.

I wave him off dismissively, while indecision and insecurity gnaw away in my gut. "Whatever," I say. "I'm gonna have fun and eat cake."

His dark eyes rove over me and he sighs. "Not too much cake, I hope, or you'll need to up your workouts. You're not in your twenties anymore."

I fight the urge to grab the nearest object -a stuffed teddy bear wearing my favourite soccer team's jersey- and hurl it at his head. After all, the little Adelaide United bear doesn't deserve that sort of treatment.

* * *

Daisy had an absolute blast at her surprise baby shower. I'd conspired with a small group of her friends from uni to bring her by my place under the pretence of picking me up for a day shopping for nursery essentials. But, obviously, when I swung the door to my apartment open, she was greeted by more friends, a mountain of gifts, and more than enough food to feed an army for a week.

She cried. A lot. Big, happy tears as she clutched her belly and thanked us all for being so supportive.

It was a relaxed little shindig, without any tacky games (just the idea of smearing chocolate into disposable nappies makes me want to vomit) and with a whole bunch of us waiting on Daisy hand and foot. She sat in my comfortable armchair with her feet up and chatted with her friends, opened gifts, and ate the gourmet snacks I'd had catered in – all pregnancy safe, thank you very much.

When all was said and done, and her friends started to traipse out of my apartment, Daisy was wiped out.

Which brings us to the here and now, with me insisting that she stay seated while I clean up the minimal mess left behind. Let me tell you, paper plates mightn't be as aesthetically pleasing as porcelain, but there's something satisfying about an easy clean up without filling up the dishwasher. While I muse on that, Daze thanks me profusely again. I wave her off.

"You made out like a bandit," I say, gesturing to the epic pile of gifts she unwrapped over the course of the party. Between me, her friends, and Henry, she and the kid won't be needing anything for a while. There are toys, clothes, nappies, bottles, a breast pump, books, more clothes, towels, blankets, more towels, and even a cot (still in its box, waiting to be assembled in her apartment) all stacked together neatly.

"Yeah," Daisy agrees, still a little overwhelmed with her haul. "I can't believe you bought me a cot. I mean, the pram was epic enough, but...Con, you didn't have to spend so much money on me."

"I spent it on the peanut," I tell her. "Besides," my throat goes tight, "Dad would have wanted to do this for you himself. And he can't, so…"

For a woman about to enter her eighth month of pregnancy, she moves fast. She's out of her chair and wrapping her arms around me, sobbing into my chest before I can blink. My own eyes water.

For all his faults, our dad wasn't a bad guy. He raised Daisy on his own when her mum ran off, and he had to deal with my moody, scared, teenaged self at the same time. He supported us both through tantrums, trouble at school, and my inevitable coming out. Neither Daisy or I ever questioned that he loved us, and I'd give back all the money I inherited after his death if it meant having more time with him. I know Daze feels the same way.

"He would've been a great grandpa," she sniffles and I swallow hard.

"Yeah, he would have."

"If…if something happens to me…"

God, I hate it when she says stuff like this. It started when she redid her will. Talking about Dad always seems to remind her of her own mortality. "Daisy…"

She only squeezes me tighter in her determination. Her voice is tremulous, but she's insistent. "If something happens to me, you'll raise this baby, right? Not as Uncle Con, but as a parent? As…as their dad?"

The concept of losing her turns my stomach with a creeping sense of dread. It's all I can do to roll my eyes and shake it off. "Nothing's going to happen to you."

"That's what we thought about Dad," she argues. "Just… just *promise me*, Connor. If something happens to me before they're old enough to understand-"

"Christ, Daze. You know I will."

She sniffles some more and stretches the hug out even longer but seems to be content enough with my answer. Not that it's changed since the last time she brought it up. Or the five times before that.

We hold each other for a little longer before Daisy takes a shuddering breath, pulls back, and brushes away the remnants of her tears. "Tell you what; I'll be glad to have these hormonal crying jags over and done with when this little monster comes out." Her hands rub over the swell of her belly before she smirks down at it. "Yeah, I'm talking about you."

"Are they kicking?" My own hands move greedily to catch the kid in action.

I'm never going to have this for myself, not even if Ant suddenly changes his mind about fatherhood. Not unless we found a surrogate who was cool with being manhandled every time the baby moved.

As if she's reading my thoughts, Daisy gives me a soft smile and moves my left hand to the side of her belly where, sure enough, a tiny pair of feet give my palm a good pummelling. "Oh, they're gonna be a soccer star for sure," I tell her with a laugh.

"They can be whatever the hell they want," she shoots back, "as long as they stop trying to burst out of there *Alien* style."

I give her stomach a sympathetic pat. "Not long now."

"Ugh. You realise this is the easy part, right?"

I know she's terrified of what will come next. Of being a single parent. Of the sleepless nights, the colicky cries, the nappies, and the tantrums. Of being judged by others for being so young -not that twenty-three is *that* young- and being alone. But she's not going to be. She's got me. She's got her friends. She's even got *my* mum, because mum never held the destruction of her marriage against an innocent kid, and so Daisy sometimes stayed at mum's with me when Dad needed a break or if he had to go away for work. Of course, my mum moved to New Zealand when I went away for uni, so her support is more moral than physical. But it's there nonetheless.

"Yeah, well, you know what's not gonna be easy?" I ask her, keeping my tone light.

"What?"

"Fitting all this shit in my car."

She laughs.

* * *

I refuse to let Daisy help me carry anything down to the car, but she insists on at least bringing down some of the stuffed toys. So that's what she does while I tried to lug the giant cot box into the lift and out to my car, having left the biggest, bulkiest item for last.

I'm still struggling with it in the foyer of my apartment building when an amused, American-accented voice calls out, "Do you need a hand?"

I turn to face the owner of the voice. I recognize him as our upstairs neighbour, though we haven't really spoken, except to nod at each other in passing.

He's dressed in what appears to be part of a firefighter's uniform. A tight black t-shirt and industrial cargo pants in that tell-tale mustard yellow colour, which are grease stained, hard-worn and insanely masculine, with thick red and grey suspenders hanging in loose loops from his narrow hips.

This man is incredibly attractive. He's got to be at least ten years my senior with his silver fox beard sharply trimmed, accenting his angular jawline and making those steely grey eyes pop. He has crow's feet beside those intense eyes, belying how often he smiles, and dark hair atop his head, which is cropped neatly at the sides, but longer on top and wavy, with the most beautiful curl dangling over his forehead. This man is sin personified. I can't help the way I take in those broad shoulders, the tapering of his form to his slim waist, and those thick, strong thighs.

I want to climb him like a tree.

"No," I tell him, "I've got it. Thanks."

He comes to help me anyway, tucking his just-retrieved mail into the rear pocket of his pants before he lifts one end of the ridiculously heavy box like I might lift a pillow. The casual display of strength throws me off for a moment too long while I can't help imagining what it might be like to be handled by someone so strong.

These musings distract me so much that I miss him asking a question and Daisy has to say my name to get my attention.

"Sorry," I apologise, feeling my cheeks heat. *Stupid pasty complexion.* "What was that?"

"I asked whether you're moving out," he says, sounding just as amused as he did a few moments ago. Once again, I'm enamoured by his accent. It doesn't sound overly regional so, with my not-exactly-vast knowledge of American accents, I guess maybe he's from California? Maybe? "Y'know, 'cause we're carrying this thing *out* instead of *in*."

"Oh," I heft my end of the box to try and redistribute the weight, "No. I threw a shower for her in my apartment. I didn't think this part of the plan through."

"Ironic," Daisy taunts.

"Shut up," I respond.

Sexy Fireman's eyes seem to light with understanding as he looks between us. "Siblings?" he questions.

Considering Daisy and I look nothing alike, and the age gap often throws people off, I'm impressed and I tell him so, craning my neck to look back over my shoulder as I back my end of the large box through the door that leads to the parking lot outside the complex.

He chuckles, "Well, it's like that between my kids."

Some part of my stomach drops a little as he mentions having kids, because that usually means a partner of some description.

Not that I should care if he's involved, considering I'm not single.

Focus, Connor.

"Kids, huh?" I ask him, hoping I sound casual. "I haven't heard the usual kiddie noises coming from upstairs."

He laughs, and I'm pretty sure he knows I'm fishing for information. "Well, the boys are almost thirty now, and they each have their own place, so I should hope not."

I almost stop midway to my car. "No way are you old enough to have thirty-year-old kids."

My sexy fireman winks. He fucking *winks*. "Flattery will get you everywhere," he teases. Then, while readjusting his hold on the box, he shrugs, "But I was nineteen when they came along. Twins," he adds, by way of explanation. Out of the corner of my eye, I watch Daisy shudder. Then he continues, "I was such a cliché. This you?"

"Huh?" I'm thrown by the abrupt change of topic, and I want

to know exactly what he means by 'I was a cliché'.

We've stopped a few feet away from my car and he juts his chin towards it. "Is this your car?"

What is it about this man that makes my brain revolt? I try not to blush as I nod. "Uh, yeah. Sorry. It is. Thanks."

I hear Daisy snigger and I just know I'm going to be teased for the entire twenty-minute drive to her apartment. If I wasn't still holding on to my end of the box, I'd kick her shin, pregnant lady or not.

"Need help getting it in?" My fireman asks, setting his end of the box on the footpath, and I do the same.

I know he's talking about the box. I do. But that's *not* where my brain goes, so my breathy, *"Yes,"* is kind of humiliating. Especially when his lips twist wryly, like he knows exactly what I was thinking.

The guy's probably straight as an arrow, Connor. Reel in your desperation a little.

"Pop the trunk, lay your rear seats down flat, and we'll get this done."

Have I mentioned that I love a guy who can take charge of a situation? I mean, yeah, I'm bossy by nature and my job warrants it, but that's all the more reason for me to want to sit back a bit in my personal life.

Trying not to imagine him commanding me in other situations, especially those requiring less clothing, I scramble to obey. I fumble getting the keys from my pocket, pressing the button to unlock the Rav. The lights flash, highlighting the charcoal grey of the chassis orange momentarily, and then I step forward to pop the boot. The rear seats are already pushed down, and I thank my past self for having the forethought to pre-empt the necessity for the additional cargo space.

My fireman gently nudges me out of the way and lifts the box by himself, sliding it into the back of my car in yet another display of effortless strength. I swear that alone is enough to get me half hard, and I do everything I can to will my cock to behave itself.

You have a boyfriend, damn it, I think down at it. *No ogling the hot fireman.*

My silent admonishment doesn't do a thing to calm my libido.

It's all over too soon, with Daisy's haul packed away in the boot of my car and my fireman dusting off his hands and backing away.

Jesus Christ, I have to stop calling him 'my fireman'.

"Thanks," I tell him again, holding out a hand to shake, hoping the action comes off more natural than it feels. "Uh...?"

"Will," he finally introduces himself, gripping my hand in his larger one. His skin is warm and dry, his palms and fingers calloused from years of a labour-intensive job. His grip is firm, but not in that dickish 'trying to out masculine you' sort of way. "Will Bradford."

"Thanks, Will," I repeat myself, smiling as I end the hand-shake. I gesture to myself. "Con. Well, Connor, but everyone calls me Con. Uh, Stark." I add my surname belatedly, because I'm apparently the king of awkward introductions at this point. Shaking the moment off, I gesture towards Daisy, who is now leaning against the closed boot of the car, rubbing her rounded belly. "This is Daisy."

"A pleasure to meet you both," Will practically purrs, and I wonder if it's just wishful thinking when I feel like it's pointed in my direction. He takes a step back, inclining his head in

Daze's direction. "I'll let you go. I remember how exhausted my kids' mom got during the last couple of months. Good luck with everything. See you 'round, Con." The fucker winks again, then turns on his heel and saunters back towards the main door of our apartment building.

I can't help watching the perfect curve of his arse as he goes.

Daisy whistles, low and appreciative. "That man's something else, huh? Enough to give a girl Daddy kink."

Oh no, I don't like the possessive jolt her words inspire. Not at all.

With my cheeks burning, I turn back to her and huff, "Get in the car."

She laughs for half the drive back to her place, then, as expected, teases me for the rest of it.

My sister is damn lucky I love her.

Chapter Two – Will

Lusting after my downstairs neighbour is wrong for many, many reasons.

Firstly, he doesn't appear to be all that much older than my sons. That's weird, right? Or is it a sign I'm going through some sort of ridiculous mid-life crisis? I've dated men in my own age bracket, so it's not like I'm one of those creeps who *only* chases after men half his age. But…he's *young*. Probably *too* young.

Ignoring that, there's also the fact that he's in a relationship. And, yeah, this probably should have been my main concern. I've seen the guy he's living with around the building: tall, attractive, always wearing designer suits. He seems like a stick in the mud in comparison to Connor.

Not that I've spent any amount of time with either man, but I rarely ever read people wrong.

Nevertheless, Connor is in a relationship with the stick in the mud. Hell, he's *living* with the guy. So wondering what those perfect, plump lips would feel like wrapped around my cock is very, very wrong.

We've crossed paths a few more times since I helped him move his sister's crib out to his car. Each time we do, we stop to talk. I ask about his sister and the baby, he asks me about work, we touch on the usual small talk points like the weather or upcoming public holidays, and it's nice.

Don't get me wrong, I'm not a hermit and I'm not desperate for social interaction, but I can't help looking forward to these little moments with Connor.

It's not like my attraction to him is one-sided, either. Even though he obviously won't act on it, I've seen him eyeing me over with blatant appreciation. It's flattering, considering there's gotta be at least a decade (if not more) between us. I'm inching perilously close to middle age, so having a hot younger man like Connor size me up with interest does magical things to my ego.

But...where was I? Oh, yeah. It's *wrong* to lust after him.

Doesn't stop me from doing it, though.

Like right now, for instance. I've just *accidentally* bumped into Connor at the mailboxes again. I've just come off a shift (okay, I came off the shift over an hour ago but, wouldn't you know it, traffic getting home was a bitch) and he's just walked in from his daily visitation with his sister.

"Hey Will," he greets me with a distracted smile, thumbing through the envelopes he just plucked out of his mailbox.

"Hey," I paste on my patented easy-going smile, "how are you doing today? How's Daisy?"

Connor brightens at the mention of his sister. He's told me before that he's proud of her for going through the whole pregnancy alone, but anyone with half a brain can see that he's been right there with her the entire time. He's endearingly excited to become an uncle, and I'm more than happy to give him an outlet to talk about it. The last time we spoke, I walked away with the impression that his boyfriend isn't as into the topic as Connor himself is.

Stick. In. The. Mud.

Connor launches into today's update: she's hit the thirty-seventh week, so could 'pop' at any time, and has taken to begging the kid to make its appearance early. I chuckle at that.

"My ex made it to thirty-six with the boys," I find myself telling him, realizing as I do that I haven't really told him much about myself. Then again, our chats only last a few minutes at a time, and aren't exactly deep and meaningful conversations. "We were told thirty-five's the average with twins, so it wasn't a shock. But they spent a couple of weeks in the Special Care nursery because they were tiny and Jack refused to latch properly, the little shit, so…" I shrug and stop myself there, acknowledging that I'm starting to ramble.

Connor snorts at my description of my son, but his eyes are full of empathy as he reaches out and puts a hand on my bicep, a fleeting touch to relay sympathy. My skin tingles as he moves back into his own bubble of personal space. "That must have been stressful and scary as fuck."

"Yeah," I nod, thinking back to those early days. Jen's utter devastation when she was discharged from the hospital three days after giving birth, sent home without her babies. The terror and frustration I felt at being a new father at nineteen, simultaneously feeling helpless and useless to do anything for my kids or my ex. Navigating the awkwardness of living with Jen in separate bedrooms, my first months of officially being out were so different to those of the other gay men I knew.

Thank God for Jen's understanding. For her patience and

support and love. Even after I knocked her up and, upon being told that I'd done as much, blurted out my truth at the worst possible moment.

She was a damn good friend. Still is, even though she stayed behind in California when the boys and I moved to Australia once they'd graduated high school.

I should probably call her. Touch base and all that. It's been a while and, last I heard, her youngest daughter, Roxy, was giving her absolute hell.

I give myself a shake when I realize that my thoughts have gone off course and that the silence between me and Connor has dragged on just a little too long to be comfortable.

"Sorry," I apologise sheepishly. "Got lost in thought there."

Connor dismisses my apology with a wave. "We all do that." After a beat, he starts to say something else, but is interrupted by a sharp, agitated barking of his name.

We turn in unison to see his boyfriend -Anton? Andrew? Alex?- striding down the short corridor from the elevator. The guy looks the same as he has every other time I've seen him. About my height, lean and toned, the smooth lines of his body emphasised by the perfect tailoring of his no doubt expensive as fuck suit. He's got dark hair and eyes, and his handsome, cleanshaven face is set into an unimpressed scowl.

"The fuck are you doing?" he demands of Connor as he gets closer, ignoring me entirely. He makes a show of checking his shiny silver coloured watch. It's probably also ridiculously expensive. "We've got dinner with Michaels and the O'Rourkes in thirty fucking minutes and there's no way in hell you're wearing *that*."

Connor's cheeks flush and he tears his gaze away from me, his embarrassment palpable. I want to reach out, hold him close and assure him that the only person who should be embarrassed right now is the asshole berating him.

What a douche.

"Sorry," Connor murmurs, and I feel a pang of tumultuous emotions when the light in his eyes seems to dim. His shoulders slump inwards and his smile turns brittle. "I must have lost track of time."

The douche huffs impatiently then, after a beat, widens his eyes and gives an incredulous shake of his head. "*Well?* Hurry your arse up."

Jesus Christ, who the fuck does this guy think he is?

I clear my throat. Two sets of eyes turn on me. One hazel and cautious, the other dark brown and irritated.

Good. Let the fucker be irritated. I raised two rambunctious boys through their terrible toddlerhoods and even moodier teen years – this guy can't rattle me.

Pasting on my smarmiest smile, I extend my hand to the douche in a suit. "I'm sorry, I don't think we've met properly. I'm Will. I-"

"Own the apartment directly above us, yes, I'm aware." Douchey McDoucheface makes no move to take my hand. He trails his gaze over me with a practiced sort of arrogance, starting at the worn sneakers on my feet, over the grey station-issued sweatpants and black t-shirt, then finally to my face. He seems to find me wanting, but I couldn't give a rat's ass. "Can I help you?"

Connor groans. "Anthony," he chastises, "*you* interrupted *our* conversation. Don't be a dick."

Anthony swivels his head back sharply and snaps, "Why aren't you heading upstairs to get dressed yet?"

I grind my teeth. What the ever-loving fuck does Connor

see in this guy?

I want so badly to put Anthony in his place, but one look at the dejection on Connor's face stops me. It's not going to make things any better for him if I tell this dick that he can't order his boyfriend around. So, as badly as I'd like to demand Anthony treat Connor with more respect, I bow out gracefully.

Clapping Connor on the shoulder, I tell him I'll see him around. "Give Daisy my best, too," I add as I make my way to the stairwell. I hope the three flights of stairs will help burn off some of my anger. It doesn't work, and the sounds of the two men arguing in my wake follow me up until I reach the first landing.

Nevertheless, I am feeling marginally calmer when I reach my apartment. I fish my keys from my pocket and let myself in, dropping the keys into the glass bowl on the side table just inside the entryway.

I love my apartment, even though my boys maintain it's too big for just me. Three bedrooms, one large bathroom, and an open plan kitchen, living, and dining space, with views of the ocean from the living room and little balcony.

I'd bought this place when Jack, Wes and I first moved here. The exchange rate worked in my favour, and property on the Gold Coast hadn't yet boomed. It's scary to think that, in the decade since then, this apartment has more than doubled in value. I'd suggest it's even tripled. I have zero interest in moving, though. As more high-rises and hotels spring up along the coastline, even replacing some of the houses that once stood in the same street that I live in, my little apartment in Burleigh Heads is exactly where I want to be.

It's a short walk to the beach -maybe fifteen minutes at a

slow stroll- and even closer to the hustle and bustle of James Street, which has become the central hub of boutique stores, cafés, and restaurants for the area. Yes, the walk back up the hill is a pain at times, and street parking can be a problem, but I'm happy here.

I've been even happier since I renovated the bathroom and kitchen and converted the room that once belonged to Wes into a home gym. Jack's old room is now a guest room, but it doesn't see a lot of use. Jen and her husband, Mitch, used to crash there when the girls were younger, but nowadays, if they travel over, they stay in a local hotel suite. Occasionally, one of the guys from the station will stay if they've had one too many beers, or Wes and his girlfriend might stay a few nights in summer, but I'm otherwise generally alone here.

Beneath me, I can hear the muted strains of Connor and Anthony arguing under my feet. They're usually quiet neighbours, but I won't lie and say I don't hear their occasional fight. In the past few months, 'occasional' has felt more like 'regular'. They're not screaming, though. Their voices are raised enough that I can hear the general tone, but I can't make out their words. That might change if I open my windows or step out onto the balcony, but I won't do either of those things.

As drawn as I am to Connor, I'm not going to nose my way into his business.

There are the dull thuds of doors being slammed and the sound of the argument travels in the direction of the front door. Silence seems to reign once the final thud sounds out.

I wince. It doesn't seem like Connor's evening will be a pleasant one at all.

I can only hope it improves for him.

* * *

I don't see Connor for the next couple of days. I wind up working double shifts because Pete broke his leg attending a house fire, and Scott's kid brought gastro home to him.

"Hey, Dad," Jack says, nodding at me as he walks towards his locker, clocking on for his shift, "you look rough."

I roll my eyes at him. "Thanks, kid. Just what everyone wants to hear."

"Just callin' it as I see it," he shrugs easily. Then he stops and looks me over properly. "Seriously, though, Will. You look like shit."

"Thanks, Jack." It took me a long ass time to get used to my kid calling me by my name when we first started working together. Even longer to start seeing the gangly teenager I'd brought over to Australia with me as a man. But that's certainly what Jack is now – all six feet and three inches of him. He and his brother were born identical, but once they hit their teens, Jack started working out at the gym while Wes dedicated himself to academic pursuits. They might be the same height and have the same face, same skin tone, same hair, and same eyes...but that's about where the resemblance ends.

"You've been working OT again, haven't you?" he pushes. "Aren't you getting too old for that?"

I snort. "Fuck you. I'm forty-eight, not eighty-eight. Jesus." I pat my abdomen, where the abs I've worked hard to maintain through the dreaded onset of middle age paunch are still going strong. "And I'm in the prime of my life, I'll have you know."

"Uh huh," he stows his bag into his locker and runs his hand through his dark hair -slightly longer on top, but shaved short on the sides- as he gives himself a glance in the mirror hanging on the inside of the metal door. "That's why you spend all your time working instead of dating, right?"

I close my own locker shut with a bit too much force. "Drop it."

"Uh oh," a new voice cuts in, and Jack and I glance over towards the doorway to find the Station Officer, Chase, grinning at us. "Your kid giving you grief again?" He doesn't pause to allow an answer. "What about this time?"

Before I can open my mouth, Jack's answering, "The old man won't date," he says matter-of-factly. "Says he's in the prime of his life, but spends his entire life *here*."

Chase, older than me by a few years, arches an eyebrow at my son. "Is there something wrong with here, Bradford?"

Jack hesitates, and it's clear he's trying to gauge whether he has actually offended our Station Officer, or whether he's being messed with. He errs (mostly) on the side of caution. "No, sir. I just think he could do with a good-"

"Don't finish that sentence," I tell him, holding up my index finger in warning. We might be colleagues, but talking about my sex life with Jack always makes me uncomfortable.

Jack laughs and holds his hands up in surrender. "*Time*! I was gonna say time!"

"Bullshit," I shake my head, unable to hide my grin.

When I was nineteen, I never would have imagined having this sort of relationship with my boys, but I'm glad that I do. I'm glad that we're close. They know they can tell me anything, ask anything of me, and I'll be there for them no matter what. I always wanted to be the kind of dad I didn't have growing up. I didn't want them to be fearful of me as an authority figure or feel like I could never understand them.

I like to think I've succeeded.

Jack and I go our separate ways to attend our rostered tasks and chores, and I wonder if tonight's shift will drag as slowly as the day shift did. That's not necessarily a bad thing: a slow shift for us means fewer disasters for anyone else.

It's just after nine o'clock when the bell rings and the alarms blare.

I'm on the response crew alongside Jack and two other guys, and we suit up, take our positions in the truck and head out with the lights flashing and sirens sounding. We're on route to a nasty car crash on the M1, which isn't exactly an uncommon event. As we near the crash site, carefully making our way through two parted lanes of traffic, my gut clenches with dread at the vision ahead.

It doesn't matter how many years I've been doing this. Fatal accidents always get under my skin.

A ute (after over a decade living here, I'm resigned to the lingo, even if I want to call the vehicle a pickup truck) with red provisional plates is parked sideways across both southbound lanes, its bonnet crunched up where it made contact with the driver's side of a cream-coloured Nissan Micra. The Micra has crumpled inwards, forming a strange V shape with the chassis, its other side having slammed hard into the cement guardrail at its left.

The cops have started easing the traffic down past the accident, directing the slowly amassing line of vehicles down one of the two northbound lanes. Because it's late for a weeknight, there's not as much congestion as if this had happened during peak hour, but it's still quite busy.

My heart stutters as we approach the cars with the Jaws of Life at the ready, catching a glimpse of a baby seat in the back of the Micra, strapped in and tilted unnaturally sideways with the movement of the chassis.

The seat is thankfully empty.

The driver's seat is not.

Worse still, I recognise the driver. I recognise her long, dark hair. The slope of her narrow, feminine nose. The greying-olive tint to her previously radiant tanned skin.

"Fuck," I breathe, feeling sick.

"What?" Jack asks from my right.

"I know her." My thoughts feel almost jumbled as my heart beats rapidly in my chest. Should that be 'knew her'? She's not moving. Not breathing. I think of Connor, his excitement about the baby. Shit. The baby. "She's pregnant," I tell Jack, "like thirty-seven weeks. Maybe thirty-eight now? I don't know. Someone get the EMTs over here. The ambos. Whatever."

I'm flustered now, jumping between the terminology I grew up with and Australian slang for the paramedics. I need to get my shit together if I have any hope of helping Daisy or her unborn child.

The paramedics are already on their way and at the ready, and I reiterate what little information I know. Jack works the combination tool to cut and spread the compressed, crunched up car chassis, pulling away the crumpled door in record time. Then we both step back to allow the paramedics to get to work.

I should be helping with the ute. I should be hosing the site free of debris, oil, and gas.

Petrol. *Whatever.*

I should be doing anything other than standing stock still, watching as one paramedic kneeling next to the wreckage shakes his head solemnly at the other.

Things get worse as a commotion on the other side of the wreckage catches my attention.

A man has pulled his SUV over on the side of the road a few hundred feet away and has abandoned his vehicle with its hazard lights flashing. He's currently yelling - screaming, actually - as he fights against the hold of one of the local police officers, trying to make it past them. I catch sight of his stricken expression in the glow from one of the police car's flashing lights.

Connor.

The very idea that he might have witnessed his sister's accident, or even just driven past it by chance, makes my stomach roil again. Before I know what I'm doing, I'm striding around the wreckage towards him.

"Will!" He cries as soon as he sees me. Tears are streaming down his face. My heart aches for him. "Will! It's Daisy! That's Daisy's car! I need to get to her! I need-"

"You know this guy?" the cop asks me, and I tear my eyes from Connor's to answer him.

"Yes. He's a friend. And…" I trail off, not wanting to be the one to break the news to Connor, even though it won't come as a surprise to him.

The police officer cocks his head, a look of understanding dawning in his eyes. He grimaces in sympathy, before he schools his features. "We can't let him past."

"I know," I nod, and Connor starts protesting again.

"Dad?" I don't know when Jack approached, but I just about jump out of my skin. I'm clearly not covering my own shock right now, because Jack *never* calls me anything but my name when we're in the field.

I turn to him, and he jerks his chin in Connor's direction.

"He's in no state to drive, and the ambulance just left." At that, both Connor and I jerk our heads up and watch the lights travelling in the opposite direction, sirens blaring as they go. "It's heading to Robina. You take him," Jack gestures back to Connor, "and I'll let the guys -and Chase- know you've clocked out early for personal reasons."

I've never been more proud of my level-headed son. Even though I feel terrible for leaving the crew shorthanded, I don't think I would have been much good to them tonight anyway. "Thanks, Jack."

Jack claps his hand on my shoulder and squeezes. "Call me later," he says, then turns and heads back to where the other fire officers are doing their jobs. The job I failed to do tonight.

Even though I'm still wearing my PPE, and I'm grimy and covered in fine debris from the extrication, I step towards Connor and gesture towards his car. "Come on. I'll drive you to the hospital."

Chapter Three – Connor

The whole night becomes a blur.

The drive itself is eerily silent. I can't bring myself to ask Will if he'd seen Daisy, and he can't seem to bring himself to tell me anything, either. Still, he does exactly what he said he would, driving me to the hospital and parking the car after I practically throw myself out of it when he pulls up outside the Emergency entrance.

Things start to go fuzzy as I beg the poor triage nurse for information about my sister's condition. With blood pumping in my veins and echoing in my ears, I start pacing, glancing towards the hallway anytime anyone in scrubs appears. Eventually, Will finds me and stands strong by my side, his large hand pressing into my back, keeping me grounded.

It turns out I needed that.

I need it even more when a doctor finally appears and asks for the family of Daisy Stark.

I need even more than just a hand at my back when the

doctor -surgeon, actually- leads me and Will into a quiet room and tells us that they did all they could, but Daisy didn't make it.

The doctor delivers this information with as much clinical empathy as he can, but it still breaks me.

Will catches me when my knees buckle. At any other time, I might enjoy the show of his strength, or the feel of his big, muscular arms and his firm chest and abdomen. At any other time, I might need to remind myself that I have a boyfriend and feeling up Will is disrespectful to Ant, even if I can see the end of our relationship coming. At any other time, I might think about turning an embrace like this into an opportunity to flirt. But, right now, it's not a sexy moment. It's not a fun flirtatious one. Will is only holding me because I can't hold myself up anymore.

All I can think about is losing Daisy.

It feels like I have lost a piece of my soul. She is…she *was* my baby sister. She was too young, too vibrant, too full of life to just be *gone* like that.

I'm just about to open my mouth to voice these denials when the surgeon speaks again.

Apparently, against all odds, my niece survived.

It all becomes too much to deal with, and I turn and press my face into Will's shirt, letting the grief take me over.

I don't remember much after that, either.

* * *

Low voices murmuring above my head make me groan. My warm, firm pillow makes a shushing sound and resettles me. I frown.

That's not right.

I crack an eye open and the light is ridiculously bright.

Fluorescents. Ugh.

The chemical smell hits me next, tickling my nostrils in an unpleasant way. It's the unmistakeable sterile smell of a hospital.

Why am I in a hospital?

The memories hit me in a rush and I gasp and sob all at once, and my pillow -which turns out to be Will- holds me close and shushes me again. "Hey, you're okay, we've got you."

"We?" I ask in a voice that sounds nothing like my own. It's gravelly; evidence of all the crying I did last night. I bring a hand up to rub at my eyes, which are gritty and sore.

I couldn't care less about how I look, but I'm betting it's not good.

"We," another familiar voice answers firmly.

I look up. "Hen?"

My best friend nods and offers me the ghost of a smile. I frown at him and struggle to sit up properly in my uncomfortable plastic seat. "How…?"

"Anthony wasn't answering my, well, I guess *your* calls," Will explains tentatively as he holds up my phone, like he's afraid this additional piece of information might send me over the edge again, "so I scrolled through your contacts until I came across 'BFF' and figured you'd appreciate the support."

Henry and Will exchange a look, and I somehow instinctively know it's about Anthony dodging my calls. Things between us haven't been great lately, but right now that's the least of my concerns. Before I can say anything, despite not knowing where to start or *what* to say, Henry drops down into the plastic hospital chair on my other side and pulls me in for a hug.

At first, I'm numb. This doesn't feel real. None of the night's events feel real. I was just driving home, and the pile up on the M1 wouldn't have warranted a second glance if I hadn't noticed the iconic collection of rainbow bumper stickers on the crushed car.

I don't know why Daisy was out last night, or why she was driving in the direction of my apartment, but I wish she hadn't been. I wish she'd called me. I wish...I wish...

Henry's murmuring soft, soothing words but I can't process them. I barely even hear them against the rushing of blood in my ears and the pounding of my heart.

She's gone. Daisy's gone. She was only twenty-three.

The tears come on without me even realising it. I don't fight them, don't try to hide them, don't even care that they're there. Henry squeezes me tight, and it reminds me of the many other times he's been there for me over the years.

When we were seven and I broke my leg when I fell out of his treehouse.

When I was ten and my family as I knew it fell apart.

When I was seventeen and I officially came out.

Two years ago, when I realised that I couldn't bring myself to practice law anymore.

But all of those times seem to pale in comparison to the anguish and terror wracking my body today. I can tell my best friend is at a loss for words. Empty platitudes and condolences have never come easily to him. I don't want those things, though, and I'm relieved he's not trying. Instead, he's reassuring me that he's here, that Sarah's here, that our other friends have got my back, too. Whatever I need. Whenever I need it.

There's another warm hand on my back and it takes me an embarrassingly long moment to remember Will is also here. I try to get a rein on my sobbing, wiping at my eyes as I turn to my upstairs neighbour.

He looks like shit, too. His handsome face is lined with exhaustion, his clothes gritty and grimy and his hair oily. He must be supremely uncomfortable, having folded that big, broad body into these uncomfortable little chairs and held me while I….what? Slept? Passed out? I still don't remember much from earlier.

I don't really want to.

But it strikes me that this relative stranger is an even nicer guy than I could have imagined. He left work to bring me here. He stayed by my side during the long, painful wait for updates on Daisy's condition. He caught me when my knees buckled and stayed with me when I crashed. No. Passed out. I don't think I'll ever use the word 'crash' again. Just the thought of it makes my heart seize and my throat tighten.

"Breathe, Connor," Will urges, concern crinkling his brow. His big, warm palm rubs circles on my back. "That's it. In….and out….*good*. That's good."

In any of the passing fantasies I've had of this man, this was not how I imagined having his hands on me.

I want to quirk my lips at the thought, but I'm emotionally wrung out and it feels disrespectful, somehow. Daisy just died, for fuck's sake.

Oh, and here come the tears again.

It's a struggle, but I get myself back under control and blurt, "You don't have to be here."

Will's handsome face softens. "No, I don't. But I want to."

Incomprehension makes me blink. "Why?"

"Because you're a friend and what you're going through..." he stops and shakes his head. "Nobody should be left to deal with this type of thing alone." He holds up a hand, forestalling my argument that I'm not alone. That I have Henry here now. "Henry's probably going to have to leave at some point because, as I understand it, he's got a heavily pregnant wife at home and-"

"And," Henry picks up on my other side, reaching out for my hand and squeezing it to gentle the pain his next words bring, "as your lawyer, I'm jumping straight into making sure Daisy's will is actioned and you get custody of the baby immediately. Otherwise, DoCS get involved, and dealing with the foster system's a bitch. As it is, you'll probably need to jump through hoops to prove your suitability, regardless of what the will says, but...well, I'll do what I can to make that as easy as possible."

The baby.

The baby.

Fuck.

Guilt threatens to overwhelm me.

I'd forgotten about the baby. Daisy will kick my arse if she finds...*oh*. No. She won't.

A strangled sound escapes from the back of my throat, and I don't know if it's because of my guilt over forgetting about the baby, or my grief at once again remembering that Daisy's gone, or the sudden comprehension of Henry's words.

Daisy's will. Custody. The promises I made to my sister.

I told her I'd raise her kid as my own, because she had it in her head that there's a difference between calling someone 'Uncle' or 'Dad'. I know a lot of that came from how much she missed our dad and how upset she was when she fully understood that her mother had walked out on her. I was always going to love Daisy's kid, and I don't know that a word makes that much difference, but now I'm facing the reality that I'm not just going to be fun Uncle Con. I'm going to be a father.

Hell, the kid's already been born, so technically I *am* a father now.

Will's hand starts rubbing my back again, his deep, soothing voice reminding me to breathe. He takes me through the action again. It's scary how desperately I need that. How much I need to be grounded right now.

Out of the corner of my eye, I catch Henry checking his watch. He's dressed in one of his expensive tailored suits, like he's ready to go straight to the office from here.

"What's the time?" I ask him.

He clears his throat. "Roughly three a.m."

Jesus. It was only nine thirty when I drove past the accident. Maybe ten when Will brought me to the hospital. It felt like a lifetime of waiting in the ER but was only a few hours at most.

It was a lifetime for Daisy.

I close my eyes against that thought and my breathing hitches.

Shut up, I tell my brain. *Shut up, shut up, shut up!*

"Do you want to see her?" Henry asks me softly and I recoil in horror. Will steadies me while my best mate seems to realise his error. "Not...No, Con. No. The baby. Do you want to see the baby? Your niece?"

"Daughter," I correct him, the word sounding foreign on my tongue. I swallow thickly and explain, "Daisy made me promise..." I can't finish the sentence. My throat closes up, and I squeeze my eyes shut.

"I get it," Henry replies softly. "Sarah and I had the 'if

something happens to us' talk, too. If Max is still too little to remember us…" His own voice has gone tight and cracked. Max hasn't even been born yet, but Henry adores his son. He takes a moment before he finishes, "Well, Sez's sister and brother-in-law would raise him as their own, too."

I nod, and we sit in silence for a little while longer, the ambient sounds of the hospital seeming almost muted and still for the middle of the night. Or maybe it's my grief making the beeps and quiet shuffling of the nurses and orderlies seem more distant.

"I want to see her. My…my daughter," I hear myself saying before my brain can fully catch up with what I've just decided.

"I'll find someone," Will pushes to his feet. He pauses to stretch, grimacing as his muscles crack and pop. Another flare of guilt hits me, but he's moving down the fluorescently lit corridor before I can tell him it's not urgent.

Not urgent.

This is my kid we're talking about. Shouldn't I feel a sense of urgency? Shouldn't I be demanding to see her?

Except I never actually thought I was going to be a father. Certainly not without warning. I've lost my sister and gained a daughter all in a matter of hours and I am a mess of emotions, not many of which are good.

It's not that I'm not relieved that the baby survived. It's not that I'm not thrilled that she's apparently healthy and finally here. I've spent the last seven months and counting wanting nothing more than to meet the tiny person who had taken up residence in my sister's belly. But I'm struggling with her existence now.

She's a permanent reminder of what I've lost. Hell, her birthday will forever be synonymous with one of the worst days of my life. None of that is her fault, but I'm afraid I won't be able to look past it.

What kind of dad resents an innocent baby for living?

"It'll get easier with time," Henry tells me, and I hang my head, understanding that I've just blurted all my thoughts out loud. He reaches out and squeezes my shoulder. It's not as comforting as when Will did it, and I don't know why. Shouldn't it mean more? Henry's been my closest friend since I was five, and I've spent maybe half an hour combined with Will before tonight.

I don't get much longer to contemplate these thoughts, thankfully within the boundaries of my own head, before Will returns on the heels of a doctor. It's not the same man who came to talk to us after Daisy's surgery, but he's just as professionally warm and empathetic as he leads the three of us through the halls towards the Special Care Nursery, explaining that they're keeping the baby (*my baby*, I remind myself) there for observation for a couple of days, considering the traumatic way she entered the world.

When we get to the grey swinging doors with the sign above declaring us to be in the right place, the doctor turns and gives our group an apologetic once over. "We can only allow two of you in."

Will takes a step backwards, already shaking his head, and I grab onto his bicep without thought. Then I cringe and turn to Henry. "Sorry. I just. I…" I can't explain it. I can't put words to why I'd prefer Will to be there for the moment I meet my kid instead of my best friend.

Henry just shrugs it off, though his clever dark eyes crinkle a little in the corners. It's a hint of amusement, and I know that when things aren't as raw, I'm going to cop some shit for this. He knows me too well, after all.

"Go on," Henry nudges me towards the door, "I'll get to meet the little princess later. I should call Sarah, and I'll go grab my laptop from the car. We'll get the ball rolling on making sure the paperwork to bring her home is in order."

I swallow over the lump in my throat and watch him walk away, then follow the doctor through the swinging door, comforted by Will at my side and his hand on my back.

The doctor gets us to scrub in using the antiseptic soap and makes us each wear a papery blue long-sleeved hospital smock over our clothes before he leads us through the inner sanctum of the Special Care Nursery. The lights in the main area have been dimmed, but nurses still bustle from room to room, and the sounds of babies crying filters into my consciousness. I don't peer in through the doorways of the rooms despite my curiosity. Instead, when we stop at the third room down, the doctor leads me and Will over to a rectangular, transparent plastic bassinet in the far-right corner of the space.

I take a deep breath to steel myself before stepping forward and peering down.

The tiny, pink skinned infant is swaddled tightly in a white hospital blanket decorated with pink, blue and yellow lines. She's asleep on her back, her little head covered with a yellow knit beanie. Wisps of dark hair curl out from underneath the edges of the cap.

Her skin is still wrinkled, but in her sleeping features I swear I can see Daisy and my heart *aches*.

"Seven pounds, six ounces," the doctor tells me, and I know that this is a detail I'm supposed to remember, that I'm supposed to tell people when they ask. But I just bob my head and watch the tiny creature sleep.

There are wires running out from beneath her swaddle, attached to the monitors beside her bassinet. Her heart beats steadily on the screen, and her oxygen saturation is being monitored, too.

"She's eating by herself, so we haven't had to utilise a nasogastric tube, which is an excellent sign," the doctor continues.

"Okay, that's...that's good." I manage, my voice tight and gravelly when I force it out.

Will's hand presses into my lower back again and I feel him lean forward to take a peek. "She's beautiful, Connor."

Tears sting my eyes and burn my sinuses. "Sh-she looks like Daze." I turn to him. "Don't you think?"

His grey-blue eyes radiate sympathy and concern, but he nods. "Yeah," he agrees, and it surprises me that he sounds just as choked up as I do. "She does."

Chapter Four – Will

Unsurprisingly, Jack is waiting for me when I get home. He has clearly let himself into my apartment with the spare key he keeps for emergencies and jumps up from the couch when I practically slump through the door.

I drove Connor home with very little protestation and I was thoroughly unimpressed to find Anthony scowling at him from their kitchen table when Connor finally managed to unlock the door with his shaking hands. The guy was dressed as Henry had been, in another stupidly expensive suit, a steaming mug of coffee in front of him. Considering the number of times I'd tried to call him from Connor's phone last night, seeing him like that set off something bitter and violent inside me.

Biting it back had been hard. I'd hugged Connor one more time, reminded him that I'm upstairs if he needs me for any reason at all, cast a disparaging glance towards Anthony and then left.

"Jesus, Dad," Jack curses, crossing my living room in four long strides until he's by my side, "you look like you're going to collapse."

Shaking off the arm that attempts to snake around my back as though I'm some sort of invalid, I sigh and scrub my palm over my face. No matter how shitty I look or feel, Connor is bound to be feeling ten times worse.

I open my mouth to answer when the shouting begins.

"Absolutely fucking not!" Anthony's voice is loud and echoing up from the stairwell beyond my still-open front door.

Jack and I turn in unison to face it. My son's face is lined with confusion and mild irritation. Mine probably betrays my disgust. We can't hear Connor's response, but Anthony's voice rings out again.

"No! I said no kids, Connor! Not under my roof!"

I start for the door, unable to listen to this, ready to give in to the violent urges I only bit back a few minutes ago.

Connor just lost his sister. Instead of kindness and sympathy, this is how his boyfriend responds?

I've only taken half a step when Connor's voice suddenly echoes up to us. "Lucky it's not your fucking apartment then! And if you won't show even a shred of decency, you can have your shit packed and be gone by tomorrow!" The sound of a door slamming follows, the loud *bang* seemingly reverberating up the tiled stairwell and through my floor.

"Connor!" The banging starts up. "Connor! Open this door!"

"Not likely, buddy," Jack mutters darkly. He looks at me questioningly. "The boyfriend didn't go to him? Like, not at all?"

I'd called Jack after Connor had crashed, filling him in on the basics of how I knew the woman in the car and who the guy I'd driven to the hospital at his behest actually was. I'm not surprised that he's made the connection between the yelling and the details of last night.

My sons are good men. Compassionate and thoughtful. Neither one of them would treat a partner the way Anthony has behaved with Connor.

"No," I shake my head, scowling as the banging and yelling continues. "The asshole was sitting at the kitchen table waiting for him when we got in, though. He could have called Connor at any time…" I growl at the back of my throat, both because of the racket Anthony is still making, and because I'm so pissed on Connor's behalf.

"Well," Jack begins with caution, tilting his jaw towards the door, "it sounds like your boy's not going to take his crap for much longer."

"He's not my boy," I correct him, then close my eyes and grimace. I know better than to bite when Jack's being flippant.

As expected, his eyes widen and a smirk curls his lips. "But you want him to be."

"Jack."

"Oh, you're *so* into him."

I shut the door, hoping to mute the sounds that are still coming from downstairs. "Jack, drop it."

"You wanna *date* him," my son continues in a sing-song voice, dragging the word 'date' out. "You wanna *kiss* him. You wanna fu-"

"That's enough." I cut him off firmly. Rubbing the space above the bridge of my nose against an oncoming headache, I sigh. "One – he's in a relationship."

Jack scoffs. "Which I'm pretty sure just ended."

"Two," I carry on like I didn't hear him, "he's too young for me."

"Oh *please*. He's, what, forty?"

"And three," on this point, my shoulders sag and I feel the weight of last night's events settling back over me, "his sister just died and he's taking custody of a newborn baby. I highly doubt he's going to be looking for a fun rebound from Douchebag McGee anytime soon. It feels shitty to even think that he might."

Jack's face falls. "Shit. I forgot. I just want to see you happy is all. Plus, I can tell you like this guy."

We finally start making our way into my apartment proper, and I drop onto my black leather couch with a groan. Jack nudges my leg with his. I crack an eye open, not entirely remembering when I shut them, and he points down the little hallway that leads to the bedrooms and bathroom.

"Go. Shower. Get changed. I'll cook you up some brunch and then you're going to bed."

Okay, I know I had him young in life, but which one of us is the parent here?

I glare up at him from my comfortable position on the couch. I'm close to petulantly whining that I don't want to get up.

"Dad, come on, you're all gross." Jack bends down and starts hauling me up by my bicep. "And you love your shower. It's got all those extra rainfall showerheads for the orgies you swear you don't have."

"Two. It has two rainfall showerheads and I'm not dignifying the rest of that with a response."

He snorts and I smother my own grin.

No, our relationship might not be textbook father and son,

47

but I wouldn't have it any other way. Jack and Wes are my sons and my closest friends. They both support me fiercely and spent the bulk of their formative years defending my honour from schoolyard bullies who taunted them for having a gay dad.

As far as I know, my sexuality hasn't ever bothered either of them. In fact, both boys insist that I need to date more, to settle down with the man of my dreams and live the life they believe I should have done all along.

In turn, I remind them that while nobody could argue that they were planned, I loved the life I had with them. Sure, I didn't do a whole lot of dating when they were kids, but I wasn't a monk. They just never met my hook-ups and casual flings because they were never serious affairs. Additionally, the benefit of Jen's and my custody arrangement meant that I would have every second week free to explore and indulge that side of my identity. If I had ever found a man I clicked with on a serious level, I would have brought him home and into the boys' lives, but it never happened, and I've made my peace with that.

Jack and Wes, however, have not.

On some level, I think they compare Jen's life to mine. They watched her meet the love of her life and move on to have two beautiful daughters, while I remained -in their eyes- painfully single. I never begrudged Jen her happiness. While I don't think the boys have either, I know they want me to have what she has.

And maybe, on some level, I want that, too.

But I'm not unhappy with my lot in life. I have two amazing sons who I am damn proud of. I work a job I love in a country that has quite literally become a second home for me. I love my apartment, love the neighbourhood, love the friends I've made here and the life I've built. It's a good life.

So what if I sometimes get a bit lonely? I'd rather that to a strained or bitter relationship any day of the week.

Guilt lances through me when I realise those particular thoughts were inspired by Connor and Anthony. I have no right to judge their relationship. None whatsoever. And it is doubly unfair to do so now when Connor's entire world has just been flipped on its axis.

These thoughts consume me, tumbling about in my head like they're in the spin cycle of a washing machine while Jack pushes me down the hallway towards the bathroom.

"Stay," he instructs playfully, turning around and ducking into the master bedroom across the hallway. I can hear him opening drawers and rifling through my closet. He returns a minute later with a bundle of soft cotton clothes in his arms, which he dumps unceremoniously on the bathroom counter.

"Do I need to run the water for you, or have you got it from here?" he asks.

I roll my eyes. "Enough sass from you. Get out and let me shower in peace."

"If your ass isn't sitting at the kitchen table in fifteen minutes, I'm gonna come back in here," he threatens me, jumping out of the way of my half-hearted punch at his arm with a laugh. "Come on, that threat worked *all the time* on me when I was a kid."

"Yeah, because you were terrified I'd catch you jerking off." I scrunch my nose at the very thought as the distasteful words leave my lips. I was never shy about the topic of sex with the boys when it came to teaching them the facts of life, but I'm still not comfortable joking about it with them. I'll blame the slip on my exhaustion. "Now get out."

He chuckles but obeys, and I strip out of my gross PPE pants and the sweaty, grimy t-shirt before climbing into the shower cavity. It's a large shower that fits two grown men comfortably. Yes, I know this from experience. The colour scheme in here is all natural stone in greys and mottled browns. It's modern, masculine, and relaxing.

There are two rainfall showerheads, but I only turn the taps for one, groaning when the hot water immediately makes me feel more human, washing away the grease and sweat accumulated during a double shift at work and a night spent on an uncomfortable hospital waiting room chair. The pressure of it also soothes my protesting muscles and invigorates me enough to properly lather myself up with my favourite bodywash (a sandalwood and musk concoction) and wash out my hair.

I step into the clothes Jack selected for me, glad for the comfort of the loose grey sweatpants and white cotton t-shirt. I dump the other stuff in the hamper to be dealt with later, and slide into my seat at the table just as Jack is placing a plate of toast, bacon, scrambled eggs, mushrooms and sauteed spinach down for me. The noise from downstairs appears to have stopped now.

I take one bite of the fluffy, perfectly seasoned eggs and actually moan in delight, giving my son the finger at his snorts of amusement. I don't stop to say a word, practically inhaling the meal, not having realised just how hungry I was until I tasted it.

I'm considering licking the plate clean when Jack pushes back out of the seat across from me and grabs the plate, taking it over to the sink.

"Thank you," my tone is soft and filled with genuine gratitude. "You're a good son, you know that? I'm so proud of you. And of Wes."

Jack nods and seems to put more effort into studying the plate as he washes it. "You should call him when you wake up later. He worries, too."

"I will." Wes lives a couple of hours' drive away, on the north side of Brisbane. He went to college in Brisbane and landed a job as soon as he finished his degree and has remained there since. Unfortunately, this means Jack and I don't get to see him as often as we'd like, but we're all still a tight-knit family unit. "I worry about him as well."

Jack's lips twitch. "You just want to know when he's gonna pop the question to what's-her-face."

"Giovanna has a name," I remind him, still amused that Jack is almost jealous of his brother's relationship. He and Wes were thick as thieves their whole lives, despite being polar opposites. When Wes announced that he and Vanna were getting serious, it sent Jack into a little bit of a tailspin.

"...a stupid name," he mutters under his breath childishly.

I snort, leaning back in my seat, shaking my head. I *tsk* at him. "You knew you were both going to grow up eventually. You never cared when he moved to Brisbane."

"Yeah, well, he can do better."

I arch my eyebrows. "Than a doctor?"

"Money isn't everything. Neither are brains." His sulking would be kind of cute if this was the first time we'd had this discussion.

"They're good for each other, Jack. I know you can see that."

"Yeah, but..."

Tilting my head, I wait patiently for him to finish his protest.

51

It's times like these when he reminds me of the little kid he once was, not the thirty-year-old he is now. He's always been stubborn (I have *no* idea where he gets that from), but his temper both flares and extinguishes quickly.

Jack sighs heavily and throws his hands in the air. I watch as water droplets fly around the kitchen. "Fine. I miss him. Happy now?"

I'm an only child, so I don't know what it's like to have a sibling, let alone a twin. Despite being adults and living their own lives, I know my boys' relationship has always been closer than most brothers. Wes being a couple of hours away was rough on Jack to begin with, but when they kept in touch and continued to visit each other on weekends, he settled down. Now it probably feels a little like Wes is being 'taken' from him, with Wes opting to spend more of his free time with his girlfriend than us these days.

I get up and cross the room, throwing my arm around Jack's shoulder the way I always have since he was eight and declared that cuddles were too babyish. I give him a squeeze and a reassuring shake. "It was bound to happen sooner or later," I tell him as gently as possible. I've never sugar-coated things for my kids. "But I miss him, too."

He waits a beat, resting his head on top of mine for a moment before he asks, "Is this the part where you tell me I should take a leaf out of his book and date more?"

I chuckle. "And sound like you? *Never*."

* * *

When I wake up late in the afternoon, I'm disoriented for a moment. Then yesterday's events snap back into place in my brain. I groan, once again feeling a pang of sympathy for Connor.

I wonder how he's doing and whether he has managed to get any sleep today. I decide that I'll go down to check in on him after I've made a few calls -to Wes, to Jen, to work- and then roll out of bed with another groan, my muscles having protested at the movement.

I eye my gym room warily as I shuffle down the hallway. I haven't had a good workout in a few days now and getting back into the routine is going to be a bitch. Still, the results speak for themselves, and I do love the post-workout endorphin surges. Maybe after I've made my calls and checked on Connor, I'll go for a run around the block and then hit the weights. That should settle the restless energy that's started to thrum beneath my skin.

When I make it into the kitchen, I grab a bottle of water out of the fridge and shake my head when I see the Tupperware container Jack has left for me to reheat. That boy will mother me to death if I'm not careful. Still, I grin when I peel back the lid to reveal a delicious looking stir-fry. That's ten times better than the Lean Cuisines I've got in my freezer, for sure.

I seal the lid back onto the round, purple container, bump the fridge door closed with my hip, and then cross into my living room to drop onto the couch, letting out a quiet 'oof' as I sink into the cushioned seat. I crack open the bottle of water and drink deeply, guzzling half of it before I screw the cap back on and set it down on the glass top of my coffee table. Then I pick up my phone from where I'd left it on the side table and scroll through my contacts to Wes's name.

He picks up on the third ring. "Hey, Dad."

It's always amazed me that Jack and Wes even sound alike.

I can still tell them apart, but those first few seconds on the phone are always a little disorienting. "Hi," I greet him in answer. "How are things?"

"Oh, you know, same old-same old," I can envision him shrugging. "Sometimes I think I should have gone into criminal practice instead of contract law."

"Nah," I dismiss the notion, "you like getting into the nitty-gritty of wording and stuff. Always have, always will."

"Yeah, well, I doubt it's as satisfying as saving an innocent person from a lengthy prison sentence."

"Except how many potential criminal clients are actually innocent?" I argue back. "Also, you find loopholes that save your clients thousands of dollars or worse consequences, even. That's gotta make you feel good about helping people, too."

I can hear Wes's smile in his next words and imagine the shake of his head -a mannerism he inherited from me- as he concedes, "Alright, fine. That *is* gratifying." He pauses, then sounds *just* like his brother when he says, "Jack told me about last night. Are you doing okay? How's your friend?"

Unlike his brother, Wes's last question is *not* laced with innuendo about my interest in Connor. Either he's being sympathetic of the situation, or Jack hasn't told him his suspicions about my interest in my 'friend'.

"I'm fine. I didn't know Daisy well, but it was still a shock to recognise her," I answer truthfully, sadness tingeing my tone. "And Connor's doing as well as he can be, given the circumstances." I think back to earlier this morning and the argument Jack and I overheard. Am I a bad person to hope that he has actually ended things with his asshole boyfriend?

I am.

But it's not just for selfish reasons, I swear. Anthony didn't seem to show an iota of interest in where Connor had been last night, and he certainly hadn't answered his (my) calls. Then the yelling about not having the baby in the apartment...well, I don't think he's exactly going to support or help Connor through the coming few weeks, months, or years. My heart clenches again for Connor. Things are going to be rough for him for a while.

Wes makes a sound of commiseration. "Is there anything we can do? Jack mentioned a baby? Has your friend-"

"Connor," I interrupt, thinking that it'll be easier for him to not have to say 'your friend' every time he brings Connor up in conversation.

"Connor. Noted. Does he need any help with the legal stuff? I mean, family law's obviously not my forte, but I can see if someone else in the office can help."

Once again, I'm warmed by how thoughtful my boys are. "His friend's a lawyer, too," I answer, "and he seemed like he was on top of it. But I'll let them know you're also willing to help if need be. I'm sure he'll appreciate it."

Wes makes another sound, this one more of a contemplative 'hmm', before he tentatively adds, "Jack also said you might like this guy."

"Jack needs to keep his big mouth shut," I grizzle and scrub my free palm over my bearded jaw. It's getting a little long again, the hairs softer to the touch than the bristle of neatly trimmed stubble. I prefer it longer, but it's starting to feel a little scruffy. "Also, like I told Jack, Connor *just* lost his sister and gained a newborn. Even if I do think he's attractive-"

Wes cuts in with what can only be described as an excited squeal. "You do?"

"Even if I do," I continue, ignoring him, "he's not in a position to start something new."

Wes's shrewd mind catches on to what I didn't say. "But if he was interested, you would be all over him like a rash?" He pauses. I imagine him frowning as he asks, "Even with a baby involved now?"

Closing my eyes, I lean my head back on the headrest of my couch. The cool leather feels pleasant against my skin. "I haven't thought about him like that since everything happened last night." I haven't really had time to, and it's honestly not fair on Connor if I do. It feels wrong, somehow, to lust after him when all he really needs right now is friendship and support.

"That's not an answer, Dad."

Suddenly, despite my day-long nap, I feel bone tired all over again. "It's the only one you're getting."

Wes's answering harrumph makes my lip curl in amusement, but he drops the topic and we move on to his personal life instead. He tells me all about Vanna's current work drama (who knew being a doctor in a tiny private practice in the suburbs could be so entertaining?) and then casually says he's planning on taking her away to a nature retreat for her birthday in a few weeks' time.

"And does this little vacation end with a bottle of champagne and a ring on her finger?" I can't help asking him.

Over the line, Wes grumbles. "Dad, stop it." His protest is delivered with a smile in his voice though.

I take pity on him and back away from the topic with a grin of my own. "Fine, fine. Keep your secrets. Just don't elope without telling me and Jack, okay?"

"You've met her mother," he quips, "there's no chance we'd get away with eloping if I wanted to keep my balls intact. That woman has had Vanna's extravagant wedding planned since she was in the womb."

All the more reason for Vanna to want to elope, I reckon, but I don't say it.

We chat some more about everything and nothing before we say our goodbyes. Glancing at my watch, I attempt to calculate what time it is back in the US, ultimately deciding that it might be too late to call Jen. I'll call her tomorrow morning instead.

Just as I'm considering heading into the gym for a light workout, there's a knock at my front door. I push to my feet and pad across the carpeted floor to answer it, surprised to see Connor's friend, Henry, on the other side.

"Henry," I greet him a little blankly, "Hi."

"Will," he nods, smiling softly. "Can I come in?"

Still confused, I step back and let the man into my apartment, shutting the door quietly behind him. He's dressed in the same suit pants and business shirt he wore earlier this morning, but his tie and jacket have been discarded. He looks tired, but he's probably been up since I called him at two in the morning, so it's hardly a surprise.

"Take a seat," I tell him, gesturing to the couch and matching armchairs in my living room. "Can I get you a drink? I've got beer, Coke, or water."

Henry shakes his head. "Nah," he responds, "I'm good." He chooses one of the armchairs positioned kitty-corner to the couch and seems to melt into it for a moment before seemingly remembering that he has a purpose here. He straightens and leans forward, resting his forearms on his knees, regarding me with those sharp, dark eyes as I take my seat on the couch, turning my body to face him. "Sorry to barge in on you like this."

"It's fine," I reply dismissively. "Is Connor…" I can't finish the question. Of course Connor's not okay.

Henry grimaces. "Obviously, that's why I'm here. I'm worried about him." Clearing his throat, he looks away. "I know you don't know him well, but...you care about him, yeah?" He looks back at me again. "I mean, a random acquaintance doesn't spend all night in a hospital with someone without actually giving a shit. Pardon my language."

I'm not quite sure how to answer him. I don't know Connor well enough to assure Henry that I care, but at the same time, I know that I am invested in the guy's wellbeing. In the end, I decide that after last night, it would be ridiculous to say otherwise.

"I do care," I eventually say, trying to choose my words carefully. "He's become a friend over the past month or so, even if just in passing. And what he's going through right now...hell, I can't imagine it."

Henry nods. "Good. I'm glad." He heaves a sigh. "He needs all the support he can get right now. If I didn't have Sarah at home, I'd probably park myself in his guest room. And the bastard is too stubborn to come stay with us."

A corner of my lips lifts upwards, but then I realise that Connor would be more comfortable in his own safe space, surrounded by his belongings and scents, and the knowledge tempers my amusement. Then my brain clicks. With clarity, I understand the point Henry is working towards. "I'll keep an eye on him," I tell him easily. "I was planning on heading down later tonight to check on him anyway."

Relief and gratitude war for real estate on Henry's handsome features. "Thank you. I've called his mum –she lives in New Zealand but she's going to fly over as soon as she can- and some of our other friends are already working on stocking his freezer, but it helps to know that he's got someone in the building." His expression clouds over. "Anthony's gone."

It's my turn to be flooded with relief. "I can't say I'm sorry to hear that."

Henry flashes me a shark-like smile. "Me either, to be honest, but," he's back to sombre, "that's just one more loss for Con right now."

Well, now I feel like shit.

As though sensing that, Henry waves his hand in the air between us. "Don't. Ant was a dick. It's good riddance to bad rubbish, but it's just bad timing." He waits a beat before adding, "Sarah and I are organising the funeral. There's no way Con's up to it. And with the baby…" He trails off.

I shuffle over on the couch, reaching out a hand to squeeze his knee. "You're a good friend to him."

Henry bobs his head. "We've known each other since we were five. He's the brother I never had."

"I'm sure he feels the same way," I agree, thinking of some of my closest friends. There are a couple back in California I miss like a lost limb, but I've made close bonds with the guys I've worked with for the past decade, too. "And he'd be there for you if the tables were turned."

"He would, yeah."

It should feel weird having a deep and meaningful conversation with this veritable stranger about another man I don't know well at all. It *should,* but it doesn't. Maybe that's because traumatic events tend to bring people together, or perhaps it's because I feel an affinity for Connor and, through him, Henry. Either way, I'm glad to be included and to feel useful in a time of crisis.

"I should go," Henry pushes to his feet after the silence

between us stretches on a little too long to be considered comfortable. "Thanks again for keeping an eye on him."

I walk him back over to the door and we exchange numbers in case of emergency, and he waves almost jauntily at me before he starts descending the stairs, practically jogging down them and forgoing the elevator. After I close the door in his wake, I head towards my bedroom, determined to get changed into my gym attire -loose basketball shorts and a breathable tank top- and hit the gym for a light workout.

I find the weights and stationary bike do very little to prevent my thoughts from drifting back downstairs.

Chapter Five – Connor

After fighting with Ant upon my return home, I cra—*fall* into bed and sleep fitfully for a few hours. I haven't eaten since yesterday, but I'm not hungry. My entire life feels like it has imploded. I'm untethered and feeling numb.

Daisy's gone. She's gone and she's never coming back.

There's a stabbing pain in my chest every time I think those words, but the tears refuse to flow. I highly doubt that I've cried myself dry. It must be the shock.

Is that even one of the stages of grief? I can't remember.

It's not like it matters. Nothing matters. Nothing is right anymore. It feels like nothing will ever be right again.

Henry drops by sometime in the afternoon and lets himself into the apartment with his emergency key. He finds me huddled in the middle of my bed and sits on the edge of the mattress, unspeaking. It's possible he doesn't know what to say and, honestly, I don't know if there's anything I want to hear right now. Just having him here with me helps.

"I've gotta change the locks," I blurt apropos of nothing.

"Because I let myself in? You gave me this key, dude." It's a crappy attempt at humour, but it does raise a small smile out of me, and I appreciate the hell out of Henry for trying.

"Ant..." I start, then sigh. "I'm kicking him out."

If my best friend is at all surprised, he doesn't show it. He doesn't give me any 'I told you so's, either, because he's awesome like that. Instead, he just smiles with understanding and asks, "Can I help you pack his stuff?"

This time I chuckle. It's a wet sound, but Henry looks incredibly pleased with himself. He springs back off the bed and wanders over to the built-in wardrobe, sliding the mirrored door open. He takes a step back and rubs his hands together with relish.

Realising that I need to step in before he takes pleasure in crumpling Ant's dry clean only suits, I groan and disentangle myself from my bundle of blankets. I'm still wearing my clothes from yesterday, but Henry says nothing about my dishevelled appearance or less than fresh scent. He just waits patiently after I advise him that I'm going to go grab some suitcases and garment bags, and I duck into the spare bedroom next to the master, going straight to the wardrobe.

It's only as I'm stepping back out of the room that it hits me. This won't be a guest room any more. This room, with its pale grey walls and slightly darker grey carpet, will be the baby's room. I find myself sinking to my knees just by the open doorway, trying to calm my breathing. Panic and grief threaten to overwhelm me all over again.

Daisy's gone. I made her a promise. I have a daughter.

I'm alone in this.

Ant freaked the fuck out when I told him this morning. As

far as he's concerned, I don't owe a dead woman any favours. It doesn't matter that the dead woman in question is my little sister. It doesn't matter that her baby is all I have left of her. That she's my own flesh and blood. To Anthony, the baby is an annoyance at best. He'd even suggested that putting her up for adoption would be kinder.

That was about the time I snapped.

Ant never saw it coming. We've argued, sure, but he's never seen me bereaved and backed into a corner. He's also never seen how protective I can be of my family.

And that's what the baby is. She's my family. Legally, she's my daughter now. Or she will be when the paperwork is finalised. Henry mentioned adoption at one point, but I'm honestly not sure how that all works. I'm sure he'll run me through it all again when my brain is more equipped to handle the information.

As badly as I wish things were different, that Daisy was still here and able to be the baby's mum, leaving me in my original role as Uncle Con, I'm not backing down from the promise I made. When the baby is old enough, I'll tell her that I'm biologically her uncle but, until then, I'm going to cowboy up and be the dad Daisy expected me to be. I owe both my girls that much at least.

So, the choice, when Ant laid it out for me, was simple. It was him or the baby.

I didn't even need to think about it.

But now I'm overcome by the daunting prospect that I'm a new father without a partner. I have to turn this room into a nursery. I have to get formula and nappies and prepare for a foreseeable future of sleepless nights and spit-up. I have to read as much information as possible about newborns and what to expect in the next few days, months, and years.

I have to think of a name.

God, I wish Daisy was here. I wish that she hadn't been a stubborn brat, determined to keep her name ideas to herself. I wish that I'd spent more time with her, learning the deeper hopes and dreams she had for her kid. I wish that I could tell her how beautiful her daughter is. I wish she'd never gotten into her car last night.

I wish. I wish. I wish.

"Hey, do you think Ant would have a coronary if we—*oh, Con.*" Henry's feet come into view, the shiny patent leather of his shoes a stark contrast against the soft grey carpet fibres. I feel his hands under my armpits as he tries to tug me to my feet. "Come on, get up. I'm not sitting my arse down on the floor next to you. We'll be civilised and have a breakdown on the couch."

I don't have any energy to argue, so I let him pull me up and nudge me out the door, down the short hallway and into the main living/dining area of the apartment. He pushes me gently towards the couch, a modern grey linen number Ant chose, with a low back and no headrests, and demands that I sit.

I flop down and sneer at the couch cushion beside me. "I hate this couch."

Henry nods, not even questioning the random statement as he sits beside me. "I've always thought you went more for aesthetics than comfort."

"Ant did," I grumble.

"Ah." My best friend sighs. "Well, you can always replace it. Maybe gift this to him in a gesture of good faith or something?" He frowns. "He's not going to try and come at you for half the flat, is he? I mean, you guys have lived together for over a year. De facto rules and all."

I shake my head. "Daze and my places are owned by the family trust. I don't own it directly. I..." I get all choked up, realizing that I'll have to sort out Daisy's apartment at some point. I'll have to let myself in. I'll have to clean out her fridge, her clothes, her toiletries.

I don't want to do that. I don't want to see the evidence that she just stepped out with every intention of coming home. I don't want to have to clean out her fridge knowing that she'll never eat the food she'd been craving. I don't want to have to go through her wardrobe to donate the clothes she was looking forward to wearing again once she recovered from her pregnancy. I don't want to take apart the nursery I helped her put together, even though I know I'm going to need all the things she's got ready and waiting in her flat. I don't want to rent the apartment out to people who aren't Daisy.

Without another word, Henry pulls me in for another hug. I cling to him and try to verbalise these thoughts I'm having, but it all comes out in a muddled mess. When I woke up earlier, I'd had the urge to call Daisy until the memories from last night washed over me. It's like a nightmare I can't wake up from. I feel lost and so unsure of where to go from here.

"Your mum's going to fly over and stay for a bit," my best friend's words cut through the building fog in my brain. "And me and Sez are only a phone call away. I wish you'd come stay with us-"

"No," my answer is as emphatic as it was when he suggested it in the hospital before he left for work. "No. Sez is heavily pregnant and the last thing either of you need right now is some depressed wanker in your space. And," I shake my head,

65

exhaling, "this is my home. I've got to get it ready to bring my nie—*daughter* home."

Henry pulls away from the hug, his lips thinning into a straight line as he thinks this over. Combined with my babbling about Daze's apartment, it's not a surprise when he says, "Fine. But you're going to give me your spare key to Daze's place and I'll go get the nursery essentials. I'd rather you not have to go through the pain of visiting her place so soon."

Once again, blessed relief runs through my veins. "Take my car," I tell him, "it'll fit more than yours." Just the idea of him trying to bring back a cot -even a dismantled one- in the back of his Mustang makes me smile a little.

He rolls his eyes. "Duh, Stark."

* * *

After making sure I eat, and watching me like a hawk as I do, Henry helps me pack as much of Ant's stuff up as possible and deposits it just inside the front door. He texts Ant from his own phone, telling him to collect his crap, then moves into another room to deal with the angry phone call that follows, sparing me the confrontation.

I feel a little like a child while he bears my burdens for me, but I don't quite have the energy to care.

When Henry eventually leaves, telling me he'll be back tomorrow morning with as much stuff from 'the other flat' (*Daisy's flat,* my brain fills in helpfully, despite his attempt to lessen the blow) as possible, I wander through my own flat listlessly. I know there are things I should be doing. I should be looking into funeral arrangements, researching baby names, tidying up one of the guest rooms for Mum to stay in when she arrives…but I have zero drive to do any of it.

In the end, I just sit on my uncomfortable sofa and stare unseeingly at the blank tv screen mounted on the wall. I have no idea how much time passes before there's a knock at the door. It's not brusque or aggressive, so I doubt it's Ant, whose keys are still sitting in the middle of the dining table. I'm briefly distracted by that realisation, wondering how he got to work, but then decide that I don't care. I also know that he keeps a spare set of keys in his office, so he'll just let himself in anyway.

The knock sounds again, a bit louder this time, and I force myself to get up and answer the door.

Will smiles softly at me when I swing it open. "Hey," he greets gently, "can I come in?"

I'm relieved that he doesn't open with some sort of benign question about how I'm doing. We mightn't have known each other long, or spoken much at all, but I think it's fair to say that, after last night, he knows me better than some friends I've had for twenty years. He was there with me through the worst moments of my life. That's bound to forge a stronger bond than almost anything else, right?

Wordlessly, I step aside and he crosses the threshold to my apartment, toeing off his shoes inside the doorway. He silently takes charge from there, taking hold of the door and shutting it quietly behind himself before gesturing towards the couch.

A smirk threatens to pull at my lips at that. Being invited to sit in my own home is certainly a new experience for me. Still, I go willingly, dropping back into the seat I'd only just vacated with a soft 'oof' when I bounce on the unforgiving cushion upon landing.

"Have you eaten?" Will asks, walking towards my kitchen like he owns it.

I blink and turn in my seat, craning my neck to stare after him. "Um, yeah," I answer, a bit dazed. "Henry was here a little while ago. He kind of force fed me."

Will nods and rifles through the glossy white cupboards, setting two matching mugs on the black granite countertop before filling the electric kettle and flicking the button to boil the water. "Tea okay?" he asks. "I'd make coffee but," he eyes my coffee machine warily, "I don't have a degree in rocket science."

"Tea's fine," I'm still thrown by this turn of events. "But you don't have to do that. I mean, this is my house, so-"

"Sit," he commands, not even turning around from where he's now rummaging through the pantry. How he knew I was already halfway out of my seat is beyond me. Does he have eyes in the back of his head?

Idly, I muse that Mum has that same skill. Is it a parent thing? Will I eventually learn it?

Stuck on these thoughts, I drop back down, barely resisting the urge to bark, 'Yes, sir' at him.

When he turns back around, he has two boxes of teabags in his hands, holding them up for my perusal. "Not gonna lie," he says, adorably sheepish, "I have *no* idea what the difference between these are. The station just stocks Lipton stuff and I only drink it when the coffee's more sludge than caffeine."

I actually do smile, albeit weakly, at that. "The English Breakfast is good, thanks," I tell him, gesturing towards the box in his right hand. "I drink it weak and milky with one sugar."

Will nods. "I can't stand tea without sugar," he agrees. "I'll take a good quality coffee black and unsweetened, but tea?" He shudders dramatically. "No thanks." He starts puttering around my little kitchen again, putting the tea boxes back where he found them and dropping a bag of English Breakfast into each mug. "Y'know, I've been here about a decade now, and I *never* drank tea back home. But it seems to be more of a thing here."

God, I appreciate this random small talk more than he could possibly know.

Or maybe he does know.

Either way, I grab onto the sense of normalcy with gusto. "Aren't you Americans big on iced tea? Like, sweet iced tea?"

"In some places," he bobs his head, heading to the fridge and pulling out my two litre bottle of milk, checking the expiry date before he sets it on the counter next to the mugs. "It's more a Southern thing, but…yeah." He shrugs. "I was never all that into it. Give me coffee any day of the week."

"I do prefer coffee to tea," I admit.

Will's handsome face falls and he hesitates as he holds the kettle over the first mug. "I can-"

"No, no, I still drink tea. And," I look towards the window, sighing as I note that the sun is setting, "drinking coffee now will probably keep me up all night. Not a practice I need to get into. Well, not until the baby's here."

I could slap myself as those final words leave my mouth. The grief hits me all over again, the distraction from my current situation having dissipated. But, curiously, there's also the slightest flutter of anticipation now, too.

Will hums his acknowledgement of my statement, pouring a generous amount of milk into the barely steeped teas. "You might get lucky. She might sleep like a champ." He chuckles wryly. "My boys didn't, but you never know."

He puts the milk away, then grabs the canister of sugar from next to the kettle and spoons a slightly heaped teaspoon of the little white granules into each mug, stirring one and then the other, before picking them both up and bringing them over to the couch.

He sets one in front of me, and then he puts the other next to it, taking the much more comfortable armchair to my left.

It wasn't that long ago when Daisy sat in that same chair for her baby shower, surrounded by friends and gifts. I can still picture her clear as day.

Suddenly needing yet another distraction from my thoughts, I thank him and pick up my mug for want of something to do, sipping at the weak beverage he's made me. Something inside me loosens after a couple of little mouthfuls, but I don't know if it's the soothing qualities of the tea, or the fact that Will isn't pushing me to talk. He's just *here*, and somehow, even though we were barely more than strangers yesterday, it's comforting.

"So," he says after nursing his own mug for a little while. His expression is a little pained, like he knows any topic he wants to bring up right now is likely littered with conversational landmines. But he forges ahead, meeting my gaze with his steady, grey-blue stare. "Has the hospital been in touch about sending the little one home?" He peers curiously over my shoulder towards the hallway. "I'm guessin' you don't have a room all set up yet. Can I help with that?"

Shaking my head, I answer, "Not yet. It'll be a couple of days. Henry's making sure all the paperwork's in order and that the official adoption process is getting started, so that should help." Running my finger around the rim of my cup, I sigh. "He's also getting the cot and stuff from…" A lump lodges itself in my throat, caught around my sister's name.

Will leans over from his seat and squeezes my knee. "He came to see me earlier, actually. Asked me to check up on you, as if I wasn't already planning to." I almost give myself whiplash with how quickly I snap my eyes back up to meet his. Henry's behaviour isn't a surprise, but Will's almost teasing confession has my full attention. "He's a good friend. And," another grimace twists his face as he tilts his head towards the pile of suitcases and garment bags by the door, "I'm sorry to hear about Anthony."

Unexpectedly, a snort escapes me. "No, you're not."

Even if we've never actually spoken about my relationship before now, Will's disdain for Ant wasn't something he ever disguised. Not even in passing.

"No," he agrees, a little smirk playing on his lips now, "I'm not. Not about him, anyway. But I am sorry that you've got that to deal with, on top of everything else."

My heart flips at the sincere empathy in his tone. "Better now than later, I guess," I sigh. It comes out shaky as another wave of grief hits me out of nowhere. I screw my eyes shut, inhale as deeply as possible, and then breathe out a long stream of air. "Fuck," I mutter on the tail end of the extended exhalation.

When I reopen my eyes, Will is staring at me with understanding and concern. "What can I do?" he asks.

I'm relieved that he doesn't try to tell me that things will get better with time. That he doesn't try to get me to let it all out, or talk, or start thinking about the silver lining - the beautiful little girl I'll be bringing home. But I'm also frustrated because there's nothing he can do. Nothing anyone can do.

It's on the tip of my tongue to bitterly demand that he builds me a time machine, or something equally irrational, but I bite it back. None of this is his fault. If anything, he has gone above and beyond the kind of help and support I might expect from my friends, let alone just a neighbour.

So I just shake my head in the negative. "You've done so much already," I eventually respond, then I frown. "Don't you have work?"

"I've got a few days off." Will lifts and drops his shoulders, tilting his head to the left. "I've just come off a run of double shifts."

Usually, I might comment about how busy and stressful I imagine that could be but, having had first-hand experience with his job now, I really don't want to think about it at all. Instead, I decide that helping little old ladies pull kitties out of trees is the extent of what he does for work.

With strained silence descending, Will picks up his mug and takes it over to the kitchen, washing it manually in the sink before placing it upside down in the dish drainer. "Well," he declares, slowly making his way back past me and towards the door, "I'm going to get out of your hair for now. But my number's in your phone -I programmed it last night- and you know where I live if you need anything." He stops and makes a face at the pile of Ant's things. "If he gives you any trouble, just shout out, okay?"

I'm touched by the sentiment, even if it's unnecessary. "Thanks. I will."

"Good." Will swings the door open and takes a step over the threshold. "I'll swing by again tomorrow. I'll bring lunch."

He shuts the door before I can turn the offer down or tell him that I'll be fine. Which, really, is probably a good thing, because I like him too much to lie to him.

Chapter Six – Will

When I return to Connor's apartment as promised, I'm glad to see that the suitcases and garment bags he'd set aside for his ex are gone. I didn't hear any yelling last night, so I can only assume that the hand-off was a restrained one, if not civil. I'd like to pry, but that's definitely in bad taste, so I keep my questions to myself.

Instead, Connor tiredly tells me to follow him down the hallway that mirrors the layout of my apartment and into the room nearest to the master bedroom. There I find Henry, dressed down in jeans and a pale-yellow polo shirt, sprawled across the carpet amongst the detritus of what should be a crib. There are indentations in the carpet from where a larger bed once sat, and I wonder when they removed it.

"This was easier to do when I had instructions," Henry grumbles when he catches sight of my amused expression. He throws a playfully dark look over at Connor. "And he's no help."

"Let's be honest, building shit was never my forte," Connor

shrugs.

He's looking better than he did yesterday. He's still got dark circles under his eyes, and sadness still seems to radiate from him, but at least there's a bit more colour to his cheeks and spark to his hazel gaze.

"Oh, I remember," Henry teases, lifting what appears to be one of the end pieces and squinting at it, "you failed woodwork in Grade Ten."

"Useless fucking subject that it was," Connor huffs dramatically. "At least that finally convinced Dad to let me take drama instead for eleven and twelve."

It's cute the way they reminisce about high school when they must have graduated something like fifteen or twenty years ago. It just speaks of the history they share, the foundation of their friendship running deep.

"Here," I step in, taking the screwdriver and allen key from Henry and dropping to the carpeted floor beside him. "It's been a while, but I built two of these a couple of times over," I explain, grimacing at the number of times Jen and I moved house in those early days. "So, let's see if I can't help."

It takes close to twenty minutes, but with Henry following my directions, passing me screws and holding the sides of the crib in place, we cheer ourselves once we're done. The crib itself is sturdy, painted glossy white and with rolled edges on either end in a sleigh style. It suits the décor here in Connor's apartment, which shouldn't surprise me, considering I know that he was the one who originally bought the thing. I feel a pang of curiosity, wondering if Daisy's apartment is anything like his, and whether he helped to decorate it, but to ask those questions out loud right now would be a mistake.

Instead, I grab the crib mattress, which was resting against the wall, and lift it over the side of the crib, slotting it into place easily. Henry steps in with a fitted sheet and wrestles it over the mattress while I stand back and turn to Connor. "Are we building anything else today?"

I imagine that there's a matching change table and chest of drawers to accompany this crib, but Connor shakes his head. "The rest is still at, uh…" His face falls. My heart aches. It has been doing a lot of that recently.

Clearing my throat, I give a quick nod of comprehension. "Right. Well, when -*if*- you need help with that, just…" I puff out my cheeks and expel a breath of air, finishing lamely, "let me know."

His smile is strained, but he nods. "Yeah, thanks. I will."

"No," Henry cuts in, dispersing the tension as he gestures at me, "*he's* Will."

Connor groans and facepalms at the awful joke, while I chuckle. "I've *never* heard that one before," I say with a liberal dose of sarcasm.

Henry's grin is unrepentant. "I could call you William?" I screw up my nose and shake my head. "Billy?"

I take the bait and point my index finger at him menacingly. "Don't you dare."

Our banter has the desired effect of making Connor chuckle, and we share an appraising glance and nod at each other before Henry dusts off his hands and declares that he has to leave. He knocks his fist against mine by way of goodbye, and pulls Connor in for a hug.

"We'll get you a car seat first thing tomorrow, then head over to the hospital, okay?" Henry asks as they separate.

"Or I can get a car seat?" I blurt before my brain can catch up with the offer leaving my mouth. Both men turn to look at me with raised eyebrows and I bring my hand up to rub the back of my neck, feeling a bit sheepish. "I mean, if it'll make things smoother for tomorrow? I guess the little miss is being discharged?"

Connor takes a steadying breath and nods. "Yeah. She's coming home tomorrow." He sounds terrified. I don't blame him. Been there, done that. I think I'm still somewhat traumatised by the whole newborn experience.

"She still needs a name," Henry knocks his shoulder into Connor's playfully. "I hear Henrietta's a great choice."

"That's a no from me," Connor scoffs, but he's chuckling again, which was most certainly Henry's intention.

Henry's expression turns wicked, much like Jack's before he's about to say something teasing, and he doesn't disappoint. "Wilhelmina?"

Connor snorts and shoves him. "Weren't you leaving?"

"Come on," Henry doubles down, even as he backs out of the room, "you could call her Mina! It's adorable."

"Get out," Connor laughs. It's a wonderful sound, even though we all know his momentary burst of joy will be short-lived.

Henry checks his watch and then agrees, "Yeah, I'd better." He looks at me. "So, you're on car seat duty?"

"If Con's okay with that."

Without glancing at his best friend, Henry declares, "He is. Thanks." Now he looks at Connor. "I'll be here at nine tomorrow. Your homework is to pick a name. I'm not bringing my Goddaughter home nameless." And, with that, he turns on his heel and walks down the short hallway and out of sight. We hear the front door close a few moments later.

"You don't have to-" Connor starts, but I cut him off.

76

"I want to. It's been a while since I've gone looking at cute baby stuff. It could be fun."

Surprise dances across his handsome face. "Really?"

"What?" I challenge, but my tone is light and teasing.

"You just don't strike me as the type to get gushy about baby clothes and stuff," he admits honestly. His gaze rakes over me. "The whole big, macho firefighter type seems incongruous with tiny booties and pink onesies."

I 'tsk' at him and waggle my index finger in admonishment, but I know I'm smiling. "Now, Mister Stark, stereotyping doesn't become you."

He blushes and it's such an adorable look on him that I have to catch myself before I swoop forward to hug him or, worse, claim a kiss from his beautiful pouty lips.

To correct myself, I force a shrug and smile, leaning against the wall as I explain, "Jen and I dressed the boys in a lot of hand-me-downs and Goodwill finds in those early days. Then, by the time we could afford to spoil them a bit, they were older and had developed their own tastes. Neither has kids of their own yet, so outside of buying the odd gifts for friends' kids -or for Jen's girls when they were small- I haven't really had a reason to do any baby shopping. So, this is a novel experience for me."

Connor gestures with his head for me to follow him out of the room, asking, "So, you're close with your ex?"

Am I reading too much into the fact that he's chosen to ask about Jen first?

I consider my answer as I follow him into the kitchen. "She's still one of my best friends," I eventually tell him, taking a seat at the kitchen table where I can watch him puttering about as he grabs two mugs and flips a switch on the too-fancy-for-me-to-operate coffee machine. "Which I still can't believe, considering..."

"Considering what?" he prods, and his tone is definitely forcibly nonchalant. But what does that mean? Is he just curious? Is he interested in me? I might be nearing fifty (*ugh*) but right now I feel as uncertain about how to proceed as I did in those first few interactions with other queer men once I was officially out.

Sighing, I look down at the polished surface of the table where I'm drawing invisible circles with my index finger. "Considering she was my high school beard and the day she told me she was pregnant, I told her I was gay."

A clatter of metal and ceramic on granite countertop prompts me to look up. Connor's scrambling to set the mugs and spoons to rights, but his eyes are wide as he stares back at me. "*What?*" he chokes out.

Leaning back in my seat, I shake my head. "Not my finest moment, I'll admit it-"

"No, no," Connor interrupts. He's still holding a teaspoon, and he waves it around wildly in the air between us. "I just...I thought..." His cheeks are back to being that deep red colour that I'm really coming to enjoy seeing on him. He's cute when he's flustered.

Then his words register in my brain, and my own eyes widen before I laugh loudly. "Come on, really? You thought I was...what? Straight? *How?*" For fuck's sake, I've spent weeks flirting with him, despite my better judgement. I'm only human after all.

"I...I mean...you have kids, and an ex-girlfriend and..." Once again, he motions from my feet to the top of my head and then down again. "Big, macho firefighter type," he finishes lamely.

"Because a big, macho firefighter type can't be into men?" I can't help how amused I sound, folding my arms and raising both eyebrows at him. "Connor, *really*?"

He closes his eyes with obvious embarrassment. "Yeah, I know, I just heard myself." When he opens them again, he bites his lip and looks down at the empty mugs. "I just wasn't expecting that. I hoped maybe you might have been curious at best, but…" He stops short, then glances back up at me like a deer in headlights. "Shit. Sorry. Thinking out loud."

Well now, even though the words were innocuous enough, his renewed embarrassment is telling. Connor *is* interested in me.

But do I really want to act on that knowledge when he's at his most vulnerable?

No.

So, despite wanting nothing more than to get up and claim his mouth with my own, I just wave off the apology. "Nah," I dismiss casually, "I get it. I'm out and proud, but I guess I don't advertise it." I don't mention all the (clearly failed) flirting I've been doing, partially to ease my bruised ego and partially because I know he needs a friend more than a fling right now.

Connor sighs ruefully. "Anyway," he shuffles back over to the coffee machine, fiddling with handles and settings as he asks, "you were saying…you find out you're going to be a dad and you tell the poor girl you're gay?"

Now it's my turn to feel rueful again. I scratch idly at my bearded jaw and nod, even though he's got his back to me. "I panicked. I was eighteen and had plans to head off to college where I could be myself, you know? Having a baby wasn't in that plan." I wince as I say the words, because he's going through something similar right now, too.

Connor doesn't flinch, though. He just presses a button which makes the machine spring to life, and the space is filled with the sound of the first mug filling with delicious smelling coffee.

"And she didn't kick your arse?" he asks when it's done, then reaches for mug number two.

"She cried a hell of a lot harder for a few minutes," I reminisce, feeling that old pang of guilt somewhere deep in my gut. "But after the shock passed, she was my biggest supporter." Fondness creeps into my voice as I finish out the Cliff's Notes version of my life story. "We told our parents everything together. She defended me against my dad when that went to shit, and her parents let me move in with them while we worked out a plan for our immediate future."

I think back on those bittersweet memories with warmth. To this day, I think of Jen's parents as my own. Even though I was the asshole who knocked up their eighteen-year-old daughter and then refused to marry her, they stood by me the same way Jen did. Their support and assistance saw us get a little place of our own with enough space for us to each have our own bedroom while the boys shared the room in between. It was Jen's mom's connections that landed me a spot with the local fire department, and her parents were always offering us free babysitting and home cooked meals.

"Ultimately, I'm so thankful for Jen," I continue to explain once Connor and I are both settled at the table nursing our mugs of steaming caffeinated goodness. "She's had my back almost our whole lives. Even when I finally moved into my own place, we still lived in each other's pockets until I moved here."

"What prompted that?" he asks me, his head cocked to the

side.

That's a complicated question, but I settle on the summary. "My mom died." I hold up my hand as he goes to instinctively offer his condolences. "Dad went a few years before her, and I hadn't spoken to him since the night he disowned me anyway. Growin' up in that house was rough. I was resentful. Bitter. I didn't mourn him, and my feelings about Mom were complicated. But she left me and the boys everything. The house, the cars, their life savings. All of it. The boys were finishing high school, and I asked them what they wanted to do with it all."

Now I smile, because I remember Jack's demands that we take the cash to Vegas, and Wes's eye roll and argument that they weren't twenty-one yet, so it would be a boring ass trip for them.

"Eventually, Wes said that he wanted to study overseas, and Jack wanted to be a firefighter like me but didn't care where, so we looked into all our options and Australia won out." Jack's delight that eighteen-year-olds can legally gamble and drink here prompted yet another discussion that we were not gambling their inheritance away. "We applied for permanent residency visas and, to cut a long story short, eventually went for citizenship when we were legally able to." Studying for that test was intense, and I'm pretty sure I know more about Australia than most of the people born here.

"Wow," Connor's voice is breathy and incredulous. "I think that's really cool; you uprooting your life for them like that."

"That's parenthood." The flippant response tumbles from my mouth thoughtlessly. Once again I'm concerned that maybe I'll trigger him somehow, but he just makes a soft little sound of concession and tilts his head in acknowledgement.

"True. But not all dads are as dedicated as you."

"Yeah, well," I joke, "I'm relying on my pair to put me up in a top-notch retirement home when the time comes."

Connor laughs, and we move the conversation on to lighter topics before I glance at the time. "So, how about that baby shopping, huh?"

And just like that, the mood is sombre again.

Chapter Seven — Connor

Dizziness threatens to overwhelm me after I wave Will off at the door. As promised, we hit up *Baby Bunting* for a new car seat and had it fitted in the back of my Rav. Will led me through the store while we waited, pointing out all the toys and gadgets that apparently didn't exist thirty years ago.

It was sweet watching him. Sweet and hot. God help me, but there's something about a hyper masculine man turning into a teddy bear around baby things that really gets my engines running. I don't know if I've always been this way, or if it's something I've come to find more attractive since meeting Ant because it's the antithesis of his entire personality, or even some combination of both. But watching Will tenderly picking up stuffed toys or running his fingers ever so carefully over the soft material of a sherpa-lined baby blanket with a faraway look in his eyes made my heart thump and my jeans grow tight.

Because I should definitely be fixating even more on my hot neighbour right now, I scold myself sarcastically. *It's not like there are other pressing issues going on.*

The dizziness washes over me again.

By this time tomorrow, I'll have a newborn to look after. I'm terrified. I love kids, but I'd resigned myself to the idea that I would never have them. I was okay with that. I was going to be fun Uncle Con, and that would have suited me just fine.

But I'm a dad now, and I'm already failing at that.

I haven't been back to the hospital to visit her. My kid. My daughter. What kind of dad doesn't want to spend as much time as possible with their new baby?

Me, that's who.

It's not that I don't love her. I do. I adore her. I've already memorised her tiny ski-dip nose, turned up just a little at the end, and the curve of her chubby baby cheeks. When I close my eyes, I can picture the exact shade of her dark hair, the way the wispy ends curled out from under her beanie. I know the shape of her long fingers and the dark blue of her eyes. However, I've been frozen with grief and fear.

I'm terrified of how badly I'm going to fuck this all up.

I can't even decide on a name.

All of Henry's joking aside, I know I do want to honour at least one person when I name her.

Daisy.

God, even just thinking her name makes me teary. I can't name her daughter -*my* daughter now- after her. I'll never be able to say it out loud without breaking down.

But she deserves her mother's name, and Daisy deserves to have her legacy carried on somehow.

So Daisy can be her middle name. Maybe with time, it will hurt less for me to think. To say.

But that still leaves her without a first name. Henry's right: I can't bring her home without knowing her name.

I start a list in my head of names I like, but none of them seem right. I feel this overwhelming pressure to do right by Daisy, to pick a name she would have chosen herself. To decide on something I could imagine her voice cooing to her newborn daughter.

I close my eyes and think of those perfect little features, so much like Daisy's. So much like Dad's.

And then it hits me.

My eyes fly open and I *know*.

There was only ever one logical choice.

"Victoria," I whisper into the silence of my apartment. The name seems to echo around the space anyway, and a strange energy buzzes under my skin. My lips pull into a genuine smile. "Vicky."

Victoria Daisy Stark.

It's *perfect*.

* * *

Henry's eyes turn watery when I introduce him to my daughter. At his side, Sarah's expression is equally poignant.

"Oh, *Con*," she sniffles, her pretty face, rounded and glowing with the final trimester of her pregnancy, somehow both lighting up and crumpling at the same time. "Your dad would be honoured. So would Daze."

I nod, holding the wriggling bundle slightly closer to my chest. She's warm, solid, and smells like new life and baby powder. Sweet and pure. "Yeah," I reply, choked up myself. "I think they would."

Victor Stark, my father, loved his kids. Neither one of us ever had any doubt about that. He would be over the moon to have his first grandchild as his namesake. I'm an atheist and I honestly don't believe that there's an afterlife but, in this moment, I like to think that, if I'm wrong, Dad and Daze are proud of my choice.

Sarah's fingers twitch at her sides, making little grabby motions that draw a watery chuckle out of me. "Wanna hold her?" I ask knowingly.

I've been snuggling Vicky ever since the nurse placed her in my arms. I've been given a cr—*whirlwind* course on changing, feeding, burping, and bathing. I figure Google will help me with the details I don't remember, and I've surprised even myself with how besotted I am with my daughter.

It's getting easier to think of her as mine, too. Knowing that Daisy wanted it that way helps.

Sarah tucks errant strands of her blonde hair behind her ears and smiles shyly at me. "I couldn't possibly-"

"Don't be a dick, Sez," I scoff, stepping forward into her personal space, careful of her belly. I transfer Vicky into her arms with utmost caution. "I'm going to have her, like, ninety-nine percent of the time. I can share right now."

My words are lost on my friend, though. All of her attention is zeroed in on the baby in her arms. She's smiling and cooing and looking absolutely radiant…and it's like a punch to the solar plexus when I realize that Daze would have looked just like that. Transposing Daisy's features over Sarah's in my mind, I can almost see it perfectly.

My breathing hitches and my eyes water.

God, I miss my sister.

"Wow," Henry almost exhales the word as he watches his

wife, and it brings me back to the moment proper.

Now I try to see it through his eyes, and I imagine it's a powerful image for him, too. In only a few short weeks, Sarah will be cradling *their* baby in her arms, gently rocking and murmuring sweet nothings to him. Knowing my best friend the way I do, this is making his impending fatherhood feel all the more real.

"Who'd have thought I'd beat you to it?" I tease him lightly. The mood in the bright hospital room is far too tense and serious for me to handle, so going back to our usual dynamic is comforting.

Henry snorts. "Yeah, man. The last person I thought would end up as a surprise daddy was you. Aren't gay men immune to that?"

Despite the momentary pang caused by the knowledge of how it happened, I roll my eyes and punch his bicep. "Wanker," I accuse him, but there's no heat in it.

I know that he says stuff like that purely to get a rise out of me, and not because he's at all homophobic or ignorant. I mean, Henry fights social injustice a hell of a lot harder than I ever have.

No: Henry just stirs shit because he's my best friend and that's part of the job description.

He grins at me. "You love me, Stark. Admit it."

"Oh, go back to panicking about this being your reality in a few weeks," I taunt back, gesturing to his wife and my daughter.

Henry's lips curl with amusement. "I wasn't *panicking*." He turns his attention back to his wife and his expression softens out.

This time my heart squeezes painfully for a different reason.

Has anyone ever looked at me like that? Like I'm their entire world? It sucks to say that Ant never did. And now…well, I don't know many men who would be interested in an emotional wreck of a man bringing along a newborn to boot. I mean, the newborn on its own is probably a cockblock, even though I won't ever regret having her in my life.

So, yeah, maybe my heart is breaking a little for the future I can't foresee having, too. It's the first time I've really thought of how these changes are going to impact me personally, without thinking about Daisy.

Yes, my troubles with Ant came to a head over this whole situation, but I'm not delusional enough to think that he was going to be my Happily Ever After. Our relationship was showing cracks long before this happened, and I can only feel relief that it's over. If that's not a sign that I'm better off alone than with Ant, I don't know what is.

Still, I don't *want* to be alone, romantically speaking.

Without conscious effort, my thoughts drift to Will. He's hot. He's got his shit together. He's sweet, and kind, and -perhaps most importantly- gay. He's kind of absolutely perfect, and I let myself daydream that he might be interested in me for just a moment. Just one moment. Then I shake my head and silently berate myself.

I *just* broke up with my boyfriend.

My sister just died.

I just became a dad.

I am a hot mess. It wouldn't be fair on me or on Will if I tried to throw myself at him right now. I've never been the kind of guy to want a fling, and now that I've got Vicky to think about, I need to make it very clear to anyone I date that we're a package deal. An instant family. That's too deep and too serious for a lot of people. And Will? The guy has been there and done that. He's raised two kids to adulthood and is now footloose and fancy free. I can't imagine him being interested in stepping up to play stepdad to my kid.

And *wow*.

That escalated quickly.

See what I mean about being a hot mess? I went from 'Will is hot' to 'I want him to raise my baby with me' in a span of seconds.

That's insanity. I barely know the guy, no matter how close I feel we've gotten over the past few days.

Trauma will do that, though, won't it? It's a connecting force. But I'm more than aware that my silver fox firefighter had his own life before I came stumbling into it, and he could do a lot better than me, anyway.

"Oh, that's the cutest thing I've ever seen," Sarah declares in a higher pitch than normal, scrunching up her nose and shaking her head down at Vicky, whose own face is stretched out in a huge yawn, the tiniest little squeaking sound accompanying the movement. "Oh, big yawns!" Sez continues to croon.

My heart feels like it is suddenly overflowing with affection. Because, yeah, that was pretty damn cute.

"Okay, Daddy," one of the doctors from the Special Care Nursery appears in the doorway of the room we've been waiting in, a wad of what I assume are discharge papers in hand. "Everything looks good to go. Queensland Health will be in touch to arrange a home visit in a few days' time, which is standard procedure for all new babies. The nurse will take some measurements, do a weigh in, check in on how you're faring – all standard stuff."

I nod, remembering Daisy saying something to that effect

after one of her prenatal classes.

Henry nudges me to get my attention. His expression is serious. "Because we've also started the official adoption process, you might be subject to more than one home visit. Not sure if Queensland Health nurses are involved in that, or if it's just social services, but be prepared for that, too."

"Sure," I agree, not overly concerned. I've got nothing to hide and my daughter's best interests at heart.

After confirming that I don't have any further questions, we're finally free to go. Sarah hands the baby over to me, and I carefully set her in the pram -a fancy thing with a bassinet that adapts to a seat as the baby grows, convertible so that I can also change the direction she's facing- and clip her in, tucking a soft blanket around her to keep her tiny body warm. Henry grabs the nappy bag which I put together before leaving the house this morning, and we start our slow meander back down the hospital hallways and towards the exit.

The moment we step into the bright sunlight outside is surreal in an unexpected way. I'd never imagined it would be me walking this baby outside for the first time. I'd never imagined that Daisy wouldn't be in the picture. I never imagined that I'd be a dad before my best friend, or that I'd be going it alone.

But here we are.

I take a deep, fortifying breath and smile down at the little one, who is thankfully shaded by the collapsible sun visor hood-thing over her bassinet. "Alright, Lady Victoria," I murmur softly, "welcome to the world. Let's go home."

* * *

My phone pings with a text notification in the late afternoon. It's from Will. The corners of my mouth turn upwards as I read it.

'How'd the homecoming expedition go?'

I think about how strange it felt to strap Vicky into her car seat. How tiny she looked in it. How suddenly nervous I was about driving. How I refused to think about Daisy's last drive and how that had ended, and how concerned I was that I hadn't tightened the baby's harness enough, or perhaps tightened it too much.

I think about how listless and adrift I felt after Sarah and Henry finally stopped fussing and left a couple of hours ago. How my apartment suddenly felt equal parts too big and too small. How I realised that I don't know how to entertain a baby, or whether it's neglectful to walk away when she's fast asleep in her cot. (Google assures me that it's not, by the way, even if I do feel like I should have an eye on her all the time.)

I think about how, when she woke up crying and pulled me from my book in a disorienting haze, it took me a few moments to understand what that sound even was. I consider my fumbled attempts to change her wet nappy and to get her to take to her bottle, or the fear I had afterwards when I didn't know how hard to pat her back to make her burp.

But then I remember the solid weight of her in my arms. Her sweet baby scent. The unfocused gaze as she started to look around, seemingly taking in the mess of different colours around her. Her tiny baby snuffles. Her strange little squeaky sounds.

'It went well.' I text back simply. Then, after only a moment of hesitation, I add, *'You can come meet her if you'd like? I can do dinner.'*

It's a selfish request. One I'm certain is motivated in part by my earlier crazed thoughts about throwing myself at him, wanting more from him than he could possibly be interested in. But he has become a friend through all of this mess, and he only lives upstairs. Surely it's not too much of an imposition if I invite him over for dinner?

'I'll be down in an hour.' Will's reply is accompanied by a smiley faced emoji and it sets my scrambled thoughts at ease.

I've only just redressed Vicky after another change when Will's knock sounds out. I hold her snugly against my chest as I pad across the apartment, opening the door with a smile.

"Hey," I greet him, stepping back to allow him space, "come on in."

Will smiles back at me and then his expression turns positively gooey as his eyes light on Vicky. "Oh," he breathes, reaching towards her and then pulling his hand back. "You forget how small they are when they're fresh."

A vague sound of agreement makes its way out of my throat. I haven't really had any experience with kids before now, so I have to take his word for it. "You wanna hold her?"

Those steely blue eyes widen. "Are you sure? I don't want to impose."

I nod, already carefully repositioning Vicky from my chest to the crook of my right arm, making sure her neck is supported the entire time. "Are all your vaccinations up to date? Whooping cough? MMR?"

He nods, his soft gaze glued to Vicky's petite features. "Yeah. It's a good idea with work, you know?"

That settles it for me, so I extend the baby out towards his large palms, and he accepts the transfer expertly. This is a man who has definitely done his fair share of baby wrangling, because there's no sign of hesitation or anxiety from him at all.

She's so tiny that she's almost engulfed by his hand alone, but he adjusts his hold and cradles her in those large, muscular arms, holding her close against his solid chest, and rocks gently from side to side in what has to be a practiced rhythm.

"Hey, sweet thing," he says to her in a voice so gentle and affectionate it almost takes me completely by surprise. "Did your daddy give you a name yet?"

I'm still not used to that honorific belonging to me. Will says it so easily, though, that I can't help but feel like it's starting to fit.

"Victoria," I answer his question. "Vicky."

He's still looking down on her, but he smiles wider. "A very pretty name."

"My, uh, my dad's name was Victor." I clear my throat. "He passed a few years ago. Cancer. It was sudden."

Now those eyes of his move up to find mine, but he doesn't offer commiserations. Instead, his expression turns understanding and compassionate. "That makes it even more special."

"Yeah," I agree, not knowing what else to say.

Will doesn't push for more conversation, either. He seems perfectly content just to cuddle my daughter, still swaying in place, murmuring sweet nothings at her.

I should not find it as hot as I do.

What is it about seeing otherwise tough men turning into teddy bears that does it for me, anyway? Is it the juxtaposition? Is it the silent, subtle confidence? The 'no fucks given' vibe? Is it the fact that genuine sweetness just pulls at the needy, emotional parts of me that I try to keep stifled?

Whatever it is, not only does the picture Will currently presents tug at my heartstrings, but it stirs less-than-innocent feelings below the belt as well.

And now I'm back to acknowledging that I'm a hot mess again.

Ugh.

"So," I decide to distract myself, forcing a smile that I know I can't quite make reach my eyes, "is lasagne okay for dinner?" It was one of the many, many meals currently in my fridge and freezer, and it called to me earlier. Is there any better comfort food than carbs, cheese and sauce? "I didn't cook it, but it looks good."

"Sounds great," Will answers quietly, but genuinely. He steps towards the couch and sits down, making a 'shh shh shh' sound as Vicky stirs and grizzles in protest. He pats her butt as he soothes her. "That's it, princess. We're just getting comfy." Then he looks up at me with a serious expression, those eyes of his practically piercing through me. "How's the first day been? And I mean really, Con. No bullshit."

I snort, then sigh, dropping into the seat beside him. Running the side of my index finger over Vicky's soft, tiny hand, I try to focus on how beautiful she is, rather than what her being here with me actually means. After a moment, I find my voice. "It was somehow both easier and harder than I thought it would be."

He nods, then moves Vicky to the crook of his other arm so he can reach out and squeeze my thigh. It's not a sexual touch, but it sends jolts of electricity through me anyway. Oblivious, Will says, "It *will* get better. I know right now things are raw, and there aren't any rules on how long you're allowed to grieve, but…" Trailing off, he looks down at Vicky. "I can't exactly speak from authority on this, seeing as I never lost anyone and I had someone to raise my boys with, but…ah, hell, I'm making a mess of this."

"No," I assure him, "you're not. I get it. And I appreciate it. I really do." I lean into his personal space so I can peer down at my daughter, trying to remain unaffected by the warmth his body radiates, or the spicy scent of his cologne. "I'm determined to make sure she knows how loved she is. How much Daze loved her." I still can't quite believe that Daisy's gone, but I don't say that. There's no point. A watery chuckle escapes me as I add, "Daisy would kick my arse if I spend too long moping over her not being here."

"I'm sure she'd understand…" he starts, but I shake my head.

"I owe it to her *and* to Vicky to not let it consume me." Yeah, there are going to be ups and downs. I remember the roller coaster of emotions that followed Dad's death vividly. But I made that baby a promise today. A promise I have no intention of breaking.

I can be stubborn that way.

A genuine smile threatens to pull up my lips at that thought. Stubbornness is genetic in my family. Dad was stubborn, so was Daisy. I glance back at Vicky and let the smile take over

You're going to be stubborn, too, aren't you, princess?

For the first time, when I look at her and see Daisy, there's no pain. Just amusement.

It's a start.

Chapter Eight – Will

❦

"You spent your entire week off with your neighbour, didn't you?" Jack greets me with a shit-eating grin, leaning against his locker as I walk in. He shakes his head when I don't deny it. "What am I gonna do with you, Will?"

"What?" I ask defensively, turning away from him to stuff my gym bag into my own locker. "Do you have any idea how scary it is to suddenly have to look after a newborn? Because I do. I'm still traumatised by a *certain someone's* allergy to sleep, and it's been almost thirty years."

He laughs lightly. "Wes always was a drama queen."

Snorting, I roll my eyes. "You were as bad as each other. Thankfully, Con only has the one to worry about, but that's enough. I mean, I had your mother. He has-"

"You." Jack interrupts my attempt to say 'no-one'. I turn back to face him and he raises both his dark eyebrows in challenge, his large tattooed arms folded across his chest. "Go on. Tell me I'm wrong."

"It's not the same," I deflect. "I was just helping out because I had the time. I mean, I live upstairs and he *just* lost his sister. But," I hold up my hand to forestall his protests, "his mom arrived a couple of days ago and took over." Just in time for the funeral, actually, but I keep that part to myself.

"Uh huh," my son still sounds unconvinced. "And you haven't been down to check on him since?"

"I'm just being a good friend. I'd like to hope that you'd have someone in your life to do the same if you were in his place."

Jack's eyes sparkle knowingly, but he doesn't call me on my flimsy reasoning. He pushes off his locker, swings his duffel bag over one shoulder, and claps me on the back as he passes. "Good luck with that, Dad."

I refuse to acknowledge that he's got a point.

I *am* only being a good friend.

I am.

I mean, so what if Connor is attractive? So what if we have a similar sense of humour? So what if I enjoy being someone he can rely on, or come to for help or support, or…my brain stalls.

Fuck.

Okay, so *maybe* I'm a little attached. Friends can be attached. I was there for one of the most traumatic moments of his life. That sort of thing bonds people together, doesn't it? It doesn't mean it has to be a romantic bond.

In fact, to chase after him now seems kind of predatory. He's vulnerable. I'm not the kind of man who takes advantage like that.

If I say that enough, I might actually believe it.

* * *

In a bid to convince myself that my infatuation with Connor is misguided, I pull out my phone after my shift and bring up the *Grindr* app. Before all this started, Jack was right about one thing: it's been too long since I dated, or even hooked up.

I start flicking through profiles of local men, refusing to feel guilty as I do.

What do I have to feel guilty for? I'm not in a relationship with anyone. Certainly not with Connor. We're friends. Just friends. I'm doing this to prove as much.

Flopping down on my couch, I chat with a couple of guys who have reached out in interest. One guy is a little older than me, according to his profile. Tall and lean with reddish hair on its way to grey, his photo is handsome enough, but I'm just not into it. So, I brush off his flirtatious suggestion that we meet for a drink. The other man is in his early forties (once again, that's if his profile is to be believed), blonde, blue-eyed, and every inch the Gold Coast surfer type. He has weathered, tanned skin and a smattering of freckles over his hairless chest. The name on his profile reads 'Toby' and he didn't start our chat with a dick pic, so I'm feeling marginally interested at this point.

After a few minutes of back and forth, I find myself agreeing to meet him at a place down on James Street in about an hour's time. The walk is only about ten or so minutes from my apartment, so I shower, trim my stubble, run some product through my hair and dress in my good jeans (the ones that hug my ass just right) and a black t-shirt. Pocketing my wallet, phone, and keys, I give my apartment one last look over before I leave.

The little Mexican restaurant-come-bar is nestled in the middle of the little arcade on Burleigh's eclectic main drag of boutique shops, ice cream parlours, and other eateries. It's very kitsch, with timber tables, chairs, and walls, and brightly coloured woven table runners, seat cushions and tapestries on the wall. It's a tiny, cosy space, and I know the food here is good (despite not exactly being authentic) because I'm a regular.

One of the servers, a kid named Sophie who is still in high school, greets me brightly at the doorway where the 'wait here to be seated' sign is. She's clutching a leather-bound menu to her chest and grins at me, twin dimples appearing on her cheeks. Her dark hair is braided and hooked over her shoulder, and I can't help grinning back, buoyed by her bouncy attitude.

"Table for one?" she asks, and I shake my head.

"Not tonight."

"Oh," her smile turns wicked, "hot date?"

"You're too young to be talking about hot dates, missy," I tease her back.

She scoffs. "I'm seventeen. I've probably been on more hot dates this week than you have all year."

I clutch at imaginary pearls. "Oh, *burn*," I cry dramatically, dropping into the seat she's pulled out for me. "Didn't your parents teach you to respect your elders?"

"I'm an orphan," she deadpans.

I know for a fact that's not true. Her parents are my age and visit the restaurant almost as often as I do. They like to sit in one of the back tables and heckle her service. She pretends that they're embarrassing, but her adoration is obvious.

"Liar," I accuse, then lift my menu. I don't know why I bother; I've basically got the thing memorised. "Can I get a glass of sangria while I wait?" She jots it down and tucks the little notebook she carries into the pocket of her black pants.

As she turns to order my drink from the little bar, I call out after her, "And don't steal any sips on your way back!" She gives me the finger but doesn't turn around.

Laughter, deep and rich, sounds out from the other side of my table and I glance up from my perusal of the menu to come face to face with my *Grindr* date. "Making friends, I see," he says, and his voice is surprisingly deep, too.

He's handsome, I can't help but think. Certainly more attractive in person than his profile photo was, which is possibly a horrible thing to say, but it's not like I didn't think his photo was hot. He's one of those people who just seems warmer in person.

I push to my feet and step away from the table to say hi properly, leaning in and accepting a kiss to my cheek while planting one on his deeply tanned skin, too. After that, I pull out his chair for him, enjoying the surprise and gratitude on his face.

"What can I say," I flirt, tilting my head in Sophie's direction as I retake my seat, responding to his earlier words as well as my actions just now, "I'm a gentleman." I finish off with a wink.

He laughs and nods. "I can see that."

Sophie arrives with my drink and then greets Toby just as happily as she did me, asking him, "Your usual?"

"Please," he says, nodding. "Thanks, Soph."

Ah, so we're both regulars, then. That has the potential to make things awkward should we bump into each other here after tonight.

Even as I think it, I want to frown. It's almost like I've decided tonight will fail on principle. Well, I'll show myself, won't I?

Determined not to sabotage this date, I make a concerted effort to pile on the charm. I'm attentive, I ask him questions about his life, I make sure to look him in the eye and not talk over him, and I get the feeling he's impressed. Considering most guys I've met on the app just want to meet and fuck, it's nice to have met someone who appreciates wining and dining first. Maybe it's that we're both of a certain age? Who knows.

Through all of this, I learn that Toby is not just an avid surfer but also a teacher. He teaches primary school (or, as I call it, elementary school) physical education, and volunteers at the local animal shelter on weekends. Like me, he's a single dad, only his kid is ten and wasn't a surprise like my boys were.

"And your ex?" I ask, unable to help myself. Curiosity will definitely kill this particular cat one day. But if satisfaction is said to bring it back…

Toby smiles and swirls the remnants of his pint of pale ale, staring into the bottom of the glass. "I'm a widow, actually. He died three years ago now. Freak surfing accident."

Well, shit. That's one way to guarantee that tonight won't end with any kind of satisfaction. Bring up the dead ex. I cringe. "I'm so sorry."

He shakes his head, his shaggy blond hair falling into his face. He brushes it back with his right hand. "Don't be. That's life, right? You'd know that better than anyone. I'm guessing as a firie you see more than your fair share of tragedies most weeks."

I can't help thinking back to last week and Daisy's crash. It still feels raw in a way no other accident I've come across has. Because I'd met her? Because I've become close to Connor? Because I have come to absolutely adore her daughter in the whole week she's existed? None of these are appropriate

101

thoughts for a date or a hook-up, so I do my best to smother them.

Toby's still waiting for an answer, so I make a show of sipping my third glass of sangria contemplatively. "I do," I tell him, not wanting to bring the mood down any further, but not wanting to be dismissive or unsympathetic, "but that doesn't mean it's worth brushing off, either."

My date does a much more impressive job of rallying and bringing the humour back. "*Ooh*," he flirts, winking across the table, over our plate of half-decimated shared nachos, "that's *deep*, William."

"Will," I correct him, making a face.

He laughs, and there's something pleasant about the way the skin at the corners of his eyes crinkles. But even though he's handsome and charming, and despite the fact that we get along, I'm disheartened to realise that I like him in a platonic way and not a 'take him home and fuck him into the mattress' kind of way.

So much for proving myself wrong.

Nevertheless, I see the date through to the end. Additionally, despite my better judgement, when he asks me if I want to go back to his place, I agree.

I'm unsurprised to discover that he lives nearby, too. Not up on the hill like I do, but across the highway from the 'suburban' end of James Street, in a single-storey brick and tile house a few streets into the sprawl of suburbia. The speckled tan colour of the bricks dates it back to the 70s or 80s, but inside has been renovated somewhere in the last decade or so. It is bright and modern, with white walls, large white floor tiles, and an eclectic mixture of canvas prints and photo frames on display.

"Nice place," I tell him as he closes and locks the front door behind me. The entryway we're standing in leads to a large living room to our right, and the internal door that leads to the two-car garage is to our left. He leads me straight down the wide hallway which then opens up into a generous kitchen/dining/informal lounge area. The couch in here is more worn, the walls a little more scuffed, and there's a toy chest in the corner of the lounge space which appears to be overflowing. A Nintendo Switch is docked next to the large TV, and when I turn to survey the kitchen, I note that the fridge is covered in A4 pieces of paper all decorated with childish drawings of Pokémon and other random cartoon characters I've long since forgotten the names of.

I can't help but smile, all of a sudden nostalgic for when my boys were younger and my house looked the same way. "I like the Pikachu," I say, jutting my chin towards the bright yellow drawing in the middle of the fridge's left door.

Toby chuckles and grins. "She's obsessed right now. Everything is Pokémon themed. Her room looks like a Nintendo game exploded in there."

"My boys were the same," I assure him. Wes was the Pokémon fanatic. Jack was into superheroes and sports stars. That *hadn't* been as fun when they were sharing a room and quite literally had a line drawn down the middle.

"Oh, so they grow out of it?" He leans against the counter and offers me a beer.

I take it with a grin and a shake of my head. "They just find more adult ways to show it."

Even now, I know Wes has a collection of Pokémon themed t-shirts stashed in his closet behind his array of suits, and Jack's sports obsession has channelled into joining local teams and spending an exorbitant amount of money on tickets to games or, when it comes to more American sports like NFL, NHL, and baseball, expensive streaming services so he can watch the games whenever he chooses.

Toby sighs, but his expression is one I know well. Fond exasperation. "I can live with that," he says.

We continue chatting as we move over to the couch, and this is the part of a hook-up I'm always just a tiny bit awkward about. How to transition from 'yeah, we're getting along' to 'yeah, let's get it on'.

Thankfully, Toby seems to be happy to take the lead - whether because we're in his house, or because he's naturally more assertive, I don't particularly care- and he sets his half-empty beer on the coffee table in front of us. I follow suit, the tension in the air between us ramping up. I rub my palms on my thighs, and then Toby leans forward and presses his mouth to mine.

It's a nice kiss. He tastes like beer, and the scent of his aftershave is spicy and comforting. His lips are firm but pliant, and his tongue teases mine in a way that should curl my toes.

Should.

But it doesn't.

When he pulls away, I keep my eyes closed for a moment too long, not looking forward to the conversation I can feel is coming.

"That was..." Toby starts, and I sigh, already apologetic.

"Yeah." I clear my throat and force myself to meet his surprisingly understanding blue eyes. "Sorry. I..." I stop. I don't know what to say to explain the lack of spark between us. I know it's all on me. I know that some part of me is just refusing to get with the program, but I can't force it. Besides,

I don't really know Toby, so I'm not going to go unloading my issues on him.

He shakes his head, a rueful smile tugging at his lips. "Don't apologise. Sometimes there's no spark." He shrugs. "It happens."

I nod, equal parts relieved and grateful. "True."

After passing me my beer, Toby clinks the neck of his bottle against mine. "And, hey, dinner was great."

"*Ugh*," I lean my head back, still feeling irrationally guilty. "Trust me when I say this is a me issue. You're a great guy, I'm just…"

"Hung up on someone else?" he hazards an eerily accurate guess and I whip my head up and around to face him so quickly, I'm certain I've given myself whiplash. His white teeth shine back at me when he grins. "I'm great at reading people," he explains with a shrug. "And, even though you didn't touch it, I saw you glancing at your phone all night."

I don't fight the groan that escapes me as I scrub my palm over my face. "I'm sorry," I say again because I honestly am sorry. He's a perfectly nice guy. Age appropriate, handsome, kind, and witty. I'm annoyed that my subconscious refuses to get with the program.

"Stop it," he laughs. "It's fine. Really. We've all been there." He gives me a little nudge with his shoulder. "Did you want to talk about it?"

Oh, sure, because that's not pathetic. Why don't I whine all over my failed Grindr hook-up about another guy?

These thoughts must be written all over my face because Toby snorts and nudges me again. "Come on," he cajoles, "I'm here, my kid's at her grandparents' place, and if I can't walk away from tonight with a spectacular orgasm or two, I'd like to at least have made a new friend."

"At least you agree that they would have been spectacular," I sass back, relaxing as he laughs.

"Honey, look at us: there's no way it would have been anything else."

Buzzing from the alcohol, and eased by Toby's blasé attitude, I figure I have nothing left to lose now. I've already turned our planned hook-up into a platonic chat, so I might as well go for broke. So I settle back into the soft couch cushions and tell him all about my cute young neighbour and the mounting drama of the past week or so. Somewhere in the middle of my story, Toby grabbed us fresh beers, and I'm probably far more loose-lipped than I otherwise would be.

Once I'm done, he offers me a sympathetic smile. "Well, I'd say you've gotten yourself in pretty deep with this guy without realising it," he observes, stretching his arms over his head. The motion pulls his shirt up his abdomen, revealing a sliver of tanned abs that should have left me salivating, but I feel nothing below the belt.

"I know," I acknowledge, letting a hint of frustration enter my tone. "But the timing sucks. And he's too young for me. And did I mention the newborn? Or the fact that he's only been single for a week? Or, oh yeah, the *newborn*?"

Toby snorts again. "You mean the kid you're already arse over tit for? That newborn?"

"I'm not-"

"Dude, you waxed poetic about her for a good five minutes there. Five. I counted."

I sigh and hang my head. "I might have gotten a little attached."

Another snort.

I lift my head back up and glower at him. "It was an intense week, okay? And Con had little to no experience with kids, while I-"

"Raised two, yeah, I got that memo, too." Toby pushes up from the couch and heads around the back of it and into the kitchen. I turn in my seat so I can watch him pulling mugs from one of the overhead cupboards. "Coffee?" He asks, lifting one of them. I nod. He continues to potter around, grabbing pods for his coffee machine and filling the milk frother with the bottle from the fridge. He leans against the counter while he waits for the machine to churn out the first mugful of hot, caffeinated goodness. "So, obviously your intentions were never romantic, but this guy's gotten under your skin. The question is," he pauses for dramatic effect, arching light blond eyebrows at me, "what are you going to do about it?"

I shrug. "The plan was to sort of forget about him…" I explain, feeling a bit sheepish as I do. But Toby doesn't seem insulted that he was supposed to be a distraction or a plan B. He just nods.

"Well, that didn't work out too well for you," he states matter-of-factly.

Shaking my head, I agree, "Nope. It didn't. And I'm-"

"If you apologise again, I'm dumping this coffee over your head." Toby holds up the first of the two mugs, now filled with a steaming hot coffee which smells amazing. "And I don't make idle threats."

My hands are raised in surrender as I chuckle. "Okay, okay, I won't apologise again. Geez."

Toby brings the mug over to me and passes it over the back of the couch. I sip at it and sigh contentedly.

"So," he picks the conversation back up as he slides his own mug under the dual spouts of his coffee machine, "with that plan failing you, what's next? Because I'd suggest talking to him."

I scrunch up my nose. "I don't like that idea."

"Why not?"

"Uh, only *all* the reasons I mentioned before." I frown, then hold up one fist, releasing fingers one by one as I list them again. "The guy is grieving. He only just dumped his ex. He's got a baby taking up all his waking hours. He's vulnerable. I'm not going to prey on that."

Toby's coffee is done, so he grabs his mug and wanders back over, sitting beside me on the couch, shifting sideways to face me properly. Instinctively, I do the same. Toby holds up his own fist, his coffee safely held in the other hand. He starts offering counterarguments, lifting a finger the same way I did for each point he makes. "Grief is a process. It sounded like they were over long before they broke up. You're already attached to that kid, and he'll probably welcome the extra set of hands. Don't leap to conclusions. *Talk* to him."

He's ridiculously mature and I hate it. But he's right, so I tell him so, and by the time I leave to walk back to my place after exchanging numbers and promising to catch up again with my newfound friend, I'm almost convinced that talking to Connor is a great idea.

Almost.

Chapter Nine — Connor

Having Mum around for Daisy's funeral and the week that followed was a godsend. She took to being Nanna like a duck to water and reaffirmed everything that Will had already told me: that I'm doing a good job, that I'm doing all the right things with Vicky, that I *can* do this by myself.

It meant a lot coming from Mum. It did. But, somehow, it didn't make me feel quite as good as when Will said those things. I refuse to analyse the *why* of that too deeply.

Mum also teamed up with Henry to clear out the last of Daisy's apartment, and three days after the funeral, she had handed me a teddy bear from Build-A-Bear that she had found in the boxes of toys and clothes, tears in her eyes.

"Press the button," she'd said softly.

After I did, I wished that I hadn't.

Daisy's voice, albeit tinny from the quality of the speaker hidden inside the toy, filtered out loud and clear. "I love you so, *so* much," she'd said. Despite the tears sliding freely down my cheeks, I pressed the damn thing again. It was a different message. "I'm super proud of you." I choked back a sob and hit it again. "You will always be perfect because you're you." After that, it had cycled back to the first little clip.

A very selfish part of me had wanted to keep the toy for myself. To somehow find a way to make the battery last forever. Then I'd facepalmed and recorded it with my phone, making sure that the recording was then uploaded to my cloud storage. I wanted to be able to preserve Daisy's messages for her daughter forever.

Strangely, though, that moment was a turning point for me. It was probably the comfort of knowing that I could, in some fashion, still introduce Vicky to her mother. And, despite sobbing piteously in my mother's arms for a good hour after listening to the bear, I felt *lighter* for having heard Daisy's voice once more. And, in some dumb way, the words of affirmation and reassurance she'd recorded for her baby also worked on me, too.

I will always continue to grieve for her, but at that moment, I felt like I could finally say goodbye.

Falling into routine with Vicky felt easier after that. I stopped feeling like I'm an impostor, and started to realise that I am really one hundred percent her dad. Mum started hovering less, spending more time in the periphery, ready to help if I asked but more content to just be my emotional support. She tidied the apartment, organised meals, and we spent hours sharing memories of Daisy's youth. It was wonderful.

So, of course, the last thing I want to do is put her back on a plane to New Zealand now.

We're standing outside the departures gate at the Gold Coast

Airport and I'm fighting back tears as I hug her close. Vicky is nestled snugly in the bassinet seat of her pram at my side, fast asleep. At two weeks old, I'm amazed by how much she's grown already, how much chunkier her little legs are and how round her cheeks have gotten.

"We're going to miss you like crazy," I tell Mum as I pull out of the hug, clearly not too proud to try emotionally manipulating her into staying.

"I'll miss you, too, honey," she replies, running her hand through my hair and down my face, cupping my cheek the way she's done for as long as I can remember. "But you can always call me. Day or night. And I want weekly Facetime calls *at a minimum* with my sweet grandbaby."

I nod vigorously. "Yeah. Yeah, of course. But, you know, you can always think about moving back here?"

She laughs and shakes her head, her mousy brown bob cut swishing around her face with the movement. "I've got the B 'n B, Con. And I'm happy where I am. But I'll come visit more often, and you can always bring the little princess over to me when she's bigger, too."

I can't help the sigh of resignation that escapes me. "I know." But the whole idea of finally being on my own with Vicky after two weeks of near constant supervision from my friends and mother has me a little anxious and clingy. Outside of Vicky, Mum's the only family I have left, and with her so far out of reach, I'm back to feeling like I'll be all alone.

Reading me like a book, Mum pulls me in for another hug and whispers into my ear, "You're going to be fine, Connor. More than fine. I promise."

I only sniffle a little bit when she pulls away this time. "I love you, Mum." I might be in my thirties, but if losing Dad and Daisy has taught me anything, it's to make sure that the people who matter to me know how much I care about them.

"I love you too, sweetheart." She bends over the pram and smiles softly at Vicky, who is still fast asleep and oblivious. "And I love you, too, Miss Priss."

I snicker a little at the nickname my mother has bestowed upon my daughter. Her night time fussiness has earned her the title, and it's likely to stick with her for life.

Mum checks her watch and then sighs. "I'd better get going. I still have to make it through customs."

"Okay," I agree, even though I don't want to. "Let me know when you're home safe and sound."

Her eye roll is fond. "Look at that," she teases, "you're acting like a dad already. You've got this, Con. Trust your instincts."

We hug one last time before she grabs the handle of her rolling carry-on and walks through the departures gate.

I miss her immediately.

Miraculously, Miss Priss herself stays asleep for the walk back to the car, only grizzles a little as I move her from the pram to her car seat, and snoozes for the entire half-hour drive home.

Okay, I think to myself, relaxing into the quiet once we're home as I place the now awake baby on the play mat in front of the couch. 'Tummy time' is apparently important, though she tends to complain her way through it. *Maybe I have got this.*

* * *

I do not, in fact, have it.

I am so far removed from having it that I don't know what

'it' even is anymore.

I don't know what I did wrong, but only two days after putting Mum on a plane, my child seemed to become possessed by a demon.

The first evening she started to scream like a banshee without any sign of stopping, I worried that I'd hurt her. She was inconsolable from around five o'clock until close to nine. No amount of rocking, singing, pacing, or attempting to feed her would settle her. She just screeched and cried and turned so red I thought she was going to burst a blood vessel or something.

Then, after she calmed down of her own volition and finally had her bottle, she settled into sleep as usual, if a little off schedule. I wrote it off as missing Nanna. After all, I missed her Nanna, too, and would totally tantrum about it if I thought anyone would care.

The following morning was back to our usual routine and I thought things were fine.

Until they weren't.

Sure enough, around five o'clock saw the screaming and thrashing start up all over again.

Google, the blessing that it is, informed me that it sounds like colic. 'The Witching Hour' some bloggers said. Hour my arse! It's close to four fucking hours every night and nothing I do seems to help.

My downstairs neighbour, Mrs Warburton, a crotchety old lady who has lived here since before I was even born, has taken to thumping on her ceiling with a broom handle. I feel guilty for disturbing her peace, and even guiltier when I think about Will upstairs. He's a shift worker, for Christ's sake!

After close to a week of the screaming, I'm starting to lose my cool. I've started to dread the clock as it ticks towards what used to be my favourite time of the day, my gut churning with unease as I wait for the wailing to start up. When, on the sixth night, Vicky starts to cry, I decide I'm going to ignore the advice on the blogs that say not to get in the habit of driving around to calm her down. I can't stay trapped in these four walls, listening to her helpless screaming echoing around me. At least in the car, I can turn up the music to drown her out.

I hate myself just a little bit for thinking so bitterly, but the lack of sleep is getting me down, too.

So I grab my makeshift nappy bag -a backpack filled with all the supplies I never imagined I'd ever need to keep on hand- and scoop my thrashing, wailing, red-tinged child up from where I'd laid her down in her cot. I carry her upright against my chest, wincing as she cries loudly into my ear, and make my way out the door. Her cries seem to increase in volume in the open space of the hallway which leads to the lift and the stairwell, and though I know the stairs would be faster, I don't trust myself to carry her down them while she's so agitated. So I pace in front of the lift after pressing the button to summon it, patting Vicky's cotton covered back consolingly.

When the doors open, I don't even look up before I attempt to walk forward into the little elevator, but Will's voice finally snags my attention over the terrible sound my kid is making.

"Oh, Princess, what's wrong?" he soothes, stepping out of the lift towards us. I step back into the hallway and the doors close behind Will. He reaches for Vicky and I hand her over with relief. The changeover seems to startle her out of crying for a moment, and she stares blearily up at him for a few seconds of blessed silence before starting her production of 'Everything Sucks and I Hate The World' all over again. "Oh, honey," Will commiserates, already rocking her. "I know. I know." Then he finally looks at me with empathy. "Colic?"

"It's the actual worst," I confirm, and I'm startled to realise that I'm on the verge of tears myself. Fuck. The lack of sleep really is doing a number on me.

Will grimaces. I look him over and can only assume he's just gotten back from work, because he's wearing his usual grey tracksuit pants and black t-shirt combo, and his hair is still a little damp from what I can only assume was a post-shift shower.

And now I'm thinking about him in the shower. *Great.*

Thank God I'm exhausted, or my body might actually give my lecherous thoughts away.

"Come on," he says, leading the way up the stairs towards his apartment, "we'll get Chinese delivered from down the street and we'll see if some of my old tricks can't help with this little monster, huh?"

I'm too tired and broken to argue with him. I've missed having adult conversations this past few days, and I've definitely missed seeing Will around. After Mum turned up and he went back to work, it almost felt as though our friendship had been temporary at best, though he was still sending random texts 'checking in', so maybe that last assumption was pure melodrama on my part.

He doesn't seem at all fazed by Vicky's howling, and he keeps up a steady stream of chatter as we head into his place. I respond with the odd 'Yep' or 'Uh-huh' or 'Sounds good' at what seems like appropriate intervals while I let the small talk wash over me.

"Jesus, Con, sit down before you fall down," he insists once we're in his flat, and he herds me towards the couch. I drop into it with a weary exhale, but he stays standing, bouncing Vicky reflexively. "You look exhausted."

I huff out a dry laugh. It's a brittle sound, even to my own ears. "I *feel* exhausted," I acknowledge. "I love her, but this," I wave a hand vaguely to suggest the caterwauling, "has been going on every night for a week now, and then she's up every three hours like clockwork…"

"It's rough. It's ridiculously rough, and it's probably even worse because there's only one of you." I'm oddly touched by the fierceness in Will's delivery, like he's daring me to argue with him. He gives me another understanding smile. "Not to mention, sleep deprivation is used as a torture device all over the world."

"Are you saying my three-week-old is torturing me?" I can't help the amusement in my own voice.

"Well, I don't think she's doing it deliberately?"

I laugh at that, a real laugh, and it feels so good. It's almost like I'd forgotten how and the sensation is brand new, which is incredibly silly to think.

He seems completely unaffected by Vicky's continued cries, bouncing and pacing with her securely held against his chest with one beefy arm, the other now holding his phone as he goes about ordering dinner as promised. When I offer to transfer him money to cover my share, he rolls his eyes and says I'll do no such thing.

"I feel like I haven't paid for food or groceries in forever," I muse, thinking over the stacks of frozen meals that have been sustaining me lately, or the fact that Mum took over for the time she was here. "Do grocery stores still exist out there in the real world?"

Will nods. "I promise, it hasn't turned into a post-apocalyptic wasteland just yet."

The mild joke is amusing and I laugh lightly at it, but I can't help but feel as though my own personal apocalypse has happened. Life as I knew it ended three weeks ago, and now everything feels strange and confronting. At first it was dismal and bleak, but Vicky has been a bright point in the debris. Even while she does her impressive banshee impersonation, she's all light and life and a reason for me to not give up.

"So, I-" Will starts, but I have no idea what he was about to say because my phone starts to ring, cutting him off and startling me.

Fishing it from my pocket, I think nothing of seeing Henry's name on my screen until I'm pressing the green answer icon and bringing the phone to my ear, only to hear his excited babbling before I can get a word out.

"He's here, Con. He's here."

"Wh-"

"Max," he rushes right over my barely asked question. I can hear the smile in his voice and can imagine the pure joy on his face. "Max is here. And he's perfect. He looks *just* like me!" In the background, I can hear Sarah's laughter and her quip about her husband's ego, but Henry's clearly lost in his own happy little bubble because he doesn't take the bait. "You have to come and meet your Godson, Con. You have to."

"Slow down," I chuckle, finally getting a word in edgewise. "Breathe for me, Hen. Firstly, congratulations. How's Sarah?"

It doesn't hurt the way I expected it might to ask about my friend's health post-birth. Even though there's still a part of me that thinks Daisy deserved to be asked the same questions, to be alive and well after the birth of her daughter, it doesn't make my happiness or concern for Sarah any less important.

"She's good," he answers, then his tone levels out to something closer to awe. "Better than good. I'm amazed by her, y'know? Glad it's not possible for men to go through that shit, though, because I don't think I'd have been able to hack it."

"Even if it were," I tell him with amusement, "you'd probably need to be having sex with another man for that to be possible anyway."

Across the room, I watch as Will raises both eyebrows to look at me. He can't hear Henry's side of the conversation, so I can only imagine what he's thinking right now. I have to smother another snort of laughter.

It's strange that this feels close to normal. That when I'm with him, I can see the light at the end of the grief tunnel. That I remember how to be human. How to be myself.

That is a powerful, dangerous kind of drug right there.

"…ot gonna happen," Henry's still speaking, and I quickly remember what we were talking about.

I choose to tease him. "Methinks he doth protest too much."

"Shut up," my best friend laughs, then asks, "So, are you going to come meet your Godson or should I tell Matt he's got the job now?"

"Fuck off," I rise to the bait, "like Matt's worthy of the role." Matt is a nice guy, but he doesn't have the history with Henry that I do. But then I look over to Will who is still trying to calm the inconsolable colic monster, and I sigh, "Listen, I don't know if you can hear the screaming, but now's not going to work, and I'm pretty sure Sarah should rest up as much as she can before you're bombarded with visitors anyway." I pause, listening to the disappointed silence for only a moment before I suggest, "First thing tomorrow, her Highness and I will be there to meet our newest family member, all right?"

There's another short stretch of silence before I hear Henry exhale. "Yeah. Yeah, you're right. I'm sorry, I-"

"Hey, no. None of that. If my kid wasn't auditioning to play every horror movie victim ever written, I'd be right there with bells on." Another soft smile curls my lips. "This'll be you in a couple of weeks."

"Ugh, no. Max wouldn't do that to us. He's too perfect."

We both laugh at that pronouncement. With the soundtrack of his imminent future squalling behind me, I ask Henry a few more questions -Max's weight, length, whether his apgar score was good, all the parent stuff that the internet suggests is important- and then I congratulate him again before I hang up, closing with a request that he give my love to Sarah.

"So you're officially Uncle Con, then?" Will asks me with a wide smile.

The question hits me a little hard. I was supposed to be Vicky's uncle. But then, Henry's been referring to me as 'Uncle Con' in relation to Max ever since he announced Sarah's pregnancy, so it's not as strange as it really should be. It just makes me a little emotional, but a lot of things do that these days.

I nod and soothe myself by recalling the pure joy in Henry's voice. "Yeah. And this one," I jut my chin towards the bawling demon child, "is going to have a built-in best friend to grow up with."

That is something that does excite me. Knowing that my kid is going to grow up alongside my best friend's fills me with a myriad of feelings I can't quite put into words. I can only hope that Vicky and Max share a bond like Henry and I do. Max will be her brother from another moth-*oh*.

Too soon.

Thankfully, Will is oblivious to the path my musings almost took me down because he deftly changes the subject. "Have you tried bathing her?" he asks, apropos of nothing.

Scrunching my nose, I offer, "Um, at least once a day?" I mean, okay, sometimes it's more just a wipe down than an actual bath, because the actual bath process is more work than I ever could have imagined it would be, but I keep her clean.

Snickering lightly, which I can't hear over the crying but I can see, Will explains his thought process. "I mean for the colic. Jack and Wes were water babies. Putting them in a warm bath, draping a wet cloth over their arms and chests while they floated, it calmed them instantly."

I shake my head. "No. I...I never thought..." I sigh and rub the back of my neck. "The blogs suggested driving around might calm her. That's where I was heading before." I wave vaguely towards his front door, knowing that he'll understand my meaning.

His handsome, bearded face lights up. "Then after the food gets here, I say we give it a shot."

We.

It should not be such a turn on to hear him put himself in the equation, if only for the evening. But I've already admitted that I have a thing for seeing big, tough men in doting daddy-type roles, so...

Whoa. No. Nuh uh. Back to the crazy hot mess again.

It's just that I'm lonely. It has to be. Most new parents have a second person to share the load with, as Will himself kindly pointed out only a few minutes ago, so I'm just projecting that need onto the first hot, single, dadly gay man I've come across. That's all.

Never mind that I wanted to climb him like a tree when I

first spoke to him months ago…

Ugh, stop it, I demand of my brain. *Come back to the real world, Con. He's being a nice guy and a good friend. Take what you can get and stop fantasising.*

But, when the food arrives and we take everything downstairs to my place, with Will still confidently holding Vicky despite her theatrics, I can't help but feel like I'm fighting a losing battle with myself.

Chapter Ten – Will

If I happen to drop in on Connor after each day shift over the course of the next couple of weeks, I tell myself that it's because I know how isolating it is to become a new parent. I definitely don't berate myself for avoiding the obvious sexual tension between us, even when I catch his eyes roaming over my arms and chest during our new colic bath time ritual.

Toby's been sending me messages every other day, asking if I've grown a pair and talked to the object of my affections. I have done my best to talk around the subject. His last message was just a series of gifs, complete with eyerolls, facepalms, and outright calling me a coward.

I didn't reply because I know he's right.

Jack has also been weirdly invested in my non-existent relationship with Connor. He's constantly asking about him, or about Vicky, and he's stopped the innuendo and insistence that I just need to get laid. And, while that should be a relief, considering how much I hate talking about my sex life with my son, I'm actually somewhat unnerved by his more serious approach.

And, all right, it's possible that I might have essentially fallen into a relationship accidentally at this point. I mean, sure, there's no kissing or sex, but seeing Connor and Vicky is part of my routine now.

I look forward to dropping in and sweeping the kid out of his arms, giving him the break he deserves. I look forward to asking him about his day and telling him about mine in return. I look forward to helping him set up the plastic baby bath and fill it with lukewarm water. I look forward to the way his expression melts every time he gets Vicky's wriggling, slippery body submerged with his forearm supporting her back and head. I look forward to the heated looks he sends me while I step in to help, gently pouring water over her exposed belly with the little plastic cup he keeps on his bathroom counter specifically for this purpose.

I look forward to afterwards, when Vicky's colicky cries have petered out, once she's dried and dressed and has been fed, when she has been put to bed and Connor and I finally share a meal at his dining table with the baby monitor placed between us.

It all feels so domestic. So new and so familiar all at once. It feels like family, like home, and I know I've gotten in deeper than I should have. Especially when I haven't actually spoken to him about my feelings for him.

Feelings which have gone from attraction and fondness to...*more.*

It's the 'more' that scares me.

How is it possible to feel so strongly for someone I've never even kissed? And, worse, what happens if I finally get my shit together and kiss him and it turns out there's no spark between us?

But tonight when I knock on his door, I'm greeted by silence on the other side and I frown. Fishing my phone from my pocket with the intention of texting him, I find a message waiting for me.

'Hey, Miss Priss has been unsettled all day so I opted to try going for a drive. No idea what time I'll be back. Catch you tomorrow?'

It's not really a brush off, but I can't help the disappointment that curdles in my belly at not seeing him tonight. Then I remind myself that I've basically just inserted myself into his life against my better judgement and a little space might be good for both of us.

'No problem,' I type back, then hesitate for only a moment before I add, *'but if you need anything before then, you know where to find me.'* I close it with a smiley faced emoji.

If he's already driving, he's not going to reply immediately, so with a final glance at his empty apartment, I head up the stairs to my own.

* * *

I startle awake in the middle of the night, unsure as to why. The clock on my bedside table tells me it's close to midnight, and my lips twist with wry self-deprecation. There was a time when midnight was 'early' to bed. But that was before children and before regular shift work. Before middle age. Now I take sleep whenever and wherever I can get it.

Assuming my brain is just having a moment, I shut my eyes again and prepare to sink back into slumber, only to hear a frantic knocking dimly echoing from down the hallway. I climb out of bed with a frown, wondering what the source of the racket is, my concern deepening when I realise that it's coming from the front door.

I have no idea what to expect on the other side of the painted timber, but I figure home invaders don't *knock*, so I twist the deadbolt and turn the handle, pulling the door inwards.

Connor stands on the other side of the threshold, pale and tear streaked. "Oh, thank *God*," he practically lunges forward, clutching the baby to his chest. "I'm so sorry," he babbles, close to hyperventilating, "I tried to call, and you didn't answer, and she's burning up and I don't know what to do. Do I take her to the hospital? Do I-"

"Whoa, slow down." Placing my hands on his shoulders, I steady him. "Breathe, Con. Deep breaths. That's it." I've said these words to him before, or at least a variation of them. He seems just as panicked now as he did the night he lost his sister. It makes my heart squeeze painfully. "Okay. Now, you said she's burning up?"

I reach for the baby who is crying pitifully, but it's not the inconsolable screaming that accompanies her bouts of colic. She sounds pained and miserable, though, and it tugs at my heartstrings even worse than Connor's distress.

Connor hands her over gratefully, worrying his lower lip between his teeth. Sure enough, when I press my lips to her little forehead, Vicky's skin feels hot beneath them.

"Any other symptoms?" I ask him, then I remember his text. "You said she's been unsettled. Has she still been taking her bottles?"

He nods. "She's been fussy, but still eating. Drinking? Whatever you want to call it."

"Good, that's good," I assure him. She's staying hydrated.

"Have you taken her temperature?"

His head bobs again. "It was thirty-eight point three a few minutes ago. That's bad, right?"

I'm not going to lie, I frown for a moment before I realise that he's talking in degrees Celsius. Damn Australians and their weird measuring systems. "It's definitely a fever," I answer, "but not a bad one."

"She's only a month old," he says with no small amount of concern. "I don't think she's even old enough for the baby Panadol yet."

"She's probably not," I agree, erring on the side of caution. I can't remember if Jen and I ever gave the boys Tylenol when they were this small. "So we're going to see if we can bring her fever down naturally."

Still cradling her warm little body close to me, I grab my keys from the bowl by the door and then gesture for Connor to go on ahead of me.

"Your place has the baby bath and all her stuff," I explain when he just stares at me with confusion.

It's only once I'm standing in his bathroom, dipping the overheated infant into a tub of cool-ish water, that I realise I'm only wearing my long, worn cotton pyjama bottoms and nothing else. I don't have the energy to be self-conscious about my shirtless state, though, and Connor's too busy fussing over his daughter to care.

She stops whimpering once she's in the tub, and, as she calms, some of the pinkness seems to fade from her skin. I take it as a good sign that most of her flush was from exertion and not fever.

"We'll dress her lightly once the water cools too much," I tell Connor, "just to make sure she's not going to overheat from the fever. And then we'll take her temperature again and see where to go from there, okay?"

His eyes are red and puffy when he looks at me, but he nods. "Thank you," he croaks, then sniffles a little. "I just…I lost it, I guess. I'm not cut out for this."

My hands are otherwise occupied, or I would have grabbed him to deliver a much-needed hug. "Stop it," I insist, using the firm tone I mastered when the boys were toddlers. "You're doing a great job. Everyone freaks out the first time their babies get sick. Especially when they're this small."

"I should have Googled." Holding up his phone, Connor reads from the search he's conducted since I started bathing the baby. "It says to do all the things you've just said. Plus, it says to take her to her doctor because she's under two months old, or to Emergency if her temp doesn't get any better after trying these things," he adds, gesturing at the tub. His shoulders slump. "I shouldn't have bothered you."

"I'm glad you did," I tell him earnestly. "Connor, I meant it when I said you could come to me anytime, for any reason. I-"

My words are interrupted as poor Vicky makes a choked, gurgling sound, throws up all over herself and my hand, and then promptly starts to wail.

Chapter Eleven — Connor

~~~

I lurch up into a sudden seated position in bed, clutching my chest to calm my rapidly beating heart. I'm disoriented and confused for a moment, because I can't hear Vicky crying and I don't remember putting her to bed. A look into the empty bassinet beside the bed has me flinging myself off the mattress and racing for the door.

I've lost the baby. I can only hope that I put her down in her cot in my sleep deprived state and that I haven't left her to smother herself on the couch, or on a pillow, or...or...

My increasingly morbid thoughts screech to a halt when I discover that her cot is empty and then they start up even worse than before. I race into the living room, tears already threatening to spill over at the fear of what I'll find, and then I skid to a stop behind the couch.

There, on the comfy armchair, reclining with his feet up, is Will. He's fast asleep, and so is Vicky, curled up on her belly beneath his chin, his big arms keeping her securely in place.

Last night's events come flooding back to me in a rush, and

I could weep with both relief and shame. Regardless of what Will said last night, I feel like I failed my first big test as a parent. I panicked when my kid needed me to stay calm, and if I hadn't given in and gone to find Will, I have no idea what I would have done. I might be a man in my thirties, but he's the adultier adult. I honestly don't think I'll be able to thank him enough for taking charge and looking after both Vicky and me last night.

I slowly make my way around the couch and carefully lower myself onto its still uncomfortable surface, my eyes never leaving the extremely attractive man across from me. With the adrenaline from this morning's shock fading, I start to notice details.

Just little details.

Like the fact that my super hot neighbour is shirtless.

Yeah.

Totally tiny, itsy-bitsy, *completely* insignificant details.

Will's broad chest is still firm and toned, which isn't exactly a surprise. His t-shirts are usually quite snug, after all. The slightly tanned skin is home to a light carpet of dark hair smattered with grey and silver. It stretches over his pecs beneath the curled form of my sleeping daughter, then tapers down towards the far-too-sexy V of his hips. It's like an arrow of deliciousness, pointing to those sinful abs and lower still, to whatever treasures lie beneath the low-slung waistband of his thin cotton pyjama pants.

I force my eyes back up towards his face again, feeling my own expression soften. He's such a handsome man and there's something special in getting to see him like this, vulnerable and unguarded in sleep.

Not to mention the way it makes my heart flip to see

him sleeping with my baby on his chest. That, more than anything, has my crush spiralling dangerously further into actual feelings. Feelings that scare me. Feelings that shouldn't be possible after only really knowing the man for a month or so. Feelings that he can't possibly reciprocate. Not when he's seen what a mess I am. When he witnessed the absolute destruction of my last relationship. When it would mean having to seriously consider having a baby in his life again. Not to mention the fact that I'm only a few years older than his sons. Would that be too weird for him?

I've had these thoughts before, and I know I'll have them again. And, even though I shouldn't, I can't stop thinking them. I can't stop daydreaming and wishing that circumstances were different. That my life wasn't quite so complicated. That I was more appealing on paper.

"Mmph," Will murmurs, that big, broad body of his tensing with a combination yawn and stretch as he shifts into consciousness. I watch as his hands tighten over Vicky, and he scrunches up his face before he opens his eyes. "Wha-?" he starts, glancing down at the bundle in his hands, then over at me. Another hum escapes him, then he clears his throat lightly. "Morning." His voice comes out warm and husky with sleep. It goes straight to my dick, but I focus on how sweet the moment feels instead.

My answering smile is soft and probably too affectionate. "Morning," I reply quietly. Then I incline my head in reference to the baby. "What happened to taking shifts?"

Will's lips twist and he looks adorably sheepish. "She settled after her bottle and fell asleep on me....and I fell asleep, too."

Guilt races through me. He worked a full shift yesterday, then I woke him in the middle of the night. The poor guy was probably exhausted. I know better than to apologise again, though. I did enough of that last night. It was what led to him sending me to bed while he took the first shift with Vicky.

So, instead of once again expressing my remorse at having bothered him, I push myself back to my feet and pad over to the kitchen. "Coffee?" I call over my shoulder, already pulling the mugs from the cupboard.

"Please," he answers.

I putter around, setting the machine to grind the coffee beans and then pour out delicious, caffeinated goodness. The milk finishes frothing in the stainless-steel jug, and I pour it in over the dark brown liquid which smells like life.

I carry both mugs back into the lounge room and set his carefully on the coffee table in front of him. Like a pro, he gets himself into an upright position, shifts Vicky to his left shoulder, and then reaches for his mug with his right.

His gorgeous grey-blue eyes flutter closed as he takes his first appreciative sip. "God, that's good."

He's talking about the coffee. He's talking about the coffee.

Why is it my brain went somewhere else? Somewhere far too inappropriate, especially when he's still cuddling my sick infant to his chest.

My brain jumps track, but it's still in vicinity of the same station. I think about more pleasant circumstances that might see me making him coffee of a morning, with him only in his pjs and his hair mussed by sleep.

After draining half of my mug, I ask, "Breakfast? I make a mean omelette."

There's a flicker of hesitation in his eyes before he nods. "Actually, yeah. I'd like that."

Mug still in hand, I use it to gesture towards Vicky, who is snuffling against his freckled shoulder but still seems to be content to sleep. "You're okay with her while I whip 'em up?"

Will nods and nuzzles the top of her head with his bearded cheek. My heart squeezes. "We'll be fine."

The urge to cross the small space between us and kiss him almost bowls me over, and I cover the resulting nervous energy by surging to my feet and hustling into the kitchen. Vicky starts to stir with a whine while I'm dicing onions and capsicum. Will's deep voice starts up, soothing her with reassurances and sweet nothings.

"Come on, princess," I hear him say, "let's get you changed and take your temperature again, hmm?"

He continues to talk to her, and I hear his voice fading as he leaves the living room and heads down the hallway.

I get the mix of eggs, cheese, and veggies into the frypan, and I wash up the chopping board, knife, and bowl while it starts to bubble and cook. While the kitchen is filled with the mouth-watering aroma of the quick meal cooking, I am once again struck by that feeling of how this could be a 'morning after' breakfast. Or maybe something sweeter. More domestic. Regular.

My stomach fills with butterflies when I consider how appealing the latter thought is.

I carefully fold the omelette and flip it, humming to myself while I grab plates and cutlery, and then set about getting a bottle of formula organised. It's been a long time since I've cooked breakfast for anyone, and it feels right to be cooking for Will. After everything he's done for me, it's the least I can do to show my appreciation.

I'm sliding the plates onto the dining table when Will reappears, still chatting to Vicky conversationally. Once again, my heart flutters and I'm pretty sure my stomach flips when he looks up at me and grins. "Her fever's come down," he says, and my shoulders slump with relief.

"Thank Christ," I breathe, then reach for her. Our hands brush as he transfers her over and I swear I feel an electric shock go through my whole body, from the tips of my fingers to my toes.

Will clears his throat and takes his seat. "You'll probably still want to take her to the doctor," he says, then picks up his cutlery. "This looks great."

I sit down across the table from him and, with the practice of the past month behind me, I shift Vicky into one arm and pick up my fork with the other. The burst of flavour hitting my tongue is almost as sharp a wakeup call as thinking I'd misplaced the baby. I've been eating toast or cereal for the past month, so a hot breakfast -even something as simple as an omelette- feels like a treat.

Will compliments my cooking and I try not to blush. "It's hard to fuck up omelettes," I shrug.

He shoots me a grin across the table. "Oh, you'd be surprised."

"What," I begin, unable to help myself from teasing, "you can't cook? Have I finally found a flaw, Mr Bradford?"

Waving his empty fork in the air between us, he *tsks*. "I didn't say I couldn't. But let's just say some of the guys at the station have me grateful that Uber Eats exists."

I chuckle at that and nod. "Alright, point taken. I'll accept the compliment with grace, then." And, because I've clearly lost my mind, I wink at him.

We eat in companionable silence and then Will gathers both plates and all of our cutlery, taking them into the kitchen behind me while I grab Vicky's bottle and situate her in my arms for a feed. I hear the tap run, and I turn to tell him that it's unnecessary to wash the dishes, but the words get caught in my throat.

He looks so at ease in my kitchen. So at home wearing only his pyjama bottoms and a smile, humming to himself as he washes the plates by hand. I swallow convulsively.

"I should get going," Will says once he places the last fork into the drying rack.

I watch as he wipes his hands dry on the gimmicky tea towel Daisy got me as a housewarming present. It's bright pink and lists all the 'adulty' catchphrases we grew up with. Things like 'were you raised in a barn?' and 'money doesn't grow on trees' and 'do I look like I give a fork?'

Nodding, I wonder if I'm imagining the note of resignation in his voice, or if I'm just projecting my ever-growing daydreams onto him. "Thanks again for last night."

Will carefully folds the tea towel in half and hangs it back in place over the handle of the oven. "Seriously," he insists, "I'm glad you came to me." It's only a few long strides for him to cross back over to me and Vicky. He runs his big, broad palm over the top of her head, a smile curving his lips as she snuffles and chugs her breakfast with heavy-lidded eyes. Then that same palm lands on my back, splayed out between my shoulder blades, and his lips meet mine.

I freeze. My heart speeds up, and my eyes widen.

It was only a chaste, quick peck, but holy fuck, it was a *kiss*.

"Uh…" I swallow and look up at him as he slowly pulls back up into a standing position. I can feel my cheeks blazing with heat. I'm pretty sure every thought I've had of the man since I first laid eyes on him is now etched across my face.

"Shit," he breathes, closing his eyes and wincing. "Would you believe that's a force of habit?"

"Yeah," I answer, licking my lips and bracing myself, "but I'd prefer it if it was more than that."

A delightful flush seems to take him over, travelling up his chest and neck to his bearded cheeks. "I shouldn't…" He stops himself and clears his throat, his eyes taking on that sad, empathetic glean that I'm sick of seeing from people. "Now's not the right time…"

"For you or for me?" I ask, but I already know the answer. The pity in Will's gorgeous eyes tells me everything. I sigh. "Shouldn't I be the one to decide that?"

Thankfully, my reaction seems to drive away the expression he was sporting. Now he just seems surprised, which is altogether much preferable. I can work with surprise better than I can with pity.

"We've been dancing around each other for a little while now, haven't we?" I push to my feet, getting as close as I can to bringing our gazes level with each other. "I like you, Will. And I hope that kiss, however sweet and innocent it might have been, means you like me, too."

It feels marginally juvenile to be talking about *liking* him when we've essentially been playing house for the past few weeks, but I feel like I need to play this out as carefully as possible. For all that he's a big, strong, confident guy, the situation itself is tenuous and fragile.

I don't want him to bolt. I want him to stay and talk this out with me. And, yeah, the fact that I'm holding a baby who will ostensibly play a huge part in whether he wants to attempt a relationship with me or not is something I'm also taking into account right now.

"And here I was thinking that part was obvious," he answers wryly, which is a good sign. A very good sign, in fact.

I can feel myself brightening at the confirmation, grinning up at him in what I hope is an encouraging expression and not a manic one. "Good," I say. "So, will you stay and talk this out?"

He grimaces, and then rubs the back of his neck, gesturing vaguely at his lickable chest. "Can I get some clothes on first?"

As much as I'd love to refuse based on the eye-candy factor, I would like him to be as comfortable as possible, so I step out of his personal space and nod. "Of course. But," I swallow, feeling vulnerable, "you will come back, right?"

In answer, he crowds me back up against the table and lands another kiss to my mouth. I gasp at the contact this time, parting my lips, and then our tongues are meeting, tangling slowly, dipping and tasting and reassuring each other. He tastes like coffee and salt, and his beard tickles my skin, and the whole experience is glorious and over far too soon for my liking.

"I'll be back," he says when he steps away, and, in a daze, I just bob my head and watch him leave.

Chapter Twelve — Will

Number one on the list of things I didn't think I'd be doing today: kissing Connor stupid at his breakfast table.

I alternate between cursing myself for the rash, impulsive behaviour and praising myself for finally making my intentions known.

At least Toby will be proud of me. Jack too, maybe.

I rush through brushing my teeth, combing my hair and getting dressed into cargo shorts and a plain white t-shirt, sliding my feet into a pair of boat shoes from the little stand by the front door. With my phone and keys in my pocket, I hurry my ass back downstairs and let myself into Connor's apartment, calling out for him while I shut the door behind me.

He wanders in from the direction of the hallway, tugging a shirt over his head. His mousy brown hair is delightfully mussed, and I fight the urge to sweep him up for yet another intense kiss.

"Hey," he greets me tentatively, but with a sweet smile, "you came back."

I can understand why he might have doubted that I would, but it stings a little anyway. "Of course I did," I reply. "You think you're getting rid of me that easily?"

"I don't want to get rid of you at all." Connor's cheeks turn pink and he seems equal parts surprised and embarrassed by his own admission. "I mean..."

God he's adorable. A rush of affection threatens to overwhelm me.

Connor's speaking again before I get the chance to gather my thoughts. "So, um, that kiss was...*wow.*"

I think back to the moments before I forced myself to walk out of his apartment only a half hour ago. The taste and sensation of his tongue against mine. The scent of his skin up close. The way he melted against my attentions. "Yeah," I agree, "It was."

"And does that mean...uh, I guess, *what* does that mean to you?" Connor bites his bottom lip, then, without giving me a chance to answer, forges on, "Because I have feelings for you, Will. Probably bigger feelings than I should have, because we've only really gotten close over the last month, but I have them anyway. And I know I should be all 'oh, we can take this slowly', but I've got Vicky, so it's more like 'oh, by the way, dating me is essentially getting yourself an insta-family', so..." Trailing off, he shrugs. "I just...I know you've already done the whole raising kids thing. I mean, technically speaking, she's young enough to be your grand-"

"Okay, stopping you there," I chuckle, planting my hand over his mouth for good measure. "The 'G' word -or any derivatives thereof- is off the table. Understood?" He nods and I remove my hand. "Good." In the ensuing silence, I lick my lips, then sigh and run my hand through my hair. "I've got feelings for you, too." Tension immediately bleeds from his shoulders. "And, yeah, I have done the kids thing, but I'm barely forty-nine. A lot of people are only just starting families in their forties. Not," I hold up my hands in the universal gesture for surrender, "that I'm saying I assume I'm Vicky's *anything*, but…"

"You've been here pretty much from the start," Connor says softly. He reaches for one of my hands and squeezes it. "I mean, hell, I woke you up in the middle of the night because she was sick and you came down here and slept with her on your chest. Which, *hello*, was pretty damn hot. But…yeah. You, uh, you're already *something* to her. To me. You, um, you get that, right?"

And this is what Jack has been getting at lately. Toby as well. I've been attached since the beginning, whether I've wanted to admit that or not. But I'm not only interested in Connor because I love his kid like she was my own, and I don't love her just because I want to be with him, either. I don't know how to explain that to him, or to my son, or to my nosy new friend.

"This sneaked up on me," I admit, pulling my hand back as I try to get my thoughts in order. It's a bit like herding cats, especially when all I want to do is lean forward and kiss Connor stupid all over again. "All of it. I thought you were cute from the start, don't get me wrong, but when everything happened…well, I didn't think I'd find myself loving your kid like she's mine, or wanting this-" my vague hand flapping is supposed to take in the three of us and the apartment and last night's events "-to be a thing."

His hazel eyes go wide, but I'm not sure which part of my confession has surprised him. Maybe all of it?

"You're serious?" he asks quietly, studying me like it's the first time he's ever seen me.

I nod.

The skin between his eyebrows creases. "I don't want to sound like a broken record," he starts again, "but...you're sure? Because this is serious stuff. This isn't 'hey let's try it and if it doesn't work out, no big deal', this is 'hearts are on the line, and a little girl's future is at stake' stuff. I know that things can change down the track, and if that happens, we'll deal with it...but...are you actually serious that you want to go forward together? I'm not saying you should jump into the adoption with me or anything, but if she gets attached, even if you don't want to be with me anymore..." He pauses and shakes his head. "Well, you're kind of stuck being *something* to her for the long-haul at that point."

I don't bother pointing out that, at a month old, we still have time before that's a concern, because I get the point he's trying to make. We're talking about going from friends to a serious relationship without really dating. It's a lot to think about, and he's right to take it seriously.

"We're a package deal," he says, as though I hadn't already worked that out weeks ago. "Vicky and me. And I know that's probably a dealbreaker for a lot of guys. Still-"

"I'm not a lot of guys, Con," I reassure him gently. "And I know a thing or two about jumping into responsibilities and family life."

"Exactly! You've already raised kids. Why would you sign up for another one? It's not like dating me is going to involve many nights out for dinner or clubbing or whatever.

It'll be takeaway and *coitus interruptus* courtesy of one loud munchkin." He tickles his daughter's belly for emphasis, grinning and shaking his head at her. "One of these days, you will giggle when I do that."

"Funnily enough, I'm not deluded enough to think otherwise," I answer. "And I got attached to the little princess before I even realised it was happening. Not that I would have chosen otherwise," I rush to add, not wanting him to think I would have chosen anything else. "And, at my age, relaxing nights in are way more enticing than *clubbing*." I make a face to emphasise just how I feel about nightclubs nowadays.

"And the...uh...other stuff?"

I can't help smirking. "I believe you called it coitus interruptus."

He reaches out, lamely slapping at me for teasing him. "Yeah, well, that's a thing, isn't it?" He squints at me like I should be able to confirm the theory.

I shrug. "I didn't exactly date while the boys were babies, but...yeah, I guess so? And, anyway, she can't help it. We'll just have to get used to being quick and/or creative." I waggle my eyebrows at him, earning the laughter I was aiming for.

After his giggles subside, he exhales and looks at me with something akin to awe. "You really wanna do this? A relationship? With me?"

"If you're serious about being into a guy almost two decades your senior, and you understand that I'm a shift worker and my job is unpredictable, then...yeah. I do. Besides," I swallow, "we've basically been in a relationship for a while now, haven't we?"

"You're not almost two decades my senior," he denies with an eye roll. Then his expression softens, becoming a little sheepish. He nibbles his plump bottom lip. "But I think you're right about the relationship thing."

I am. I know I am. We've gotten to know each other well over the past month, and I've spent most of my free time with him and Vicky. It has felt intimate, regardless of the lack of kissing or sex to this point.

I nod, then circle back to my concern about our age gap. He's only three years older than my sons. "I'm sixteen years older than you. I am technically old enough to be your fa-"

It's Connor's turn to clamp a hand over my mouth, and he looks down to apologise to the disgruntled baby in his arms for the sudden movement before glaring back at me.

"No. Bad fireman. *Bad.*" He removes his hand to use his index finger to bop me on the nose as though I was an errant dog, before covering my mouth again so I can't protest. "Now, listen here," he starts, but I have other ideas.

I lick his palm.

Connor yanks his hand back with a bitten off squeal and wipes it on his jeans. "Oh," he complains, brandishing his index finger at me again, "you're going to be like that, are you?"

"And here I thought you'd be into me licking you."

His jaw drops and he makes a show of cradling Vicky closer to his chest, covering her exposed ear with his free hand. "There are children present, mister!" He's aiming for scandalised, but he can't help the grin stretching across his face, and I can't help mine, either.

"Whoops," I say, not at all repentant. "Sorry."

"You're going to be more trouble than the kid, aren't you?" The question is accompanied by a similar squinty-eyed expression to the one he used before, but then he breaks into another beatific smile that makes my stomach do a funny little flip in my belly. "As soon as she's asleep," he murmurs, leaning forward conspiratorially, "we're repeating that kiss. And," his lips quirk into a wicked smirk, "maybe taking it further? I mean," he shrugs, but he's anything but nonchalant, practically vibrating with need, "seeing as we've already been dating for the past month."

Now I'm the one who can't stop smiling.

* * *

I feel like a giddy teenager as Connor pulls the door to Vicky's room shut behind him. He leans his back against it for a moment, closing his eyes before opening them to gaze up at me from behind lowered lashes. My heart raps a staccato beat in my chest at that look.

It's a look that says he's going to make good on his earlier promise.

It's a look that says he wants to do *more* than make good on that promise.

I send a short mental 'thank you' out into the universe for the timing working out for me. I'm on my rostered three days off, having come off the week of day shifts now, which means I have plenty of time to dedicate to getting to know Connor in as many ways -and positions- as possible.

I'm about to open my mouth to speak, to tell him that we can take things as slowly as he needs, when he launches himself off the white, glossy surface and fuses our mouths together.

Like our previous kiss, this one is all heat and yearning. There's no slow build up of want or tension, just a blazing, fiery passion that ignites as soon as our lips connect. My hands go to his hips, tugging him flush against me, and I can feel his body responding as fervently as my own. His cock grows and hardens against my thigh, while mine presses into his stomach, and we groan in unison when he starts to grind his hips, seeking friction.

"God, your beard," he murmurs into my ear when we part to breathe, rubbing his barely stubbled cheek against mine, "you're so fucking hot, Will. I swear, I...*oh*."

It turns out, now that we've acknowledged our mutual attraction, I can't help myself around this man. So, while he was lavishing me with appreciative words, I shifted my hands to cup the pert, round globes of his ass and I squeezed. That breathy responsive 'oh' of his almost does me in, so I plant my feet, bend forward and then lift him from the ground.

With a startled yelp, he wraps his slender legs around me and I spin us around, heading for the door to his bedroom.

"This okay?" I ask him, albeit a little gruffly, as I carry him to his immaculately made-up king-sized bed. Those pristine white cotton sheets, probably composed of an excessive thread count, are not going to stay so pristine for much longer if I get my way. But, at the same time, I need to know that he doesn't feel rushed, even if this was his suggestion. We've gone from friends to whatever this is awfully quickly. "It's not too fast? Because we can stop. We can talk. We-"

"*Will*," he nips at my lips, his voice breathless, but with the hint of a giggle. "This is more than okay. Not too fast. Just...oh, *fuck yes*."

Grinning against the skin of his neck where I have started to suck and lick and explore whichever parts of him I can reach, I drop him to the mattress and then follow him down as he bounces in place. He shuffles back and sideways until he's lying in the middle of the bed, his head on a pillow, and I crawl over his body, relishing in his greedy hands as they explore me with equal fervour.

While his fingers slide beneath my t-shirt, I lean across to his bedside table and switch the baby monitor on, not wanting either of us to forget that his daughter is still the priority. Even though her fever seems to have waned, and Con has scheduled an appointment to take her to the doctor later today, I know we're both still concerned about Vicky. Besides, nothing about the sudden change in my relationship with Connor should negatively impact her.

"Okay, that shouldn't be as hot as it is," Connor says, shaking his head, his brown hair getting a little wild around the pillow courtesy of the movement.

"What shouldn't?"

He pulls one of his hands back out from under my shirt to point between me and the gadget on the nightstand. "That," he says, as though it explains everything.

I raise an eyebrow and he huffs out a small laugh.

"Stopping to turn on the monitor. Who knew that daddy vibes are an absolute turn on?"

My heart does that funny, faltering beat-skipping thing again. It's too early to consider myself a parental figure to that baby, but there's no denying that I've been silently playing a similar role anyway. Instead, I force a wolfish grin. "You can call me Daddy if you're into that kind of thing. I didn't take you for the kinky type." I fake a sigh. "It's always the quiet ones."

"You know that's not what I meant." With pink cheeks, Connor smacks at my bicep. I'm still holding myself over him, bracing my weight on my arms, my knees pinning his thighs between them. I shift my knees, dropping my hips down to meet his, grinding our aching cocks together through too many layers of fabric. He tosses his head back and whines.

"I know," I reply gently, in a tone completely juxtaposed to the heated actions of our bodies. I still my hips, needing him to understand. "But…that's too much right now. I'm not…I love her, but…"

"Hey," suddenly his hazel eyes are serious and concerned, and he brings his hands to my cheeks, cupping my face, holding me in place. "I get that. This is new. We're serious about each other. You're serious about her. Labels will take time. That's okay." He scrunches up his face. "Anyway, no more talking about the kid when we're about to get naked." He gives a little wiggle of his hips for emphasis, and my dick springs right back to attention again.

"Good plan," I agree, then he moves one hand to my lower back, threading the other into the hair at the back of my head, and pulls me down to meet him for another deep kiss.

His kisses are addictive. The way his mouth moves against mine. The way he takes exactly what he wants. The way he melts against me but doesn't turn at all passive. We spend minutes like this, tugging each other's clothing off as we rock together, rolling about on the bed while we catalogue one another's bodies through feel alone.

Connor's skin is still tight and pliable with his youth. It's smooth and warm beneath my searching fingertips, yielding and supple and perfect. His arms and legs are dusted with light, mousy brown hair, but his chest, back, and even ass are all waxed within an inch of his life, all in direct contrast to the veritable carpet of dark hair turning salt and pepper over my own form. Not that he seems to mind that my backside is a little furry, or that he can tangle his fingers in the hair across my pecs. If anything, I'd say he gets even more excited when he does, moaning into my kisses and bucking his leaking cock up against mine.

"How do you want to do this?" I eventually ask, when our teasing has reached fever pitch and I'm afraid I might just come all over him at the next thrust of our cocks together. I reach between us to take us both in hand, delighting in his groan and the dribble of precum he emits. "We don't have to-"

"Lube and condoms are in the bedside table. Top drawer," he rushes out, and I chuckle at the blush spreading down from his cheeks and over his pale chest. I wonder if I can make that blush extend even further.

"Okay," I say, slowly stroking our dicks together, making no effort to roll away and retrieve the items yet. "Would you prefer to top or-"

"Fuck me, Will," he blurts.

And, would you look at that: the blush *does* go lower.

I lean towards him and press a sweet kiss to his now swollen lips. "Yes, sir." Then I roll off to the side and locate the little bottle of lube and the box of condoms, eyeing the selection of toys in the drawer with interest before I check the date on the box because I'm a stickler for being safe. Happy with my find, I tear a foil square from one of the strips in the box and return to Connor's side.

He casts an uneasy glance at the baby monitor before nodding quickly at the items in my hand. "Don't, uh, don't drag it out. Y'now, just in case…" He tilts his head back towards the bedside table and my lips twitch upwards with amusement.

Still, I'm just as keyed up as he is, so I don't tease him. I uncap the little bottle with a *click* and then make short work of prepping my new lover, watching his face for any signs of unease.

But, as with everything else, he's enthusiastic and responsive, bearing down onto my slippery fingers, panting and begging for more while he grips the base of his cock but doesn't stroke it.

"Now," he urges, canting his hips up. "Now, Will. I'm good."

I suit up and toss the re-capped bottle and empty foil wrapper off the side of the bed. Connor arches his back, already gripping at the sheets on either side of his hips while I crawl back over him and line myself up.

Hot, tight perfection engulfs me as I slowly slide inside him.

"Fuck, *Will*," Connor half pleads, half praises, "more. *More*. Move. I…*oh God, yes.*"

I bend over him, bringing his bent legs with me, forcing him to open further so I can thrust in deeper and harder. He helps me along, gripping his thighs under his knees, practically turning himself into a sexy human pretzel, all the while babbling obscenities and compliments on the edge of every gasped exhale I force from him with my movements.

Between us, his cock is flushed a deep red and is spilling precum in surprisingly copious amounts, considering it has been left untouched. Connor writhes beneath me, and the feel of him clenching and squeezing around my sheathed cock has familiar tell-tale tingles of pleasure coursing through my extremities and balls.

I piston my hips harder, faster, listening to Connor's breathing hitch every time I bottom out. It's music to my ears, and I encourage him with low, panted, 'Yes, baby's and 'tell me how you like it's.

I know when I've grazed his prostate when he jerks and cries out, his 'please's and 'more's turning into a repeated mantra of "There, there, there, there!" timed with every pass of my cock.

"I'm gon-" he starts, then whimpers and arches off the mattress with a cry, "I'm gonna…oh, God, *Will*. Fuck, Will. Fuck! I'm there, I'm-" the last word cuts off, morphing into a strangled cry as he releases between us, his body clamping down around me while his cock jerks and spurts.

My own orgasm crests and hits me like a tsunami, crashing over me with a thunderous silence in my ears. I stop thrusting, instead grinding my emptying cock as far into Connor as I can, wringing every last drop of pleasure from the experience.

Then I carefully withdraw, remove and tie off the condom, and collapse in a sweaty heap beside him, breathing heavily but feeling immeasurably light.

Connor snuggles into my side, attached like a limpet, and lazily kisses my pec.

"That was worth the wait," he says, and I can hear the smile in his voice. Kissing the top of his sweaty mop of hair, I can't help but agree.

He goes quiet again for a moment, his fingers twisting and toying with my chest hair, before he asks, "No regrets?"

With the arm wrapped around him, I squeeze him closer to me. We still have to talk, but there's only one way I can answer his question. "Absolutely not."

"Good."

Chapter Thirteen — Connor

Will and I manage to sneak in a super quick shower, sadly without any additional exploration of each other's bodies, and get dressed before Vicky starts to stir from her nap. As though choreographed, Will heads out into the kitchen to sort out a bottle while I head into the nursery to scoop the baby up and get her changed. I frown when I feel that her skin feels a little warm again, and I glance at the clock, glad that she's booked in to see the doctor in a couple of hours' time.

She's fussy and whiny when I carry her out into the main living space of the apartment, and Will hands over the bottle without needing to be asked.

I still can't believe the changes that have taken place today. When I woke up, I was still convinced that he would never want me. Not with Vicky in the picture. Not with knowing that I can't do casual flings anymore. Not with knowing that anything between us will have to get serious fast.

But here we are. I haven't scared him away. I haven't freaked him out with the declarations of my feelings or my intentions for a future with him. Instead, it only seemed to bring us closer.

Obviously, we still need to talk about where we're going to go from here. We need to talk about what my idea of 'serious' is, and whether his idea matches up with it. We need to talk about how now seems to be the perfect time to trial a relationship, while Vicky doesn't actually know what's going on and before she can get too attached, just in case he doesn't want to do the stepparent thing after all.

We need to talk about the fact that I might already be too attached to him anyway.

We need to talk about how fucking mind-blowing the sex between us was, because hot damn do we have chemistry!

And, oh yeah, we should probably actually talk about whether he is okay with dating someone his sons' age. I mean, he might be alright with it, but will they? I don't want to come between him and the boys (*men,* I correct myself, because I am only three years their senior) he loves so much.

I don't have a problem with our age gap. Sixteen years doesn't really seem like a lot now that I'm in my thirties. It's not even a topic that comes up all that often, because we have similar interests and conversation flows easily between us. But I still understand that some people might look at us with raised eyebrows and concern.

Some people like his sons.

His sons who I have never met.

Well, no, I think I met Jack -the one he works with- the night of Daisy's accident, but I am not counting that for obvious reasons.

From all the stories Will has told me, Jack and Wes sound

like great guys. They sound like the sorts of people I'd get along with socially. Well, you know, if I wasn't fucking their dad. Some people tend to get squeamish about that sort of thing.

Ugh.

I don't know why this is suddenly playing on my thoughts. I don't know why it's suddenly making me anxious to consider. Will is a grown man. I am also a grown man. Ergo, there's nothing wrong with us being in a relationship, and I'm sure his rational, adult sons will be fine with it.

I hope.

Jesus, what is wrong with me?

I am sure his sons will be fine with it. But will they be okay with their dad signing up to be a stepdad to a newborn? Imagine being thirty and getting a surprise baby stepsister!

I'm getting ahead of myself again.

Besides, we can just call them Uncle Jack and Uncle Wes. It doesn't have to be a sibling thing. We can set the rules.

My brain stammers to a halt at the manic level my thoughts have reached. I tell myself I'm going to take things as slowly as possible for Will's sake and then leap into 'what is my daughter going to call his sons'. Because that's *definitely* taking it slow.

Seriously, what the actual fuck is wrong with me?!

"You all good?" Will's deep, soothing voice, so deliciously accented, pulls me back from the brink of crazy mental rambling.

I lift Vicky towards him. "Does she feel warm again to you?"

With a frown marring his handsome face, Will gently touches Vicky's forehead with the back of his hand, then nods. "Yeah," he sighs. "I'd say the fever's coming back. I'll get the thermometer. Did you want to try and get her in to see the doc earlier than planned?"

This! This right here is exactly why I keep getting ahead of myself. Because the man I'm falling for is just slipping into this with me so effortlessly. Hell, he's parenting her more naturally than I am which, when I stop to think about it, isn't exactly a surprise. He has experience. I don't. I wasn't expecting to be a dad, whereas he already was one.

It's going to break my heart if he decides that this is too much for him after all.

And I'm doing it again.

Great.

Focus, Connor.

Will re-emerges from the hallway with the fancy infrared thermometer Daisy had insisted was a necessity and hovers it over Vicky's forehead while she finishes her bottle. He hums at the back of his throat and shows me the digital screen after it beeps.

"Thirty-eight," he reads for me. "Not as high as last night, but still technically a fever."

"Here, you take her and I'll see if I can get an earlier appointment," I tell him, already passing Vicky across to him in a move that has become almost second nature to me over the past month.

I don't think about how domestic this all feels while I fish my phone from my pocket and swipe at the screen, pulling the number for the doctor's surgery up and pressing the little green 'call' icon. I don't think about how much we already feel like a family, even while I glance over at him cooing at the baby while I listen to the obnoxiously cheerful hold message. I don't contemplate whether I should add him as one of Vicky's or my emergency contacts because he's strong in a crisis and he lives in the same building.

And I certainly don't wonder about what is considered a reasonable time frame to do any of the above.

Thankfully, I'm distracted from my not-thoughts when one of the receptionists answers my call, and we chat back and forth as I explain the situation. I hear her tapping at her keyboard rapidly while she 'umm's and 'ahh's pleasantly, trying to help me out. When she tells me that I'm in luck and that there's an appointment in half an hour's time courtesy of a cancellation, I snap it up and thank her profusely. Then I tell her we'll be in soon and end the call with relief.

Will's already getting the nappy bag arranged by the time I tuck my phone back into my pocket.

"Did you, um, want to come with us?" My question comes out awkwardly and I wince and backpedal immediately. "Not that you have to. I just know you're worried about her, too. I mean, not *worried* worried. Babies get sick. But-"

"I'd like to tag along," he says, interrupting my nervous babble. However, my relief is short-lived when he shakes his head and adds, "But I have a few errands to run and calls to make. Can I meet you back here in, say, two hours?" He checks his watch. "We can have a late lunch."

I have no reason to be disappointed that he doesn't want to come to a baby's doctor's visit, I tell myself. This is all part of me rushing headlong into a long-term relationship when we've only just agreed to start dating. The man deserves a little space, and maybe I could use it as well. A reminder that, as happy as he is to be helpful with Vicky, she's not actually his responsibility. She's mine, and mine alone. At least for now.

"Sure," I chirp at him, cringing internally at just how forced my enthusiasm sounded to my own ears. I clear my throat and try again, aiming for something a bit more genuine. "That sounds good. Thanks."

He passes me the grey linen nappy bag and I sling it over my shoulder before he wraps his arm around my waist and pulls me in for a kiss, mindful of the squirming baby in his other arm. "Good," he declares, his tone warm and playful, "it's a date."

And, just like that, my spirits soar all over again.

* * *

The doctor's visit is pretty routine. When she was born, I opted for Vicky to share the same GP that I've been seeing for the past few years, a middle-aged woman with a kind smile and a no-nonsense demeanour. During today's visit, she checked Vicky over, asked me the same questions Will had last night, and typed away at her computer, noting Vicky's symptoms and my answers into her file.

"Well," she says at last, after inspecting the insides of Vicky's tiny ears, "it looks and sounds like an ear infection. Not uncommon with babies, but painful. She's over a month old, so you can treat with Panadol. I'll send you home with a script for antibiotics, too, but give it a couple of days to clear up on its own before you try that, if that's alright with you. If you don't see signs of improvement, even after a couple of days with the antibiotics, come back and see me again."

And that's that.

I thank our doctor once she hands me the printed prescription while I pull the strap of the nappy bag back over my shoulder. I head back out of the doctor's office and into the reception area to pay the bill, where I'm told the appointment has been bulk billed today. Apparently my GP always bulk bills for kids under the age of thirteen, which is good to know.

We duck into the chemist next door to get the prescription filled, and then we're able to head home.

Out in the sunshine, I chat to Vicky as I carry her back to the car.

"Well, that was worth the trip, wasn't it, Miss Priss?"

She squints up at the sound of my voice, clearly not loving the bright sunlight.

"And Doctor Walters didn't make me feel like a panicky new parent or anything," I continue, looking left and right before stepping across the pedestrian crossing between the buildings and the carpark. It's such a short walk from one to the other, that I didn't bother with the pram.

Vicky makes a quiet sound of complaint, flailing a little arm jerkily. I tsk.

"I know, I know, we'll be out of the sun before you know it."

"Connor?" A voice says my name in question as we're passing the first row of cars in the paved lot. I'm parked in the second, under the shade of a large tree. "Oh, hey! Connor!"

I stop and turn to face the owner of the voice, bracing myself for the pity and strained conversation. Outside of Henry, Sarah, and Will, that's all I've gotten from any of my original friendship circle. Well, from the half that remained my friends. Ant made off with a bunch of them during the split, but he deserves those arseholes anyway. Good riddance to bad rubbish and all that jazz.

"Mick," I greet my old friend with a pasted-on smile, readjusting Vicky in my arms. "Hey. How are you?"

As expected, his face shifts into immediate sympathy, and

he softens his voice to match. "Better than you, I'm guessing. How are you holding up? How's the little one?" He makes no move to get closer to her, eyeing her more like she's an explosive device than a baby.

His wariness amuses me, and I find myself beaming at him. "I'm good. Great, actually. And she's...well, I mean, okay, she's got an ear infection right now, but she's perfect."

Mick's a caterer friend who I met when I decided to give up my career in law to pursue event coordination instead. We've worked a few big events and parties together in our time, and I am always impressed with his food and his presentation skills. And he fell into place in my eclectic little social group effortlessly, which was a plus.

He blinks big, blue eyes at me from beneath a floppy red fringe, clearly surprised by my upbeat demeanour and happy reply. "Uh...wow. That's, well, that's great." He exhales, cocks his head as though inspecting me properly, and then a genuine smile tugs at his freckled face. "That's really good to hear, Con. We've all been thinking of you."

I nod, not wanting to say that *I'm* not the one who died and any one of my mates could have picked up the phone at any time to check in. The bitter thought isn't really fair. Life goes both ways, doesn't it? I could have reached out to them, too, after all.

"Yeah. It's been an intense month, but things are getting better." I think of Will, of the lunch date we're going to have after I get home, of the promises of more toe-curling kisses and more sex and I grin again. "What about you?" I ask, jiggling Vicky a little as she starts to sound restless, "How've you been?"

Mick shrugs. "Same old, same old. I worked that wedding

you got me booked for the other week. That was a lot," he scrunches up his nose. "Bride and groom were fantastic, but the mother of the bride needs to take a long walk off a short fucking pier." His eyes widen in horror, and he covers his mouth with both hands, looking down at Vicky. "Shit. Sorry. Fuck. Oh, God damn it."

Laughter bubbles up and out of me and I make no attempt to stop it. That's when it hits me that I've missed this: laughing with friends, feeling light, carefree, and 'normal'. I'm going to have to make an effort to reconnect with everyone. I might as well start with Mick.

Shaking my head, I roll my eyes at him. "She's a month old, mate. She doesn't understand a word you're saying, and she's even less likely to repeat it."

"I'll take your word for it," he backs up a bit, as though expecting Vicky to start swearing any second. "Anyway, I'll let you get her home, yeah? She doesn't seem all that impressed that I've kept you."

He's right: Vicky is getting grizzly. I readjust her in my arms and nod, smiling genuinely at my friend. "I'll text you, alright? We'll get the whole gang together for drinks soon." Well, what was left of the gang. I was going to be bitter about the friends who had taken Ant's side for a while. *Arseholes*.

"Sounds like a plan," Mick replies, then he leans forward again, clearly tentative, and offers Vicky a funny little wave. "It was nice meeting you, missy."

She chooses that moment to squawk her displeasure and Mick hightails it out of there. My laughter follows him, and I'm still chuckling as I make the short drive back to my apartment.

It was genuinely good to catch up with a friend, and I resolve to stand by my promise to Mick. I can't let my entire life go just because I miss my sister. She wouldn't want it that way, and she wouldn't want me to raise Vicky like that, either.

Chapter Fourteen – Will

J ack takes one look at me when he walks through the door to my apartment and smirks. "You," he declares, stretching out on the couch with his hands behind his head and his feet propped casually on my coffee table, "got laid."

"Jesus," I pinch the bridge of my nose. "Really?"

"You're not denying it," he sing-songs, completely ignoring my discomfort.

"Why can't you be more like your brother?"

Jack rolls his eyes. "You'd die of boredom if Wes and I were both uptight sticks in the mud." He shrugs. "Besides, I'm not the one who got suspended in tenth grade."

"No, but you're the one who encouraged him to free the mice from the biology lab."

He grins wickedly. "Wes is, was, and always will be a bleeding heart," he shrugs. Then he waggles his index finger at me. "But that's not going to get you out of telling me all about whoever it was that gave you that whole afterglow deal

160

you've got going on."

"I swear to God, Jack…" I feel my cheeks heating up. "I don't have an 'afterglow thing'."

"Pfft," he dismisses. "And I'm Wonder Woman."

"You'd never fit the costume."

My son laughs and shakes his head. "Fine. Batman, then."

"If you had Batman's funds, you wouldn't be working a normal job. You'd spend all your time in the gym."

"Wrong," he corrects me, "I would buy my own sports teams and put myself on every single one."

That does sound very much like a Jack plan.

"Anyway," he continues, now narrowing his gaze at me, "you're being cagey. So, I'm guessing it wasn't just a *Grindr* thing." Drumming his fingers on one of his thighs, he runs through the limited options in his head. Then his eyes widen. "The neighbour? Really?"

I can't read his tone. It's not disapproving, but there's a hint of something serious there.

"Dad," he's moved into cautious, which is so out of character for him that it makes me sit up straight and take notice, "I'm not saying it's not great, but…he's probably looking for something serious and permanent."

"And you think I'm not?" My own tone is calm and measured, but I can't help the note of steel behind it.

Jack blinks at me. "I know you're attached to his kid, Dad, but come on. This guy's my age. You're old enough to be-"

I interrupt him, not wanting to hear it. "If he doesn't care about my age, and I don't care about his, should it matter?"

The question is defensive, but I'm doing my best to keep my voice even and calm. Jack's voicing my own concerns, after all. And he's my son: I want him to get along with Connor, especially if things go well and Connor and I do decide to give a serious, long-term relationship a shot.

After a moment of staring me down, Jack shakes his head. "No, of course not. But we're not just talking about your relationship with a younger man here. He's got a baby. Are you really okay with that?" He holds up his hands in surrender before I can get even more defensive. "I'm not saying you shouldn't be. But it's a lot. You drilled that into Wes's and my heads from puberty."

He's got me there: in a bid to prevent them from becoming surprise parents early on in life, I might have gone a little hard on the sex ed talks. Jen had thought it hilarious. In hindsight, I'll admit I probably went overboard. It wasn't as though I regretted having my boys, and I certainly didn't think they'd held me back in life, but I'd still wanted them both to think before unexpectedly committing themselves to parenthood.

And that's the difference here. I am thinking about it. I'm not an eighteen-year-old who should have thought twice about having unprotected sex with his girlfriend, especially when it was a desperate attempt to hide who he was. I'm a forty-nine-year-old man who is going into a relationship with a single new dad with his eyes open.

"I did," I acknowledge with a nod. "And I appreciate your concern, but I know what I'm getting myself into." I offer him a fond smile. "If I survived you and Wes when I was a clueless kid, one tiny baby girl isn't going to scare me off now."

I watch as my son grins widely and settles back into the couch cushions, relaxed again. "Good," he declares, then asks, "so, when am I going to meet him properly, then? I've been looking forward to giving someone the 'you hurt my dad and they'll never find your body' speech."

"Don't you dare," I threaten him without any heat. I know he's only teasing. Then I shrug. "If you hang around for another hour or so, he'll turn up. He had to take Vicky to the doctor: she's been sick."

Jack's eyes light up with genuine excitement. "Holy shit," he practically bounces in his seat, and it's an amusing sight considering his bulky frame, "you're actually going to let me meet him? Damn, you must be serious about this one. I can't remember ever meeting one of your boyfriends before."

That's true as well. A testament to the utter lack of serious relationships in my past. I can't even deny it. So, in some ways, I'm not exactly going into this relationship with any more experience than Connor after all. We're on a more even keel than he realises, and I make a mental note to discuss that with him. He deserves to know that. He deserves to know that I'm probably going to screw up because I don't really know what it's like to have a life partner. A spouse? A significant other? A real boyfriend? Why do none of these words feel right?

Before I can say anything else, Jack's got his phone in his hand and is swiping at the screen, and it's too late before I realise that he's calling his brother and putting the call on speaker.

"What's up?" Wes asks, and he sounds distracted.

"Dad's got a boyfriend," Jack blurts without a proper greeting either. He sounds like a giddy teenager, as does his brother when he squeals over the line.

"What? Really?" Wes sounds more excited about this than when he called last week to tell me that Vanna had accepted his marriage proposal. "Who?"

"The neighbour guy," Jack answers readily.

"Connor?" Wes's voice offers, his memory as sharp as ever. "That's the one."

I sit back and let them gossip, just waiting for my chance to give my input. Then, predictably, Wes asks, "So, when are we meeting him?"

Proving that siblings never change from childhood, Jack relishes in being able to tell his brother, "Well, *I* get to meet him this afternoon. If you hadn't moved over an hour away, you could have, too."

I swear, it's like they're still six years old sometimes.

At least Wes doesn't squawk about how unfair that is. He just sighs. "Then you're going to have to report back to me. Make sure he's good for Dad."

"Oh, for fuck's sake," I mutter. "If the two of you could trust my judgement and remember that I'm the parent here, that'd be great."

Realising that he's on speaker and that I'm present for the conversation, Wes launches into a series of questions similar to Jack's. It's not the first time he has broached the topic of the baby being in the picture, but this time, knowing that Connor and I are actually involved, he's far more serious.

"You're really okay with doing the baby thing all over again?" he asks and sounds so much like Jack that I want to laugh.

"I think so," I answer honestly. "Vicky's been a package deal from the start. And I love her. But, like I told your brother," I pause to shoot a pointed glance at Jack, "we're taking this slowly and talking about everything as we go. She's not old enough to get too attached to me yet, so if it doesn't work out…"

"She won't remember," Wes's tone softens. "But you and Connor can still hurt each other, Dad."

"That's true of any relationship," I argue. "If I let a fear of getting hurt -emotionally or otherwise- stop me from living, I'd be a hermit."

Wes chuckles at that. The sound is a little tinny through the speaker of Jack's phone. "Okay, that's a fair point. But if you're serious about Connor, I want to meet him, too. Maybe Vanna and I can come visit next weekend?"

I stifle a snort at the way Jack petulantly rolls his eyes at the mention of his brother's fiancé. "What," Jack wheedles, "you can't do things separately anymore? You're one of those nauseating couples who lives in each other's pockets?"

"If you stopped whoring around and actually tried being serious with someone," Wes snipes back, "you might actually understand."

Watching the bitter twist of Jack's features has me stepping in before they can start arguing for real.

Children, I think to myself as I say, "Okay, that's enough. Yes, Wes, bring Vanna next Saturday and we'll do lunch. I'll be on night shift, but I can make it work. Maybe we can go to the Mexican place down the hill? And stop calling your brother a whore. Jack," I point my index finger at him, "you stop teasing your brother about his relationship."

There's a pause before they both sigh and say, "Yes, Dad" at the same time, in the same voice.

Then Jack catches my eye and smirks, "You really wanna sign up for this all over again?"

I think of Vicky, of how tiny and perfect she is, colicky nights and all, and I consider all the horror stories from Jen over the years, especially as her girls hit their teens.

"Yeah," I nod. "I really do."

* * *

Jack's still loitering in my apartment when Connor knocks at the door. I've just thought that I really should get him a key when I realise just how many steps forward I'm leaping with that thought. But our situation isn't your standard dating relationship and I'm not going to pretend otherwise.

"I've got it," I tell Jack before he can spring off the couch and scare my lover off with his enthusiasm. Wandering across the living room, I pull the door open and step out into the hallway so I can properly greet and warn Connor.

"Hey?" He greets me with curiosity as I pull the door gently closed behind me. He happily accepts the chaste kiss to his lips, though. "What's up?"

I pluck a grizzling Vicky from his hold and tuck her up against my shoulder. "I know I promised you a late lunch date, but Jack wanted to meet you properly, and I didn't have the heart to say no."

What I don't tell him is how invested I am in seeing them get along. He doesn't need the added pressure, and I know that he's already a bit anxious about being practically the same age as my kids.

"He's your son," Connor shrugs lightly. "I wouldn't ever ask you to choose between spending time with them or me."

"I know. But…" I cringe, "he can be a lot. So, brace yourself."

That earns me a snicker. "You've met Henry. If I can handle him on far too many red bull and vodkas, I can handle anyone."

I search Connor's eyes to make sure he really is okay with having this sudden 'meet my family' moment sprung on him. "Just know that I won't blame you if you need to fabricate an excuse to escape." I pause. "Maybe we should have a safe

166

word?"

This time, Connor outright laughs. "I don't need a safe word to get out of a conversation with your son, Will."

"All the same, I suggest 'pumpernickel'."

He shakes his head, still amused. "I'm sure I can work out a very natural way to slip that in, too," he teases with light sarcasm. Then he gestures towards the door with his chin. "Come on, you coward."

"I'm not a coward," I protest, though it does seem as though I'm more anxious about this than he is. I wonder if that's just because I want this to go well, or whether I'm concerned that he's putting on a front for me. Maybe it's both.

Nevertheless, I turn back around and use my free hand to turn the handle of the door, asking Connor over my shoulder, "How'd the doctor's visit go?" as Vicky continues to fuss in my hold.

"Ear infection," he sighs. "Doc said to give her Panadol and, if there's no improvement over the next day or so, she sent her home with some antibiotics, too. But, because of her age, and because the symptoms are mild, she wants me to hold off on those if we can."

I nod and rub Vicky's back soothingly. "Poor princess," I murmur.

Jack has clearly been watching the entire interaction, but he stands up to greet Connor properly once we're fully inside my apartment with the door closed.

"Hi," he says, smiling down at Connor with his hand extended, "I'm Jack. it's great to meet you. Dad talks about you and Vicky non-stop."

Connor blushes and looks at me to verify or deny the statement, and I shrug as he takes Jack's hand and gives it a quick shake. It's not like Connor hasn't been a big part of my life for the past month or so, after all, and he knows I care about him a lot.

"It's nice to meet you, too," he replies to Jack, then he steps back and closer to my side.

Ah, so not as confident as he pretended to be, then.

I tug him against me with my free hand and Jack makes grabby motions towards the baby I'm holding at my shoulder.

"May I?" Jack asks, and it surprises me because I've never known my son to be at all interested in kids, especially babies. I glance down at Connor and he bites his lip, but he nods all the same.

"She's a bit fussy," he tells Jack. "She's got an ear infection. I stopped in at my place and gave her Panadol and a bottle before we came up, though, so it should be kicking in soon."

Jack bobs his head in understanding and I carefully transfer the baby into his arms, blinking when he settles her head in the crook of one arm and starts to rock gently. It hits me that I've never seen either of my boys interacting with kids, and Jack seems perfectly at ease like this.

"Don't go getting any ideas," he says playfully without looking up. "I'm not interested in making you a grandpa anytime soon."

I scrunch my nose at even the suggestion, and Connor laughs, wrapping his arm around my waist. "Oh, I like him," he says. "Is Wes just as funny?"

"Nope," Jack answers before I can, still smiling down at Vicky, "Wes is boring. I'm the fun one."

Connor snorts.

"Have you eaten?" I ask him, remembering my original promise for a late lunch date. He shakes his head. "What do you feel like? I can whip some sandwiches up?" It's hardly romantic fare, but I can make up for that later when Jack is gone.

"I'm fine," Connor says, but Jack 'tsk's.

Connor's about to discover that my son is every bit the mother hen I am and then some.

"You've gotta eat, man," he tells my lover, finally looking up from the baby and pinning Connor with a serious stare. "You're probably not sleeping properly, so you've gotta get your energy boosts somewhere."

"I can grab a protein shake from downstairs later," Connor waves a dismissive hand. "I feel like all I've been doing for weeks is eating and sleeping at any possible opportunity." He cringes and looks down at his body. "I haven't seen the inside of the gym since before…"

Connor's words trail off with a tinge of sadness. It's not hard to understand what the *before* references.

"You can always use Dad's home gym," Jack offers easily, redirecting the conversation before the melancholy can set in, but also not dismissing or ignoring Connor's upset, either.

I'm once again filled with pride, and I wonder how Jen and I raised such amazing people. While I'm lost in that thought, Jack keeps talking.

"It's basic, but at least you can bring the baby up here while you work out. And I'm sure if he's not working, Dad won't mind looking after the Vickster here while you head out to the real gym, too."

I feel a little guilty for not offering to look after Vicky on my own sooner, to be honest. I'm sure there are plenty of things Connor would like to do without carting the baby around. And I haven't asked him about his job, either, or how the adoption process is going.

My thoughts snowball while Jack keeps Connor occupied. I leave them both to it and head into my kitchen, pulling out the fixings to make sandwiches for all three of us.

We eat around my dining table when they're done, and by the time Jack's making sounds about having to leave, he and Connor are thick as thieves.

"You've got my number," Jack says as he heads towards the door. "You should totally think about joining my indoor soccer team. Dad'll look after Vicky on those nights."

"I'll give it a go," Connor nods. "I do need to get active again. Can I bring a friend?" He looks at me and smiles a conspiratorial smile. "Henry might be grateful for a reason to leave the house."

I nod, then explain for Jack's benefit, "Connor's best friend also has a newborn at home. He's, what, two weeks old now?"

"Yeah," Connor says, "something like that. I need to go visit again."

"You've had a lot on your plate," I remind him, "and now Vicky's not well, either. He'll understand better than you think."

"True," Connor muses.

Jack clears his throat, bringing the conversation back on track. "Anyway, sure, bring your buddy along. The more the merrier."

They chat about it some more as Connor follows Jack to the door, and I can't help but feel like I'm the luckiest guy in the world.

170

Chapter Fifteen — Connor

D ating Will is almost too easy. I honestly can't recall any of my previous relationships working this well. Nothing about our schedule really changes over the next few months. We still work around his shifts, but when he's on day shifts, he spends evenings at my apartment helping with Vicky, having dinner at my dining table, and then making love to me in my bed. Some nights he even stays over, though most see him heading home upstairs as I drift off to sleep.

I do join Jack's soccer team and Henry tags along every other week. On those weeks, Henry usually tells me he can't believe I manage raising Vicky on my own, and I gently remind him that I have Will to help more often than not. We've stopped pretending that he's 'slowly' trying out being a parental figure again, because it's more than obvious to anyone with eyes and ears that he's all in with Vicky.

Will's other son, Wes, is also a nice guy. I've only met him in person a couple of times since Will and I started dating. Even so, he seems as kind as his brother, and his fiancé, Vanna, is a delight. Sometimes, though, she reminds me a lot of Daisy in her mannerisms or feisty attitude, and the pang of missing Daze hits me hard. Will gets it, though, and he never pushes me to talk about it until I'm ready.

When I follow through on my plan to reconnect with my friends, he's equally supportive. Some of them are surprised when I introduce him as my boyfriend, but he's charming and they can all see how happy he makes me. So by the end of our first casual get-together, where both of his sons are also in attendance along with a handful of his friends and colleagues, our two groups seem to have melded into one.

Life is good.

By the time Vicky is six months old, I can't remember it being anything else. Of course, this is also the time that I realise I have to look at restarting my business again. Between my inheritance from Dad and Daisy's life insurance, I can afford to be a stay-at-home dad for a lot longer, but I don't want to. I've finally leased out Daisy's apartment, and the funds from that are going directly into a savings account for Vicky's future. Financially, we're set, but I'm starting to feel like I've lost myself.

So I bring the idea up with Will.

Unsurprisingly, where Ant poo-pooed my aspirations as an Events Coordinator, Will supports them.

"You do a lot of the work from home, right?" he asks over dinner. He and I are eating grilled chicken with asparagus and a side of spiced brown rice, but Vicky is sitting in her highchair, mashing her chubby little fingers into what remains of her pureed vegetables.

I cringe at her, but the dimpled, toothless grin she throws my way makes the clean-up I'm facing all worthwhile. Then I turn my attention back to Will and nod. "Yeah, most of it. I do have to visit venues and clients occasionally, but a lot of the actual organising can be worked from here."

The internet is a beautiful thing indeed.

"That should help with daycare issues. At least until she's toddling and into everything." Will sets down his cutlery and reaches for the ever-present tub of wet wipes in the middle of the table.

My apartment is a far cry from the minimalist oasis it was six months ago. Now, there's a brightly coloured plastic playpen in the middle of my living room, the coffee table long gone. The light grey linen couch has been replaced by a much more comfortable, but less stylish, dark grey sofa. There are toys of all shapes and sizes and colours scattered around the space, and I know that as Vicky becomes more mobile, that's only going to get worse.

Will wipes down Vicky's grubby hands and cheeks while I swipe at the mess on the plastic tabletop of her highchair.

"It won't be that long until she's crawling," I acknowledge. "That's bad enough."

Will knows my complaints are half-hearted at best. I have been excited over every single milestone she's hit so far. Smiling, rolling over, sitting up by herself: every little thing she achieves is something to marvel over. Thankfully, Will has celebrated each one with me. Crawling is a big one that I'm looking forward to.

"Then maybe daycare is something we should look into anyway?" Will suggests, and I love the way he includes himself in these decisions now.

For the first few months, it was awkward drawing lines about just how much I should include him when it came to

Vicky. I knew that he cared -that he even loved her- but was he going to be a stepparent, or a passive observer unless otherwise asked, or was he going to acknowledge the fact that he's been raising her since birth just as much as I have? I didn't want to push him, and it's only been the last few weeks where he's started to accept that he's her dad as much as I am.

And, while we've only been together for five months, I'm tempted to ask him how he feels about me updating my will to name him as her guardian should anything happen to me. Right now, Henry and Sarah are on the paperwork, but Vicky adores Will. Some days, I think she loves him more than she loves me.

And it won't be long before she starts to talk, either.

Do I really want her calling him Will? The number of times I've almost slipped and referred to him as Daddy or Papa is ridiculous.

Hell, even Jack calls us Daddy Con and Daddy Will when he's talking to her. Surely if Will had an issue with that, he'd say something, right?

"Con? Sweetheart, are you with me?"

I give myself a little shake and offer Will a rueful smile. "Sorry, I was lost in thought. You were still talking about daycare?"

His eyebrows furrow. "Yeah," he answers cautiously, letting Vicky grab and slobber all over his hand while he continues to feed himself with his other one. "What's wrong?"

"Nothing, honest. Just...thinking."

The way he arches one of those greying eyebrows is too sexy for such a simple action. "Uh huh." He doesn't sound convinced.

I lick my lips anxiously. "You're happy, right? I mean, with

174

us? With how things are going?"

Will's gorgeous blue-grey eyes widen, and he sets his fork down, pinning me with his whole attention. "Where's this coming from?"

That wasn't an answer, but I'm not insecure enough to think that he's deliberately avoiding the question. I've just taken him by surprise, and now I need to put it all on the table. I hadn't been planning on doing this so soon, but the thoughts have been swirling around in my head for days -weeks, really- and if I don't put them out there, my brain might explode.

"I'm thinking of updating my will," I blurt, cringing at the clumsy way I'm handling this conversation. "I mean, if you're okay with it."

"I don't think that dating you for a few months gives me the right to tell you what to put in your will."

"Ugh," I facepalm, "I'm fucking this up." I push my plate out of the way and force myself to look my handsome boyfriend in the eye. "If something happens to me, I want Vicky to stay with her other dad, Will. Not with Henry and Sarah."

His expression scrunches into confusion as he silently repeats 'other dad', his mouth forming the words a couple of times before I watch the penny drop. "*Oh*," he inhales, and his eyes take on a wet sheen that he blinks away quickly. "But I-"

"Have literally been there since she was born," I finish for him. "I know we said we'd take this slow, but can you honestly tell me you're not her dad too? I mean honestly, Will?"

As if to punctuate my statement, the little princess slams her pudgy fists down on her highchair table and squeals.

Will laughs, but it's a fragile sound.

"I don't want to rush you," I try to reel it back, but he reaches

175

for my hand across the table and shakes his head.

"No, I love her," he insists as I place my hand in his. He squeezes mine. "Con, I love *you*. I love you both."

Now it's my turn to inhale sharply, because we haven't exchanged those words yet. Not until now. I'd always imagined that we would do so in bed while he was slowly rocking into my body, a veritable romantic cliché. But this? This impromptu, unexpected, completely random moment shared over a meal I threw together within half an hour after a day trying to entertain an increasingly cranky infant?

This is *perfect*.

"I love you, too," I tell him earnestly. "*We* love you. It's why I asked…no, it's why I want you to know that you are her dad in every way that counts. I want her to call you Dad. Or Daddy. Or Papa. Or…whatever. I want you to know that you're my equal in this. I would have been lost without you, you know that, right?"

Okay, so maybe I won't avoid all the romantic clichés after all.

Will's Adam's apple bobs as he swallows roughly, and then he's standing up and tugging at my hand, pulling me up with him. He walks behind Vicky's highchair and then yanks me against him, taking my mouth in a forceful kiss that leaves nothing to the imagination. It's deep and passionate and full of promises that guarantee a sleepless night in all the best ways. His tongue tangos with mine, his beard tickling my skin, and I give the same energy right back to him.

"Move in with me?" I pant as we separate. "Make our family whole?"

It's a lot to ask after only a handful of months, but Will doesn't hesitate. His smile is wide and beaming as he nods.

"Okay."

There are logistics we'll need to talk about. He has quite the bachelor pad set up upstairs, and I know that, when the shine of the moment we've just shared wears off, losing his home gym will be unpalatable to him. But I don't need a guest bedroom here anymore, and I'm happy to make sacrifices and compromises to ensure that Will knows that this is his home as much as it is mine. I don't think he'll want to sell his apartment, but will he consider renting it out? And what about all his furniture and his TV? These are all concerns for later.

For now, I want desperately to consummate this new development in our relationship. It feels so much bigger than any step I've ever taken with a lover before. Sure, Ant moved in with me, but that never felt this significant. This feels more binding. More formal. More like an actual commitment.

I guess, in many ways, it is.

He's just agreed that he's my daughter's other father. We're officially co-parents, even if the adoption still hasn't yet been finalised on my end and we haven't spoken about him also adopting her, too. Those legalities aren't as important as the intent of our words to each other. Not to me, anyway.

Sadly, though, as much as I want to get naked and celebrate with him, the whining six-month-old beside us demands my immediate attention.

"Later," Will practically purrs into my ear, as though he's reading my mind.

A thrill of anticipation races through me.

Later can't come soon enough.

* * *

"Thank fuck colic is a distant memory," I declare after Vicky is safely sleeping in her cot. We've recently moved her out of her bassinet for good and, while I'm slightly anxious not having her right by my side, it's better for my sex life this way.

And what a sex life it is.

Will's mouth is sucking and licking a path down my neck and bare shoulder. We shed our clothes on our way down the short hallway and into the bedroom, leaving a trail behind us. But it was worth it, because now we're naked and pressed up against each other, and it is just as wonderful as the first time we did this.

As I have done so many times before, I drop to my knees in front of my hot fireman and nuzzle my face into his crotch, breathing his musky, masculine scent in as I tease his heavy, hard cock with my cheek.

Will's broad palm lands on the top of my head, his fingers threading into my hair. He groans as I pull back a touch to tease the head of his straining erection with tiny kitten licks. The taste of his precum, slightly salty and so damn appealing, tantalises my tastebuds and I want *more*.

He rewards me with exhalations of praise and encouragement as I take him into my mouth properly, wrapping my hand around the base of his cock when I know I can't deep throat the whole length. I suck, and I slurp, and I moan around him, fondling his fuzzy balls with my free hand. He rocks his hips into the motion I set, while I close my eyes and relish the moment.

This is not how either one of us is going to come tonight, but I can never get enough of this man. The taste of him, the scent of him, the *feel* of him.

Even though none of this is new to us now, I can't help

but think that it still feels different tonight. We exchanged declarations of love and pretty much committed to being parents together forever, and that's kind of epic. I feel closer to him now, like the remaining barriers between us, no matter how thin they were, have been torn down.

This man means everything to me.

That is a startling realisation to have when you've got the guy's dick down your throat, but I'm able to blame the way my eyes well up on the blow job rather than the wave of emotions that washes over me, so that's something.

Not that I'd really hide my emotions from Will. He wouldn't judge me for them.

"Con, sweetheart, your mouth," he's muttering above me, still rocking his hips gently. "I love your mouth. *Fuck*, the things you do to me…"

He is far too coherent, but then I'm not trying to drive him out of his mind with lust right now. This is closer to a lazy blow job than anything. It's just an excuse to taste him, to have him in my hand and mouth. To let him know how much I want him.

He lets me continue for a little while longer before he growls and pulls me to my feet, and his hand wraps around my leaking, aching prick. He kisses me ravenously while his hand slowly strokes me, spreading my sticky precum all over my own shaft.

"On the bed, ass up," he commands, and even five months in, I still love the way his accent curls around words like arse. I'm a proud Aussie at heart, but there are certain words that just sound better in a sexy American accent. (Condom's another one, but that particular rant is one I'll save for another time.)

I do as he says, stifling a squeal when his big, open palm lands on my left butt cheek with a stinging smack. We don't exactly practice anything kinky in the bedroom but, as with every other touch of his skin against mine, excitement rattles through me all the same.

Then both his big hands are squeezing my cheeks, fondling them and spreading them. His thumbs dip into my crack and tease at my hole and then the tickle of hair and the lightest press of his lips to my left cheek alert me to his intentions.

I thank my early evening past self for showering before dinner, especially when the first brush of his warm, wet tongue swipes over my entrance.

"Oh fuck," I bite out sharply, then bury my face in my pillow to prevent myself from getting any louder. I do *not* want to accidentally wake Vicky up tonight.

"Good boy," Will murmurs, his deep voice low and sensual, and I groan into my pillow, the sound extending into a muffled cry at another swipe of his magical tongue.

I lose myself to the pleasure of him eating me out. He works my rim with patience, swirling his tongue and spearing me with it while I writhe and rock back into his delicious attentions. When he adds a finger and crooks it *just so*, teasing my prostate with precision, I have to push my face further into my pillow to cry out in ecstasy.

I beg and whimper and babble obscenities, but Will doesn't change his pace or show any indication that he's in a hurry. I simultaneously adore him and hate him for it.

My cock is aching, leaking as it leans its weight against the inside of my thigh, and I can feel the precum trickling down my leg. But I'm gripping the pillow to my face tightly with both hands, my fingers clenched against the onslaught of pleasure and sensation, and I can't get my brain to work properly. If I could figure out how to adjust my balance and reach for my own cock, I would, but it's too much. Too good. Too...*everything*.

Will's working me open with a couple of fingers now, his tongue still licking and lapping and fucking me, and *God*, it's the best thing ever. I never want him to stop, but I'm also desperate for him to replace his fingers and tongue with that gorgeous cock of his.

"I need..." I try to explain, but the words are muffled by the pillow at my face and I forget where I was going with them when Will toys with my prostate again, making me see stars.

He chuckles, and because his tongue is still inside me, I swear I feel the vibrations of the amused, sexy sound inside me.

"*Will*," I turn my head to beg. My voice is thin, needy, close to breaking point. I want to sob with desperation. This is so damn good. "Will, *please*..."

He doesn't ask what I need, because he knows. I whimper in dismay as he pulls his fingers and that perfect, sinful, decadent tongue of his away, but I watch through bleary eyes as his strong form passes between me and the bedside table to grab the lube and a condom.

"No condom," I blurt, and he stills.

Then he's lying down beside me, his eyes searching mine. "You sure?"

We've been exclusive the whole time we've been together, and I got myself tested after I kicked Ant out, so I nod. "I'm sure. I love you. I want...*need* to feel you. Just you." Tears brim in my eyes, and I don't know why. Well, no, that's a lie. I do know why. "I've never..."

Will's eyes widen. "Never gone bare before?"

I shake my head.

"Not even with-"

"Nope." Some of the fire and desperation has leeched out of me, but this is so important for Will to understand. I offer him a watery smile and a half shrug: it's an awkward manoeuvre with my butt still in the air and my face still smooshed against the pillow. "I don't think I ever trusted him." And maybe that should have been a red flag, but I came to my senses when it counted.

Will's palm cups my cheek and he leans down to kiss me deeply, turning my head a little uncomfortably to get the right angle. Some guys might get squeamish about kissing their lover only a few moments after being thoroughly rimmed, but I don't care. I can taste myself on his tongue, but it just turns me on more, remembering how good he'd made me feel.

When he pulls back, he rests his forehead against mine. "I love you," he tells me softly.

The moment is sweet, but it's starting to feel heavier than I'd like, so I quirk my lips and demand, "So fuck me already."

The skin at the corners of Will's eyes crinkles with his answering smirk. "Yes, sir."

The mattress shifts as he moves back into position behind me, and the *snick* of the cap of the bottle of lube has my cock hardening back up again in a response so ingrained now that I swear it's Pavlovian.

His slick fingers return to my hole, and I can't help grinning into the pillow. Will is a stickler for prepping me properly, no matter how much I rush him. He doesn't want to hurt me, which is sweet, but right now I just want him inside me.

"Will," I whine and buck backwards onto those perfect probing digits. "*Now.*"

"Have I ever told you I love how bossy you are?" he teases,

182

but his fingers withdraw and the hot, slippery head of his cock replaces them, teasing the tight ring of muscle at my entrance.

"Will!" I demand a bit louder, raising my head to glare over my shoulder. "So help me, if you don't—*oh, fuck, yes.*" My complaints melt away as he slides inside me with little resistance. There's still a burn and stretch, but it's minimal and it feels amazing.

"Fuck," he breathes, sounding awed. "Con, you feel so good like this. So hot. So tight. You fit me like a glove, baby."

I groan, egging him on. He's not usually as vocal in bed, and I don't know whether the change is emotional or whether the newness of going bare after months (or, in my case, a lifetime) of always suiting up has shocked the words out of him. Either way, it's driving me wild to hear his thoughts spilling out, and I want as much of that as he'll give.

He doesn't disappoint. "You were made for me," he mutters on another thrust. "Made for my cock. You take it so well, don't you, baby?"

"Yes," I turn my head to hiss, the 's' in the word turning sibilant with my need for more. "Yes, Will. More. I need more."

More words. More thrusting. More Everything.

And he gets it.

He slows his pace but drives harder and deeper. "That better?" he asks, sounding so fucking pleased with himself when I smother my howls of delight with the pillow. He's managing to hit my prostate with every slam of his hips and it's overwhelmingly good. "You like it when I fuck you harder?"

He knows I do, but I nod and murmur my agreement, my brain turning back into mush with the overload of how good this feels.

"God," he declares, his voice turning raspy, and I know he's getting close to the edge from that sound alone, "I can't get over how good you feel wrapped around me like this." Then one of his hands moves from its grip on my hip, reaching underneath me to circle my cock, and I stifle another cry into my pillow.

"You close, baby?"

"Yes," I all but sob, and I know he can read the tells in my body as well as I read his own now. My balls are drawing tighter, my back is straightening, and my breaths are coming out in short, sharp pants. I can hear how slick my cock is from the precum I've been dribbling, and the sound of the jerks of his fist over it are wet and almost obscene. "So close."

"Me too," he breathes, and his hips move faster, matching the pace of his wrist. "I'm gonna fill you up, baby. You want that?"

My brain short circuits and that's all it takes for the bubble of insane pleasure to reach bursting point. I come hard, shouting into the pillow, shaking and jerking through the waves of white hot bliss. I clench around his cock and then he's slamming home one last time, collapsing over me with his chest to my back as he empties his balls inside me.

The sensation of it forces a couple of additional weak spurts of my own pleasure out of me, and I practically melt into a puddle of satisfaction, barely paying attention as Will carefully pulls out and climbs off the bed, heading into the bathroom to run a couple of washcloths under the tap.

He comes back and wipes me clean, kissing my lips while he takes care with the cloth over my skin. As much as I love the sex, I adore these moments shared with him. He's sweet and considerate and everything I had only ever dreamed of in a partner before he came along.

"Penny for your thoughts?" he asks me after he tosses the damp cloths onto the bedside table and settles into bed beside me, neither one of us concerned with our mutual nakedness.

I snuggle up against him, resting my head on his bare chest, immediately bringing my hand up to toy with the hair that continues to fascinate me. "Just thinking of how perfect you are," I answer honestly, and he snorts.

"That's the orgasm talking, sweetheart."

I roll my eyes even though he can't see the expression. "No, it's not." With regret I move my head back so I can look at his handsome face. "Some days, I can't believe you're real, or that you're mine."

His expression shifts from amusement to something far softer. The corners of his lips tug upwards and his eyes light up with affection. "The feeling's mutual, Con. You know that, right?"

"Yeah," I answer, "I do. But," I can't help grinning cheekily up at him, "it's nice to hear it every so often."

He tickles my sides and I try not to squeal too loudly.

Life is good, I think to myself.

And that, as it always does, proves to be a mistake.

Chapter Sixteen – Will

I am fully moved in to Connor's apartment within the month. Jack and Wes both leaped at the chance to help, the pair of them beyond ecstatic that my serious relationship only seems to be getting more serious. They love Connor, including him in any and all family get-togethers, and have made no secret of how happy they are to see me 'domesticated'. It's been something they've both wanted for me ever since their mom settled down, after all.

So, between the four of us, it didn't take long to swap the furniture from Connor's guest room with my gym equipment, or to bring down my clothes and my TV, considering my entertainment system was better than Connor's. I will miss my bathroom, but nowhere near enough to regret my decision to move in with the man I love and his -*our*- daughter.

That last bit is still taking some getting used to, I'll admit it.

I know that Connor says I've been there from the beginning, but he still did all the hard work with Vicky while I flitted in and out for my job and my own life. Even after Connor and I started dating, I still lived separately, so it feels strange to just declare his daughter my own, even if I love her as such.

I talked to Jack and Wes about it, too. Despite being thirty now, I owed it to them both to have some variation of the 'this baby doesn't replace you' speech, which amused them both to no end.

"Dad," Wes had said, sipping at a beer and shaking his head, "we've seen this coming since the beginning."

"And," Jack had added, nodding along with his brother, "we already have two half-sisters anyway. What's a third?"

Wes had called him insensitive after that, and then they'd devolved into bitching at each other as they are prone to do. But it was still nice to know that they do accept Vicky as a sibling, no matter how strange the age difference might feel – both to them and to me personally.

Because it is a strange feeling to be starting all over again thirty years later. It's been a long time since anyone called me Daddy (and, as much as I joke about it, that's never been my kink, though I don't judge anyone who enjoys it), and a part of me does secretly worry that I'm too old to be a new dad again. I'll be fifty within six months, and that number is daunting.

I am technically old enough to be her grandfather. Even now, I'm not oblivious to the looks Connor and I get when we're out on family dates. They don't exactly bother me, but I worry that in ten or twenty years' time, Connor might realise he's backed the wrong horse. After all, what guy my age would be at all interested in bedding a geriatric?

I might have gotten a little drunk with Toby and raised these concerns, only to have him scoff and tell me that I can't possibly know what the future holds. He'd even suggested that I might be a hot seventy-year-old.

I'd confiscated his beer after that. He was clearly much more drunk than me.

So…okay, maybe the age difference is still a concern for me. I know it doesn't bother Connor right now, but it might in the future.

Then again, if my job has taught me anything, it's that nothing is guaranteed. So I guess Toby was right. I need to live in the present and not worry about what may or may not happen.

Which is why I fully embrace moving in with Connor. It's a bit of a change for both of us, with him having to get used to my odd hours and me getting used to having my personal space occupied when I get home exhausted. He starts working at a part-time capacity, too, and schedules meetings with clients, venues and other event suppliers on days when I'm rostered off working at the station so he can leave Vicky at home with me.

It works out well for both of us, and it's not long before I've adjusted to my new normal.

It's a Wednesday when everything comes crashing down.

I only just kissed Connor goodbye twenty or so minutes ago when there's a knock at the apartment door. It's insistent, and I wonder if maybe it's Anthony returning for yet another shot with Connor. He's been mostly silent these past few months, only rearing his head via text messages to Connor after he'd heard through their mutual friends that Connor's doing well and has moved on. Anthony was sharp enough to realise that it was with me and he sent a few snarky messages, but he has otherwise stayed away at Connor's urging.

I sit Vicky down in her brightly coloured playpen, which contains an equally brightly coloured squishy vinyl floormat, and head over to the door. I swing it open with a frown, fully prepared to stare down my boyfriend's ex, but a stranger stands in front of me.

He's young, maybe mid-twenties at most, with dark brown hair that flops into equally dark brown eyes. There's a smattering of freckles across his nose and cheeks, but his skin is otherwise pale and flawless. There's something familiar about him, but I can't pick what it is.

He blinks at me in surprise, then cautiously questions, "Connor?" His tone is disbelieving. "I thought you'd be a hell of a lot younger."

"Not Connor," I shrug. "Can I help you?"

He doesn't actually know Connor, so he's obviously not a friend, acquaintance, or colleague. He's also not a potential client or business associate, because Connor never gives his address out to anyone unless it's for social reasons. If this guy can't pick Connor out of a line up, it's doubtful he's been invited here.

The kid straightens his spine. "Does Connor Stark live here?" He checks his phone screen and then squints up at me. "This is the address Rach gave me."

I don't know who 'Rach' is, either, but I won't lie to this guy. "He does," I answer slowly, "but he's not here right now. Is he expecting you?"

"No," shaking his head, the uninvited guest sighs and then rubs the back of his neck. "I…"

Vicky starts to cry out, having lost patience at being left to her own devices. She's starting to get frustrated at not being able to move around and grab things, and rolling only gets her so far, especially when she's limited to the few feet of space within her playpen.

The visitor's eyes practically bug out. "*Oh*," he says, craning his neck as he tries to peek into the apartment, "is that...is that Daisy's kid?"

I can feel my frown deepening as I observe the guy. He seems to have gone paler, his freckles standing out more sharply on his face. His strangely familiar face. A gnawing sense of dread picks up in my gut.

"Sorry," I prod, "who did you say you were again?"

He's still trying to peer around me, his eyes straining towards the source of the crying. My heart is squeezing because Vicky's got me wrapped around her little finger and her anguished wails make me want to just abandon this dude at the door and lift her up for a cuddle. But my internal alarm bells are ringing, and my gut rarely ever leads me astray, so I hold firm.

"I didn't," he answers. "Shouldn't you be seeing if the kid is okay?"

"The kid," I respond drily, aware that he has about as much information about 'Daisy's kid' as he did about Connor, "is fine. I can see the playpen from here. The crying is just frustration because crawling is still a couple of months away."

He narrows his gaze at me and looks me up and down. "If you're not Connor, what are you, then? The babysitter? Bit old for that, aren't you? And you can't be Daisy's dad: he died a few years back. She told me that much."

I'm younger than Vic would have been had he lived, but, yeah, I'm old enough to have comfortably been Daisy's father. Not quite Connor's, though. Not comfortably, anyway. Still, the words make me bristle.

Agitated already by the sound of Vicky's cries, I hold the edge of the door just a bit tighter and cut to the chase. "I don't see how any of that is your concern. If you won't introduce yourself or your business here, I'm going to have to ask you to lea-"

"That's my kid in there," he interrupts me sharply, puffing his chest up and straightening to full height. I'm still taller than him, and broader than his lanky frame, but his declaration has me shaken.

"*What*?" I exhale. I have about a thousand questions, but no more want to come out.

The guy sighs. "When Daze told me I'd knocked her up, I did a runner. Then I found out she'd died and that her poof-er, *brother*," he censors himself quickly at my sharp glare, "was raising my kid and I had to set that right."

"She's not your kid," I spit out, incensed beyond measure that this kid has shown up unannounced, questioned my parenting and used a homophobic slur all within a few minutes. And then to insinuate that there was something wrong with a gay man raising the baby? No. Hell no. I am not having any of it.

His eyes widen. "She?"

Fuck.

I grit my teeth. "Yes. She. Now," I start to close the door, "if you'll excuse me, she needs my attention more than you do."

His hand flies out and pushes back against the glossy white surface that separates us. "No. Please. Can I...can I see her?"

"You have no rights here," I take great pleasure informing him of the fact. I can't hide that. My smirk is smug. "You walked away early on in Daisy's pregnancy. She documented that in her will. You're not listed on the birth certificate per her wishes. You haven't been involved for the past seven and a half months, either. So I'd say you're shit out of luck...if you even are the father. You haven't even introduced yourself by

191

name."

"Brandon," he says, and now he's frowning deeply at me. "Brandon Waters. And what do you mean she didn't want me on the birth certificate?"

I shrug. "She stated it in her will. You'd walked away. As far as she was concerned, you gave up your rights when you did."

Vicky's still screaming for my attention, but I'm going to stare Brandon down until he gets the message.

"Prove it," he juts his chin out and *damn it*, I've seen that exact expression before. Vicky's inherited the stubborn set of his jaw, and maybe even his nose. As much as she looks like Daisy, I don't think a paternity test would come back saying this guy isn't the father.

"Prove what?" I demand right back.

"Prove that I walked away. Prove that it was my choice."

My heart starts to race because the only 'proof' Connor and I have is Daisy's will and a statutory declaration she made while she was pregnant. They're just words on paper, and a lawyer might argue that Daisy made them up. She's not here to defend herself, and neither Connor or I were there when Brandon left her pregnant and alone.

It's his turn to look smug, as though he can read my thoughts. "Exactly," he says. "So, let me meet my daughter. Or do I need to get lawyers involved?"

"Damn straight you need to get lawyers involved," I argue back. "You think I'm just letting some random guy walk into my apartment and manhandle my kid?"

"*Your* kid?" Brandon repeats, his expression twisting with confusion. "But you said you're not Connor."

I relish telling him, "No, I'm not. I'm Connor's boyfriend, and I've been raising Vicky with him since he brought her home."

He's not fast enough to hide the scrunch of distaste on his face and I hate him. I hate him so much it's almost physical. My gut clenches with it. I force myself to keep my hands gripping the door and the door frame respectively, so I don't pull my right hand back and clock him in his irritating face.

When he opens his mouth, I'm braced for the homophobia. I'm not braced for what he actually asks. "The hell kind of name is Vicky? She's not a 50-year-old woman."

"It's short for Victoria," I have no idea why I'm telling him any of this. Dimly, I'm aware that Connor may just kill me for it. "In honour of her late grandfather, Victor."

"Right," Brandon says slowly. It's clear he's not a fan. "That's not the choice I would have made."

I make a show of looking him over scornfully, from his worn sneakers, his ill-fitting jeans and the t-shirt and flannelette over-shirt combination, to the messy hair on the top of his head. "No," I drawl. "But then, the choice you made was to leave a woman to deal with her pregnancy alone, so that says a lot about your choices, doesn't it?"

His face goes red and Vicky's still crying.

"Go get a lawyer," I instruct him, done with the conversation. "You're not stepping foot in here until you do."

I enjoy closing the door on him, and I make sure to lock it securely before I hurry back across the living room and scoop Vicky up into my arms, hugging her close. My heart is pounding, and I feel sick. Brandon's words echo in my head.

Prove it. Prove that I walked away.

Things are going to get messy.

* * *

After doting on Vicky, spending a little extra time playing peek-a-boo (her favourite game right now) and giving her apple puree instead of veggies, I get her to go down for a nap and then I drop down heavily at the kitchen table with my phone held in my shaking hand.

My attempt to call Connor earlier went to voicemail, and I hesitate between dialling Wes or Henry. Ultimately, I decide to get them both on a conference call. I have to Google how to do that, but then I manage it using Facetime. Wes picks up first, sounding cheerful but distracted. That's unsurprising considering it's just gone noon on a Wednesday and he's at work. I prop my phone up against the decorative bowl in the middle of the table so I can talk hands free, and so the others can see me properly.

"Hey, Dad, what's up?" He smiles into the camera.

"I need your professional advice," I tell him, and I can hear how strained my own voice is. God only knows what my face looks like. "I'm also patching in-"

"Will?" Henry's confused face appears on the screen. He's become a good friend over the past few months, him and his wife both. Connor and I have spent a lot of time in their company, and it really does look like little Max and Vicky will grow up just as close as Con and Henry did.

"Hey, Henry," I greet him, and Wes does the same. They've met before, during one of our big social gatherings, and they got along well, from what I recall.

"What's going on?" Wes asks, leaning closer to his camera. His face, a little thinner than Jack's and clean-shaven, is lined with concern. "What's wrong?"

Henry also gives me his undivided attention. I can see that he's in his office in Palm Beach and not his home office. His back is to the window which looks out over the oceanfront. I catch a glimpse of blue sky behind him and it feels like it's mocking me.

Taking a deep breath, I launch into recounting the confrontation I'd had literally on my doorstep. I try to reiterate it word for word, cringing when I admit the details about Vicky that I'd let slip. Wes assures me that this guy would have learned them all anyway and that I didn't do anything wrong, and Henry steeples his fingers and touches them to his lips, looking pensive.

"This is not my area of expertise," Wes says, deferring to Henry, "but if I were defending the guy's rights, I'd say he makes a valid point. It's a classic he said/she said and she's not here to prove that he walked out. He could argue that she kept the baby from him for no good reason and…" He trails off. "The adoption isn't finalised, is it?"

Henry shakes his head, looking pained. "These things can take forever. Even with the will in place, the system is slow. On average it's six to nine months, so…" He sighs. "This guy's timing is going to delay things. If he proves to be Vicky's biological father…"

"I'm pretty sure he is," I admit, feeling dejected. Tears threaten to well up in my eyes and I blink rapidly to beat them back into submission. "Even before he started talking, I thought something about him was familiar."

This is going to kill Connor.

He's still grieving Daisy but having Vicky has helped him to keep going. The threat of losing her, too, is going to do untold damage and I have no idea what to do to help or prevent that from happening.

I don't think I can prevent it, and that makes me feel

powerless.

Not to mention the fact that I don't have any legal standing where Vicky is concerned. Yes, Connor has updated his will to include me as her guardian in his absence, and I'm one of her emergency contacts for any medical issues, but I haven't adopted her. I haven't been granted legal custody. At the end of the day, I'm just her dad's boyfriend.

Wes and Henry are debating the best ways to prepare for the legal battle which is looming when Connor's keys jingle in the lock. I freeze and look towards the door, and I know the expression on my face gives me away as soon as Connor steps inside the apartment.

He shuts the door quietly behind him and drops his satchel by the door. He moves to head over to me, but I point back at the door. "Lock it," I tell him, and the voices coming through my phone speaker go silent.

Connor's eyebrows raise, but he does as I've asked, and then he comes to sit beside me, pulling his chair around to be closer and reaching for my hand. His eyes search mine. "What's wrong?" A sound from my phone catches his attention and concern mars his pretty face. "Uh," he says to Henry and Wes, "hi?"

Their matching sombre expressions make the furrow between Connor's eyebrows deepen. "What's wrong?" he asks again, this time with a bit more force.

I lick my lips and squeeze the hand holding mine. "We had a visitor today," I start slowly. "It was a guy…he must have been mid-twenties, maybe? Said his name was Brandon Waters." I search Connor's face for any sign of recognition but there isn't any, so I continue. "He said he's Vicky's biological father. He-"

"No!" I don't get to finish my sentence. Connor wrenches his hand out of mine and lurches out of his chair, pacing the floor between the kitchen and dining table. He runs his hand through his mousy brown hair and rants all the same thoughts that have been running through my head. "He can't have her. He can't…he can't just waltz in after abandoning Daze and just…*no.*"

I stand up, ignoring the Facetime call, and try to pull him into my arms. "I know, baby," I try, but he shakes his head and evades me for more pacing.

"If he suddenly cares so much, where was he when Daisy was pregnant?" Connor demands, and his voice is shaky with emotion. "Where was he for her funeral? Where has he been for the last seven and a half months of his daughter's life?"

"These are all questions we'll pose in court if it comes to it," Henry tells his best friend, sounding every bit an attorney right now. Connor finally stops storming around his kitchen and looks down at the phone. The fight seems to leave him and he slumps down into the seat he'd only recently abandoned.

I resume my own next to him and take his hand in mine again.

Connor sighs and looks to Henry and Wes. "You don't think the adoption will come through before then? We're so close."

"I know family law wasn't your thing," Henry says gently, "but you know how these things go. If he's serious about this, he'll get a lawyer on it today or tomorrow, and it'll pause the adoption while he contests it."

I wince as Connor screws up his face and growls, "Fuck."

"I've already reached out to Optus on your behalf to get her text records to back up her stat dec," Henry says. "She was smart, Con. She got him to rescind his rights in writing. It's just going to take some time to prove that he had no intention of being involved."

"That's well and good," Wes cuts in with an apologetic grimace, "and, look, this isn't my specialty either, but if I was his lawyer, I would argue that he might have had a change of heart. They allow it for birth parents in adoptions that fall through, right?"

"But-" Connor starts, only for Henry to speak over him.

"We'd argue that his absence speaks for itself."

Wes shakes his head. "Except he would say that Daisy disappeared on him or denied contact...and then we're back to a classic he said/she said situation."

I love my son dearly, but right now I want him to just stop talking.

Then again, Connor was a lawyer, too. I'm sure he's already thinking of all the possible arguments and defences we're going to face.

"At this point," Henry speaks when nobody else does, "I'm going to bank on the fact that a judge and the welfare officers in Vicky's case aren't likely to rip her away from a stable, loving environment and the only family she's known for her life so far. We might have to steel ourselves for the possibility of joint custody because he is her biological-"

"That is bullshit," Connor seethes. "The guy dumped my pregnant baby sister, missed out on all the hard work and colic and poop explosions and everything else and, what, he gets to just come in and disrupt our lives? Disrupt Vicky's life? Fuck that. *Fuck it!*"

This time when he surges from his seat, it's with enough force to send the whole thing clattering to the ground. He doesn't stop to pick it up and set it to rights, though. He just storms off towards the bedroom and then slams the door behind him.

Vicky's cries start up a few seconds later.

Taking a few calming breaths of my own, I shoot an apologetic glance to my phone screen. "I'm gonna…" I gesture over my shoulder.

Both men on the screen nod.

"Keep an eye on him for me," Henry says, and I roll my eyes.

"You don't need to ask me to do that anymore," I remind him.

His smile is soft. "I know. Look after yourself, too, man. I'll let you know if I hear anything."

I thank them both, tell Wes that I love him and I'll talk to him later, and then I end the call.

Chapter Seventeen — Connor

B randon Waters is a dick. I hated him on sight. It doesn't help that the first time I met him was in court when he and his lawyer filed a motion against my adoption, bringing the whole thing to a standstill mere days after he turned up on my doorstep while I wasn't home.

Now, a few days after that less than delightful experience, I glare across the table in the swanky meeting room where our lawyers are attempting to mediate the situation. Vicky's at Henry's house with Sarah, and Will's at my side, having taken the day off work so we could present a united front. The room we're in is bright and airy. It has a huge floor to ceiling window looking out over Surfer's Paradise, with a glimpse of ocean in the background.

Bitterly, I think that the offices in Henry's building have a much nicer view, even if they are located in Palm Beach instead of the more affluent suburb of Broadbeach. Henry's offices are also in a dated brick building of only four stories in height. These ones are in a much more modern skyscraper. Henry's have character. These are soulless – all glass and chrome and shiny white surfaces. Where's the timber? Where's the dark leather and rich carpeting? I decide that I hate this place as much as I hate the man across the table.

He's brought a girl with him. Well, a woman. She's very pretty, but nothing like Daisy. She's slim where Daisy was curvaceous, blonde where Daisy was dark haired, brown-eyed where Daisy's were blue. It feels like he's trying to make a pointed statement, but maybe I'm being a touch too sensitive about it.

Either way, the woman he's brought with him is doing a good job of helping him present an image of a stable, nuclear environment. Cis-gendered, heteronormative expectations for the fucking win, right?

I want to scream.

Instead, in a lull in the custody negotiations I want no part in, I lean over the table towards the woman, offering her a false as fuck smile.

"I love your dress," I tell her, and that part, at least, is honest. It's a sleek, pale pink pencil skirted thing, with a high scooped neck and cap sleeves. It makes her look demure and respectable, and the tiny gold cross on a thin chain around her neck is the icing on the freaking cake. The whole set-up is giving me the shits.

"Thank you," she says, a little cautiously.

She has every reason to be cautious.

"It's designer, right?" I prod, unable to help myself.

Her nod is slow, her perfectly bouncy blonde waves moving around her shoulders like something out of a Pantene commercial.

"Dry clean only?"

201

Brandon rolls his eyes. "Is fashion really more important than talking about my kid?"

Will's hand gripping my thigh tightly is the only thing that prevents me from launching myself over the table to strangle the smug little arsehole.

"Well," I answer as calmly as possible, "I was just thinking it would be a shame if the dress got ruined. I don't wear any of my designer clothes around Vicky anymore. Not after the third poop explosion." I shudder dramatically, then cast Brandon's companion a very fake conspiratorial smile. "But it won't be an issue for you, will it?"

Her pretty face is scrunched up in disgust. "Uh…"

"Of course not," Brandon answers for her, pinning her with a look I can read all too well. I used to get that look from Anthony.

Shut up and be pretty.

When Henry leaps on the topic and starts demanding to know just how prepared for the realities of having a baby in their lives they actually are, I pat myself of the back. I know it won't do much to change the inevitable outcome of Brandon's custody claim, but a cruel, sadistic part of me is pleased to have set a cat among the pigeons. If all I achieve is making the couple argue, that's at least marginally satisfying.

I know, I know: if I believed in hell, I'd probably have to admit that that's where I'm destined to end up.

* * *

I am definitely not a ball of sunshine when we get back to Henry and Sarah's place. They live in a single-storey home in Elanora, situated on Tallebudgera Creek. It is brick and tile and fully renovated, painted in bright splashes of colour inside, with Sarah's artwork hung proudly on the walls. I've spent a lot of time here over the past few years, especially in summer, because their backyard is home to a beautiful swimming pool which overlooks the creek.

Will doesn't push me to talk about the results of the mediation, and I feel a little bit like a dick for not letting him put voice to his feelings, either. But I feel as though I'll scream if I have to think about it.

Sarah greets us at the front door once we've parked in the paved driveway and let ourselves through the front gate on the left-hand side of the double garage. Their front yard is surrounded by a tall brick fence matching the house proper, giving it a feeling of security and privacy. Already, Henry's building Max a little playground in the lush green space, and I imagine Vicky playing here with him.

Of course, that'll only happen on the weeks where I'm allowed custody, because Douchebag McDoucheface is being awarded far too many rights, as far as I'm concerned.

"It didn't go well?" Sarah asks softly, and I'm guessing my thunderous expression has given me away.

Beside me, Will shakes his head. "Not as well as we'd hoped, no."

I clench my jaw and my fist. It's not fair. None of this is fair. I feel so powerless and angry, even more than I did when Daisy died. That had been an accident. This? This just feels like the guy that fucked my sister over is being malicious.

Sarah's eyes water and she steps forward to pull me in for a tight hug. Tears prickle my eyes and burn in my sinuses. Ever since Daisy's death, Sarah's hugs have been the closest thing I've gotten to a sisterly embrace. Right now, they are simultaneously the last thing I want and everything I need.

"I can't imagine," she sniffles quietly. "If someone tried to take Max..."

The strangled sound that escapes my throat is inhuman.

She clutches me tighter. "We're all here for you, Con."

"What if he takes her?" My greatest fears come tumbling out in a whisper. I'm dimly aware that I'm shaking. "Do you know how many times that happens? A kid goes to one of their parents for a scheduled week in their custody and then that side of the family packs up and takes them out of state or out of the country, never to be seen again."

I've been reading a lot of traumatising material on the internet lately.

"That's not going to happen," she assures me, still not letting me go.

"You can't promise that!" I'm aware that I'm becoming *slightly* hysterical.

Sarah finally releases me, sighs, and then makes a soft 'tsk'ing sound. "Why don't we head inside and have a cuppa, hmm? Was Hen far behind you?"

I shrug.

Honestly? I don't want to sit down and wait for my best friend to show up.

The shock of having Henry sit at my side and agree to a temporary trial shared custody arrangement is wearing off, and I'm not sure I can look him in the eye right now, even though he was just doing his job.

I need to blame someone, need to lash out at someone.

If I lose her...

No. No, I can't think that way. Or, at least, I shouldn't think that way. It's impossible not to, though.

Daisy hasn't even been gone a year yet and already I've failed her. She hadn't wanted her kid to go to their biological father. She'd wanted *me* to raise them. And now I'm being forced to hand my daughter -*Daisy's* daughter- over to the guy who had held his hands up in surrender and walked away.

There's a tiny, *tiny* part of me that is tempted to do exactly what I'm afraid Waters will do. To grab Vicky and run. We could move interstate. Hell, we could move to New Zealand. Or America. Or, better still, somewhere with no extradition treaty.

Where did Christopher Skase run off to back in the 90s? Was it Spain? I'm pretty sure it was. Spain sounds lovely, really...

But, no. I don't have it in me to follow through on those fantasies. No matter how tempting, I can't actually abandon my life here. My friends are here. Yes, Mum is in New Zealand, but I doubt she'd appreciate me rocking up on her doorstep with a technically kidnapped child. Nor would she be impressed if I legged it to Spain.

Besides all that, Will wouldn't come with me, either, and I can't fathom walking away from him.

Oh, yeah, and there's also the fact that I'm not actually all that criminally minded. The idea of constantly looking over my shoulder doesn't appeal.

These thoughts are nothing more than my brain's attempt to reconcile with the shitshow that is my current situation. I can daydream all I like about taking my baby and running away, but that's all I'm doing. Daydreaming. Mentally escaping from reality for a bit.

"I think," Will answers Sarah when I don't, "that we might just take Vicky home. It's been a trying day."

I snort derisively and, under my breath, I mutter, "That's a fucking understatement."

Will's hand rubs consolingly at the small of my back. I know I'm not in the best place emotionally, because I have the fleeting thought that he probably doesn't understand just how devastating this whole situation is for me, and then I immediately feel guilty because of course he does. One look at his drawn expression and the tightness of his shoulders confirms that he's just as upset as I am, he's just holding it together a bit better.

Thankfully, Sarah doesn't push the issue. She steps back inside and we follow her through the house, into the carpeted lounge room where she has the kids sprawled out on play mats. It's clear they've been rolling around, because they are on opposite sides of the space, and Max is on his back, wedged halfway under the couch. His round baby belly is probably the only thing that prevented him from getting himself the entire way beneath it.

"You little rodent," Sarah chides him with affection, pulling him out from the awkward spot. She props him up on her hip. "I legit left you two alone for two minutes. I'm going to have to start putting you in baby jail." She points towards the disassembled play pen.

Usually, I'd chuckle and explain that it's exactly what we've been doing, but I don't have it in me. Instead I'm already scooping Vicky up, greeting her with kisses and trying not to cry at the thought that I have to share her with a stranger.

Oblivious, Vicky starts babbling excitedly at me, and that makes the ache in my chest grow even sharper.

Will thanks Sarah for babysitting on our way back out the door. He's got Vicky's nappy bag slung over his shoulder and the silence between us is tense as we get her settled in her car seat in the back of my car. By now, we've bought an additional seat for Will's car, but we tend to drive mine around more than his. It's easier to get a squirming baby in and out of the SUV rather than his lower-to-the-ground sedan.

For the first time since the day we properly met, I have no idea what to say to Will. I'm not feeling flustered by his presence like I was back then, though. This time I feel shattered. I feel almost like I did when Daisy died: like a piece of my heart is being torn away, leaving a gaping hole in its wake.

We make the fifteen-ish minute drive home in silence, with even Vicky seeming to pick up on the tension. Usually, her adorable baby babbling can be heard over the low hum of the radio, but today she's quiet. With Will driving, I turn in the passenger seat to peer over my shoulder, just checking that she hasn't fallen asleep. Now is not her scheduled nap time, and I don't need a cranky baby on top of everything else we've dealing with today.

Thankfully, she's not asleep. She's just quiet, her little round face scrunched up in a moue of irritation. She reminds me so much of Daisy in this moment that it makes my heart squeeze painfully.

I'm losing her.

I don't care that it's a 50/50 arrangement and that I will still have her every second week. I still feel like she's being taken from me. I feel like she's being taken from Daisy.

It *hurts*.

It hurts even more because Waters showed no interest in being a dad until he realised it was *me* raising the kid.

I mean, for fuck's sake, the guy didn't know me. Until a handful of days ago, we'd never even met. But just knowing that a gay man was raising his kid had been enough to set him on this course of action and that rankles.

I have been providing Vicky with a stable, loving home. With or without Will, she's grown up the way Daisy had intended her to if she couldn't be there for her. She has known nothing but love and support and I'm so afraid that having her routine disrupted is not what's best for her.

And, yeah, there's a part of me that worries about what kind of homophobic bullshit Waters will fill her ears with during her weeks with him.

He's already made noises about how weird it is that Will and I have been calling ourselves 'Daddy' around her. It didn't matter that Daisy had been insistent on my doing so in her absence, Brandon's staunch argument that he's in the picture now so I can go back to my rightful place as Vicky's uncle is one he's still carrying on with.

Thankfully, he has no legal rights to get us to change the way we talk to Vicky. But, on the flip side, I don't have a right to police what he says to her, either.

As far as I can tell, her life going forward is going to be stressful and confusing. She'll be shuttled between homes on a weekly basis, and likely subjected to vitriol and contradicting information any time she's with her biological father. A biological father who had zero interest in her for the first seventh months of her life, or the pregnancy preceding them.

It hurts. It hurts and I'm angry.

Henry's doing his best to put together a case that proves that it's in Vicky's best interests to stay with me and Will, with the only family she's ever known, but the justice system in Australia seems kind of unjust right now. I'd had my issues with it when I left my career as a lawyer behind, but now I'm even more disillusioned.

"It's not as bad as America," Henry had tried to joke way back when I first floated the concept of leaving law for a less depressing job, and those words echo in my brain now.

I can't help but think he was wrong. As far as I can tell, there's no such thing as justice at all. At least, not where Brandon Waters is concerned.

I know that I'm bitter and upset right now. I know that, for the most part, Australia's judicial system is practical and fair. But, right now, I want to go full Katniss on the place. I want to tear the whole establishment down and rebuild it to be fairer.

Well, fairer to me, at any rate.

Because this isn't fair. It isn't fair that my daughter is being taken from me purely because her sperm donor has reappeared. It isn't fair that, once again, I'm losing someone I love and I can't do a damn thing to prevent it from happening.

Is this the universe trying to tell me that I'm not allowed to love people? Should I just cut my losses and become a hermit now? At the rate I'm going, I'll lose my mum, Henry, and Will soon, too.

"You're spiralling," Will says quietly, and he reaches across the centre console to place his left hand on my thigh. My car is an automatic, so he can spare his hand while he drives. His touch grounds me, and some of my panic starts to fade.

Only some of it, though.

Most of it lingers because my situation remains unchanged.

A lump lodges itself in my throat and I can't quite swallow around it. I close my eyes and lean my head back against my seat's headrest, trying to breathe.

"This fucking sucks," I croak out. Even to my own ears, my voice is tight and on the verge of breaking.

Will's hand squeezes my thigh. "It really does."

I don't open my eyes, so I can't see his expression, but he sounds just as broken as I feel. That shouldn't make me feel better, but it does.

I'm not alone in this.

No matter how badly I want to rail and scream and push everyone away, I also don't want to be alone. I want to be held and comforted and reassured that things are going to be okay, even though I know they won't. Not like this. Not for a long time. But knowing that Will's not unaffected –that even though he has no legal or biological claim to Vicky, he still sees her as his– settles some of the storm raging inside me. I still have him. We have each other.

"You're not going anywhere, right?" I ask him, my eyes still firmly shut.

"No." I can feel his hand tense up for only a second before it squeezes down again. "We're in this together, baby."

I'm relieved that he doesn't ask me why I would even think to question him about whether he'll stay. He knows me well by now. He's seen me at my absolute lowest and he knows my insecurities and fears better than almost anyone. Hell, possibly even better than Henry at this point.

The tightness in my throat hasn't eased up by the time we pull into my designated car park under the apartment complex. It won't take much to push me over the edge, and I'd like to be inside my safe space when it happens.

Will collects Vicky from the back seat while I grab the nappy bag, then we head across the small underground car park and into the lift. I lean against Will's other side on the ride up, the tears still threatening to fall.

"Coffee?" Will asks as we finally make it inside the apartment.

I shake my head.

I just want to sit on the couch and cuddle my daughter and my boyfriend. I want to pretend the rest of the world doesn't exist.

"Con…" he starts, then stops. I know he wants to comfort me, but this time there are no words that could possibly help.

I just nod. "I know," I tell him, because I do.

I know that he wants to assure me that things will be okay. I know that he's feeling just as hurt and powerless as I am.

I know that he wants to believe that we'll get through this.

But I appreciate that he knows me well enough to understand that I don't want to hear it. At least, not right now.

Chapter Eighteen – Will

T he past few days have been rough. Scratch that. The past few weeks have been rough. But the past few days have been the hardest so far. Ever since the mediation between both parties in the custody battle, Connor has been a wreck, and I can't say I've been much better.

For the first time since we started dating, things have felt strained. Even after he lost his sister, I never felt as though I was at a loss with what to say or do. But this is different because I'm in it with him. I'm frustrated and hurt and powerless beside him. I can't be his anchor or even lend him strength, because I am breaking right alongside him.

Despite things being tense, though, we're still communicating. We hold each other tight and talk about how much this fucking sucks for both of us. He tells me about his fears that Daisy would hate him for letting her ex take her daughter and, in turn, I tell him that I'm worried my presence is only going to make things more complicated while he continues to fight for his right to adopt the baby. I love them both so much that it aches to think they might be better off if I stepped aside. He tells me I'm stupid for even considering it, and I agree.

Initially, I was worried that Connor might lash out and tell me I couldn't possibly understand because Vicky wasn't really mine, but that hasn't been the case. He hasn't once made me feel as though my lack of a legal or biological claim makes my feelings invalid. In fact, he's acknowledged that he thinks that might make it harder for me, because I'm the one who has the most to lose here.

I don't completely agree with that assessment, but I can see his point.

If something happened to him, even with his will in place, it would be harder for me to retain custody of our girl. Or if he were to break up with me...

No, I can't think that way. He wouldn't. Even though things are hard right now and emotions are high, we're still a united front together. Our love for each other is not in question.

Nevertheless, even loving each other might not be enough to weather the pain of the custody dispute and having to give our baby to her biological father every other week, which is why communicating is so important. Neither one of us can afford to wallow in our fears and frustration if it means pushing the other away.

So we have been talking. It has been hard, and tempers have flared more than once, but we've been pushing through.

Until today.

Today presents the biggest challenge we've ever had to face. Today is the day Brandon will be taking Vicky for the first time. I can't pretend that I'm okay. I've had every awful thought possible. What if he neglects her? What if he gets angry and shakes her? What if he doesn't have a safe car seat, or doesn't buckle her in properly and they get into an accident? What if, like Connor fears, he decides he doesn't want to share custody and he runs away with her?

What if, what if, what if.

Logically, I know that it's not likely that any of the above will happen, but it's the tiny possibility that frightens me. After all, bad things happen all the time. I've seen enough of them at work. I don't want to see more bad things happen to the man I love, and I certainly don't want them to happen to my kid.

Neither one of us slept last night. We held each other close and tried to reassure each other that we're going to make it through this. When Vicky woke up at two in the morning, wet and hungry, we broke our own rules and brought her into bed with us once she'd been changed. Then we cuddled her together, the both of us watching her sleep, unable to do so ourselves.

It breaks my heart that she's not going to understand what's happening. She's not going to understand why she's with strangers instead of her dads. She's not going to understand that we want nothing more than to have her at home with us, and that none of this was our choice.

Just the thought of her being out of her routine and distressed makes my throat tight.

Connor's mom, Leah, offered to come and stay for additional moral support (after half-seriously threatening to have Waters "taken care of"), but we managed to talk her down from that ledge. It's not that she's unwelcome here, but there's not a lot she can do other than listen to Connor and I rant and rave about how unfair the situation is. She and I get along well, even if it was awkward to acknowledge that the age gap between me and her is smaller than the one between me and Connor, but having her here would feel uncomfortable, especially at a time when Connor and I are going to struggle to begin with.

"There's still time," Connor says with a shaky voice, pulling me out of my thoughts. His face is pale and there are dark circles bruised into the skin beneath his eyes. "We can take Vicky and move to Aruba or something."

"Don't think I'm not tempted," I respond, then pull him against me for a much-needed hug.

We turn to watch Vicky smashing the keys on a floor mat piano with her chubby little hands, her fingers splayed as wide as she can manage. A mishmash of sounds comes out of the mat, and she squeals and babbles happily, oblivious to our turmoil. Connor sobs and turns his face into my chest, his shoulders trembling.

It's all I can do to hold it together so I can try and soothe him.

"Is it too late to have Waters offed?" I ask, trying to lighten the mood.

It doesn't work.

"Not as far as I'm concerned," Connor mutters darkly against my shirt.

I don't know how to respond to that, so I just squeeze him again, and we both jump when there's a sharp knock at the door.

Our time has run out.

Connor makes no move to answer the door, so I extricate myself from our embrace with obvious reluctance. When I open the door, Waters and his girlfriend are waiting on the other side expectantly.

Ignoring every ounce of my upbringing, I don't greet them

with words at all, nor do I invite them inside. Connor is slowly getting Vicky organised and I'm content to stand here and glare Waters down.

He sighs. "Look, until I can get sole custody, we're going to have to at least be civil."

"There's no way in hell you're getting sole custody," I manage to get out from between clenched teeth.

He just lifts a shoulder and drops it. "We'll see." He glances at his watch and then back up at me. "You're eating into my time with my daughter, dude."

"Con's changing her," I answer, the lie falling easily from my tongue. "I can tell him not to bother, but-"

"It's fine," the girlfriend cuts in, her expression a little green. She hadn't seemed thrilled about the realities of childcare when we'd discussed it during mediation. Usually, I'd be empathetic, but I have no such compulsion with this pair. "We'll wait."

"Bec," Brandon says in warning, but she glares at him and he shuts up.

I don't bother to disguise my smirk of amusement, though I instantly feel guilty that Connor and I are sending Vicky off into what is potentially a volatile relationship.

Eventually, after taking his time scooping Vicky up and snuggling her close, Connor brings her over to the doorway. I take her from him and smother her with kisses of my own, unable to prevent the tears from leaking down my cheeks as I tell her how much I love her and how desperately I'm going to miss her.

We haven't packed a bag for her. Connor had wanted to, but I argued that making Waters foot the bill for any necessities she needed while she was with him was reasonable. We've fed her extra foods -both solids and formula- this morning, and she's wearing an outfit that is plain but also adaptable should the weather change. The only caveat to my argument about not sending toys was to provide a spare of her favourite stuffed toy: a plush Batman doll with a bulbous head which Henry bought her when we'd taken the kids for a day out at *Movie World*. Now we have three (inclusive of the one we're sending along with her today) just in case it ever gets lost or needs a trip in the washing machine and dryer.

"Be a good girl, princess," I tell her as I hand her over to her increasingly impatient father. My voice is shaky and I immediately want to snatch her back. She stares at the stranger holding her for barely ten seconds before her adorable little face scrunches up and she lets loose a wail.

Watching Brandon bounce her and unsuccessfully try to shush her is painful, but this is what he's signed up for. I grab at Con's bicep to prevent him from lunging forward to comfort our girl.

"We'll pick her up in a week," Connor reminds Waters as he and Bec turn to go. "She, um, she loves *The Wiggles,* especially the Emma years, and her favourite food is pureed apples. You have to steam them first. She hates bananas. Um…" After a moment's hesitation, he says, "if you need to know anything else, just call me. She loves it when you sing *The Itsy-Bitsy Spider.* If you do the hand movements for her, it'll cheer her up." His voice finally breaks and he curls himself back into my chest in a mirror image of the embrace we'd shared before Waters knocked at the door.

Holding his daughter *–our daughter–* awkwardly while she continues to cry and reach for Connor, Brandon nods. "Thanks. We'll be fine," he adds dismissively. Then, with slightly more empathy, says, "See you next week."

Then he and his girlfriend head towards the elevator and I drag Connor back into the apartment, shutting the door on our baby's cries before we both give in to our own.

The apartment is silent. It feels empty, like something vital is missing.

Someone vital is missing.

My heart clenches, and I have no idea what, if anything, I can say to try and ease some of the pain we are feeling.

Connor sniffles and his fingers dig into the soft cotton of my t-shirt, wrapping the fabric around their lengths, pulling it tight around my back and shoulders. "Will?"

My voice is gruff and I have to clear my throat to get it to work properly. "Hmm?"

"I…" breathing hitching, he says, "I need to forget. Make me forget."

I blink down at him, taken aback. His big, hazel eyes are wide and wet with tears, and his imploring expression is one I can never deny.

Sex between us has never been angry or sad. It's always been loving, joyful even when fiery or intense, and I hesitate. My eyes flicker between his, trying to determine if this is a wise move. "Are you sure?"

He nods. "I need it hard. Rough. I need distraction. I need-"

I slam my lips over his.

I know what he needs because suddenly I need it, too.

* * *

We tumble into the bedroom, our kissing frantic in a way I've never felt before. We've torn our clothes off along the short trip from the lounge room, leaving a trail of debris in our wake. I've never seen Connor like this before: reckless, wild, *angry*.

He practically vibrates with a frustrated energy that I can feel echoed in my own soul, and we press hard, bruising, biting kisses into each other's mouths, our tongues fighting for dominance.

There is nothing romantic about this. Nothing sweet or loving, even though we definitely love each other. Though I could never have imagined being turned on while I was so upset, my cock takes over and aches to be buried inside my lover.

This is probably not the healthiest way for either of us to deal with our grief, but I couldn't turn Connor down when he begged me so sweetly to help him forget, and I didn't want to.

He pulls me onto the mattress, rolling himself sideways to rummage through the bedside drawer for the ever-present bottle of lube, and he tosses it at me before getting to his hands and knees. Over his shoulder, he instructs, "Minimal prep. I want this to hurt."

A shudder of unease travels through me. "I'm not going to hurt you, sweetheart. Not even while we're feeling like this."

The sound of frustration that travels from the back of his throat is almost animalistic. He squeezes his eyes shut and takes a deep, calming breath. I'm almost concerned that I've said the wrong thing. That this is wrong. That we should stop and talk it out instead of delaying the inevitable with angry sex.

But then Connor snatches the lube away from me.

I watch as he sits up onto his knees and pops the cap on the bottle. He drizzles the liquid onto his fingers almost carelessly, clicking the cap back down and tossing the bottle back on the mattress beside him, where it rolls into the divot beside his calf muscle. He plants his feet and spreads his legs wider, then reaches between them to prep himself gracelessly.

It's hot, but not as hot as it is when he puts on a show to tease me. Right now, my pleasure isn't what's driving him, and that's okay. Still, as he works two fingers in and out of himself, his shoulders lose a little bit of the tension they were carrying, and he closes his eyes, sighing into the heated air between us.

"Sit up against the headboard," he demands, and I scramble to comply.

I appreciate that he's taking the reins here. That he's taking what he needs from me, but not allowing me to feel as though I'm at risk of doing him any actual damage. As he straddles my thighs and sinks down on my dick, he hisses with discomfort, but his own cock strains and leaks with the evidence of his enjoyment.

Then he leverages himself back up and almost off before dropping down again in a move that forces my own breath out of me in a *whoosh*.

He sets a punishing pace, riding me with his eyes squeezed shut. My fingers grip his hips of their own accord. I'm afraid I'm going to leave bruises, but he doesn't seem at all concerned. If anything, I think it plays into what he needs from me right now. The physical pain distracts from the emotional, giving him something new to focus on, if only for a few minutes.

Sweat glistens on his pale, freckled skin as he continues to rise up and slam back down, hitching sobs leaving him on every exhale as he lands in my lap. It's breathtaking and heartbreaking all at once, and even though my cock demands

220

release, I'm nowhere near ready to come.

But he's starting to tire out. I wonder if the adrenaline of his rage is passing, or if the sleepless night has finally caught up with him. Either way, I know he's also not close enough to go over the edge, and I want to help prolong this for him.

For us.

The next time he rises up, I push my hips down into the mattress and pull out completely, shushing him when he complains.

"Get up," I tell him, leaving off the endearments I would usually include. I throw one of his high, firm pillows onto the edge of the mattress and jerk my chin towards it. "Bend over that."

His eyes light up with understanding and he rushes to follow the instruction.

A few heartbeats later, and I'm standing behind him, his body positioned at the perfect angle for me to drive into him in a single thrust. His legs are spread, his feet planted firmly on the carpet on either side of mine, and his face is pressed into the soft Egyptian cotton of our sheets.

This time, I set the pace.

I'm unafraid of hurting him now, more confident that I know what he wants and how much he can take. This is still different for us -not the position, but the emotion- and I can't help but miss how vocal and encouraging he usually is.

But this isn't about us as a couple or what we mean to each other. Instead, this is about us giving each other an outlet for our mutual anguish and frustration. This is about how powerless we both feel, and about being there for each other in a new and surprising way. It's about letting go and knowing that we're there to catch each other during the hard times and the ugly times as well as the sweet and beautiful ones.

In its own way, it's still beautiful.

Connor will always be beautiful to me.

Right now, as he cries out into the mattress every time I slam home inside him, with his body flushing pink and my dick driving in and out of his perfectly rounded ass, he's just as beautiful as the first time I slowly made love to him face to face, whispering words of adoration between us.

I can tell when his orgasm nears, the tensing of his back and the way his thighs tighten against the oncoming wave give him away. His neglected cock is pinned between his lower belly and the pillow, and I expect the push and pull of my brutal thrusts are giving him enough friction that neither of us needs to reposition to stroke it.

I know he's crying, and it's bizarre to realise that I am as well. We're both truly letting go and being vulnerable, even while we aggressively fuck. It's the strangest mix of emotions I've ever felt, but it's good. It's so good, I couldn't stop even if I wanted to. Well, not unless Connor told me to.

His howls of pleasure, tinged with pain and exertion, morph into the panted breaths that usually herald his release and it's not a surprise when he raises his head, planking on his elbows, to push back roughly against my next hard thrusts.

"*Yes,*" he cries, repeating the word every time I crash back into him, "yes, yes...oh, fuck, yes!"

On the last one, his hips jerk and his channel clenches around me, and he practically sobs out his release. I piston into him twice more as my own orgasm rockets through me. Once I've carefully pulled out, we collapse together over the side of the bed, a sweaty, tear streaked, sticky mess of boneless limbs.

Our mutual breaths are ragged in the stillness of the room, and my heart feels like I've run a marathon.

"Thank you," Connor croaks out, rolling over onto his side so we're face to face. "I needed that."

I nod and cup his jaw in my palm, smoothing my thumb over the remnants of his tears. "Me too," I answer softly.

It was perhaps the most emotional sex I've ever had in my life, even if we didn't share many words through the entire exchange. Even if it wasn't gentle or loving in the romantic sense of the word.

I feel broken and raw, but also a hell of a lot lighter than I did beforehand.

"I love you," Connor's declaration isn't new, but there's an added degree of gravity to his words now.

It's like we've taken yet another step in solidifying what we mean to each other, though moving in and agreeing to raise a baby together honestly seemed like the biggest commitment we could ever have made.

I kiss him with all the tenderness and feeling I can muster as warmth swells in my chest. "I love you, too."

He blinks slowly as we part from the chaste kiss, and his serious eyes bore into mine. His voice is firm and decisive when he speaks: "Marry me."

Chapter Nineteen — Connor

❧

Okay, so my proposal might have come off a little impromptu, but I've been thinking about this for weeks. Months, actually, if I'm being completely honest. Yes, the moment I've chosen to blurt the demand –not even a question– is emotionally charged, and probably not at all romantic enough, but after everything we've gone through, I can't imagine a future where Will isn't by my side.

Hell, if I lost him now, I would probably be tempted to step in front of an oncoming tram.

Melodramatic? Sure. But that's how I feel.

If I'd had any doubts about how much he loved me or how much he loved our daughter, today would have blown them out of the water. He's just as devastated to have handed her over to Brandon as I am. He's just as lost without her, and struggling just as badly as I am.

And, even though he'd been uncomfortable with the idea of fucking our frustrations out, he went through with it for me.

I can't help but think it only brought us closer. I don't

think I've ever cried during sex before. Certainly not the ugly, heaving sobs I spilled out today. But I'd needed that. I'd needed to have angry, rough sex to push out all of the hurt and the pain I couldn't put into words. It was cathartic and healing in a way I can't properly verbalise. Additionally, the fact that Will not only seemed to understand how badly I needed it but also got to the same emotional breaking point with me just proves how perfect we are together.

Will stares at me in surprise for a long moment and my heart squeezes. I wonder if maybe I've pushed him too far, too fast. But, I mean, I asked him to raise a baby with me. That's more serious than marriage, right? And he jumped into that feet first. After all, divorce is a thing, whereas Vicky will be a permanent fixture in his life, regardless.

I'm opening my mouth to backpedal, or to assure him that it's nothing we have to rush into, when he finally responds.

"I'd marry you today if I could, baby."

I can't describe the feeling that sweeps over me. It's a mixture of joy, relief, excitement, and contentment. My heart somehow speeds up and slows down all at once. The fear of rejection melts away. My shoulders loosen up and warmth spreads to my extremities.

"Yeah?" I ask, unable to keep the disbelief from my tone. "Really?"

My big, sexy fireman cuddles me close to his chest, his deep voice rumbling and vibrating into me, "Really," he says firmly. "I love you."

I could cry all over again if I didn't think I'd already emptied my body of tears today. I clutch at him and swallow roughly. "It's not too soon?"

His answering chuckle is dry. "We're raising a kid together," he says, and it's only the fact that I'm pressed tightly against him that allows me to hear the snag in his voice when he mentions her. "I'd say the timing is just fine."

How is it possible to be so happy and so sad all at the same time? I'm ecstatic because *holy shit,* we just got engaged. But I'm also miserable because my family feels incomplete right now and will remain so for the entire week,

How am I going to survive this week? And how am I going to keep on repeating this process every second week? Will has taken this week off work to mourn with me, and we're both so grateful that his boss is super compassionate and that Jack was willing to step in and pick up half his shifts, but he won't be able to do this next time. Or the time after that. And then I'll be left to ramble around the empty apartment wondering what I ever did with my life before Vicky existed.

Will eventually nudges me out of bed and we strip the sheets together, tossing them into the laundry hamper. Then he guides me into the bathroom and we spend far too much time under the soothing heat of the shower's spray, washing each other and exchanging soft, worshipful kisses.

By the time we're dressed, it's already past noon. My stomach growls. I glare down at it, wondering how I can possibly be hungry when I'm so emotionally bereft.

"Let's get lunch," Will says.

I school my instinctive reaction to shake off the suggestion. Starving myself isn't going to make the situation any better. If anything, it will make things worse.

I head into the lounge room in search of my shoes, freezing in place at the sight of the empty playpen. Turning to face the kitchen doesn't help because there I find the empty highchair.

"Come on," Will places his hand on the small of my back and

226

guides me towards the door. He pulls our slip on boat shoes off the shoe rack and I mindlessly step into mine before he pushes me out into the small hallway.

"I can't do this," I tell him as we start to walk towards the stairs. I haven't taken the stairs in what feels like forever because I usually have the pram with me or I don't want to risk tripping down them while carrying the baby. It feels strange to be leaving with Will but without our loud little companion. "How am I supposed to do this?"

"Right now," he admits quietly, but his voice bounces off the tiled floor in the stairwell, echoing around us, "I'm pretending she's at a playdate with Hen and Sarah. I'm just trying to take every hour as it comes."

I nod. It's not a bad strategy. It's certainly better than my current headspace anyway.

When we're out of the building, I stop on the footpath and take a deep breath. The air is crisp and clean. In a couple of months, it will be warm enough to head down to the beach for more than just walks. I've been looking forward to taking Vicky. I think she'll love the sand, and she'll be old enough to sit on the water's edge and squeal as the remnants of the crashing waves tickle her tiny toes.

There I go again. Suddenly, I realise that I'll only really have half the summer with my daughter. With a frown, I start to calculate dates, trying to work out who will have custody over Christmas. Or over Vicky's birthday, which is in January.

My stomach sinks when I realise that I'm probably going to miss out on one if not both events.

"Con?" Will's voice is calming, as is the hand at the small of my back. "Talk to me."

My current train of thought comes spilling out, along with

a fresh wave of tears. The idea of not sharing my baby's first Christmas or her first birthday (which coincides with the first anniversary of her mother's death) is too much for me to handle. Will pulls me tightly against him, holding me while I bawl.

I don't care that we're standing on the street where passers by can see us. I don't care that people probably think I'm a lunatic. I don't care that the perfect weather is mocking me with its blue skies and light breeze.

I don't care about anything anymore.

Chapter Twenty — Will

"How is he?" Henry asks me as soon as I answer his call.

I'm back at work, and Vicky is back at home with Connor. Our first week without her was absolute hell. Connor's belated realisation that this arrangement is going to fuck with Christmases and birthdays was the last straw, destroying the tenuous hold over his impending breakdown.

I've felt powerless to help.

When the boys were growing up, I didn't really have to worry about not sharing major milestones or events with them. Jen and I were best friends, so I was always welcome at all family events. Even after she started seeing Mitch, I was still included at all gatherings, so this is new to me, too.

"Not great," I answer with a pained exhale, scrubbing my hand over my face. "He needs to talk to someone, like a therapist or something, but he won't."

I sound frustrated to even my own ears.

Henry makes a commiserating sound. "We're still fighting

for the adoption to go through," he tells me, but his tone tells me everything I need to know about how well that's going.

"Yeah, well, we're not counting our chickens."

There's a beat of silence. "Have *you* thought about talking to someone?"

Licking my lips, I nod though Henry can't see me. "The station has a service," I tell him. "It's technically more for the pressures of the job, but I've made an appointment." Having distracted or stressed-out firefighters isn't ideal, after all.

"Good," Henry says, "that's good."

He hasn't spoken to Connor. He feels guilty for the terms we came to during mediation, and Connor's still hurt that Henry agreed to the 50/50 arrangement at all. It's hard seeing the two best friends at odds with each other, but I know better than to meddle or push.

"You're taking care of him, right? I know this is shit for you, too, but…" Henry's sentence hangs for a moment while I gather my thoughts.

Sitting in the poky station break room, I look at the chipped Formica counter and the electric kettle which have seen better days. I consider making myself a cup of coffee, but I've really come to hate the instant crap. Connor's spoiled me on the coffee front.

"Of course I am," I try not to snap at Henry. Suddenly, my determination not to meddle vanishes. "But you know what might also help him? His *best friend* swallowing his pride and reaching out."

There's a sharp intake of air, audible even down the phone line. "Will…" Henry's tone is one of warning.

"No. You're all he has left, Henry. Outside of me, Vicky, and his mom, you are all he has. You're the brother he never had and he's hurting. One of you needs to make the first move to fix things and, I'm sorry, but with the way he's feeling right now, it's not gonna be him." I breathe deeply, hold it and then release it slowly. "I'm sorry," I repeat. "I know it's not fair. You were just doing your job. On some level, Con knows that."

Someone else walks into the break room and I raise my eyes to greet them. It's Pete, and he gives me a knowing, compassionate half smile. We've never been close, but I know he's also been through a custody battle of his own, and we've worked together long enough that his silent support is bracing. I nod at him, he nods back, and then he goes about making himself a coffee. I shake my head when he holds up a second empty mug. He shrugs, then turns his broad back on me to focus on his task.

Henry finally starts speaking again midway through this entire interaction. "I know," he tells me softly. "I miss him, Will. You get that, right? But I figure he's got a right to be pissed with me."

"For doing your job?" I repeat, this time sounding incredulous. "No, and he knows that. We both do. He's hurting. He needs you. Just," I drum my fingers on the plastic tabletop in front of me. It's from one of those cheap outdoor sets from a big chain store, but it does the job in the break room, "talk to him, okay?" I glance up at the clock. "Anyway, my break's over. I've gotta go. Call Connor. Please."

We exchange goodbyes and I clap Pete on the shoulder as I pass him.

* * *

The alarm goes off twenty minutes before the end of our shift, and we all suit up and climb into the truck without complaint. There's no time to send off messages saying that we'll be late home, and those of us with families and significant others know that they expect this to happen from time to time.

Still, I can't help feeling uneasy as we drive towards the warehouse fire in the Burleigh industrial estate. With Connor's fragile emotional state, I don't need him worrying about me. I tell myself I'll buy him his favourite Thai food on my way home later to make up for it before my attention is drawn to the plumes of dark smoke billowing into the late afternoon sky.

The Burleigh station already have two trucks on the scene as we arrive, but they'd called in back up due to the wind causing issues. We pull up and Pete, taking lead, barks out our tasks. Within minutes, we have the hoses out and aimed at the building.

Over the noise of the rushing water and the roaring and crackling flames, I swear I can hear a faint cry.

"The building's empty, right?" I call over to Pete.

He nods. "Supposed to be," he answers. Our SCBA (self-contained breathing apparatus) masks are fitted with com units that make these interactions a hell of a lot easier than the days when I first joined the service.

I strain my ears. There it is again! It's faint, but it's a cry for help.

"There's someone in there!" I insist.

Pete shakes his head. Our proximity to the burning building has waves of heat licking us, but our PPE gear keeps us safe. "They said it was clear. We need to contain the fire."

"*HELP!*"

This time, the voice is carried on the wind and Pete hears it, too. His head shoots up from the nozzle end of the hose and he scans the area for signs of life. "Shit," he curses. "There's someone in there!"

Before I know what I'm doing, I pull away from my spot behind Pete and move towards the flames. They're bright orange and red, with ominous black smoke only emphasising their flickering.

"Will! The fuck do you think you're doing?!"

I'm a rule follower in general. I don't break rank, and I don't disregard procedure, but the warehouse in front of us is already bowing and swaying as the flames weaken its structure. I can't ignore the cries for help, and we're the only unit on this side of the building.

"Bradford!" Pete barks into his coms. "Pull back!"

Knowing that I'm going to get in a lot of trouble for this, I race forward in my clunky PPE gear as the next cry sounds out. I follow the general direction, squinting through my mask, as though that's going to help me see better through the smoke and flames.

"*HELP!*" the voice calls out again, and as I near the building, I catch sight of movement in the second storey window.

Fuck.

Pete is still berating me as I lumber through the first gap in the flames I find, and my heart races when I understand just how monumentally stupid and unsafe the decision I just made was. But as I make it up the creaking, swaying stairs and through the smoke to the corner room where I'd seen the movement, my stomach plunges for a different reason.

There are two small bodies huddled together in the corner. They're filthy -from the smoke and likely homelessness- and neither could be older than thirteen or fourteen. They're just kids, and one of them isn't moving.

The conscious kid, presumably the one who had been calling for help, starts to sob when they see me. The sobs turn into hacking coughs, and I scan the room for my options, even as I'm already relaying my find over the coms. Pete cusses and curses and tells me to hold tight while they get the ladder or life net in place, and I head over to the kids and crouch down in front of them.

The conscious one is shirtless, and he's holding his shirt over his prone companion's mouth and nose. I pull out a spare dust mask from my kit, knowing that it's not going to help much, but the kid needs to cover their own face as best as possible.

"Hi," I say as I hand it over, keeping my tone calm and level. "I'm Will. We're gonna get you both out of here, okay?"

"He's too heavy to carry down the stairs," the kid in front of me sobs and then coughs some more. "And I burned my feet trying to get help. My thongs melted, too."

I look down and, sure enough, the kid's feet are bare and not in a great state.

"Easy, easy," I soothe, "we'll get you all fixed up in no time. What's your name?" From somewhere in the building, there's a loud crash. The whole building shudders. The faint roar of the familiar sound of a large burst of oxygen feeding the flames follows.

Pete's voice in my ear tells me one of the walls has come down and that I need to get my ass out now.

Having jumped and flinched, the kid's wide, terrified eyes try to meet mine through my mask. "J-jack," he answers my earlier question, and my heart clenches.

"My son's name is Jack," I tell him, ignoring the ominous way the room is now swaying, no matter how subtle it is. "I need you to hold on just a bit longer, okay? The rest of the team are working to get a ladder up here."

Jack shakes his head. "Mason can't climb. He passed out. He..." More hacking coughs wrack his thin frame.

"I will get him out of here, Jack. I promise."

The kid sniffles and nods. The building makes more ominous sounds as the fire continues to destroy it from the inside out. Thankfully, Pete tells me that the ladder and life net are both in place and I shield both boys after confirming that we're out of the way of the window. Whoever is at the top of the ladder shatters the glass and clears out the frame, and I coax Jack to head out first.

The floor beneath our feet groans.

I help Jack out through the window, my heart squeezing as he cries out at the drop to the life net below. He hesitates, but Cam, on the top of the ladder, finally gets him to jump.

I waste no time scooping Mason up, though it is awkward trying to get him through the window unconscious. With the flames and damage travelling through the building, though, I can't risk trying to take his unprotected body back the way I came up, assuming the rickety stairs are even still there to begin with.

Cam confirms that he's got him, and I let go, climbing through the window myself. Just as I'm about to leap, the wall itself gives way. Something hits me in the back of my helmeted head, and then I'm freefalling.

Chapter Twenty-One — Connor

I'm sprawled out on the floor in the lounge room, surrounded by brightly coloured Duplo blocks and about a billion plush toys. Vicky's sitting on her padded butt in front of me, gnawing on one of her blocks. She's chosen bright green today. Drool dribbles down onto her chin, and I scrunch up my nose in mild disgust.

I don't think I'll ever fully be okay with how sticky and gross babies can be.

We're having a conversation about the best way to build a castle (I say connecting the blocks works, she says mashing it with her pudgy fists is better) when my phone rings.

Lifting the device up, I smile at the picture accompanying Jack's contact name. It's a photo of him and Vicky, the pair of them wearing matching teddy bear ear headbands. He's ridiculously good with her, which I appreciate. He's also become a pretty good friend to me over the past months, something I know Will is over the moon about.

I press the green answer icon and put him on speaker so I

can keep playing with the baby.

"Hey Jack," I greet him warmly. "To what do I owe the-"

"Connor," his tone is serious as he cuts me off. A chill runs down my spine.

"What's wrong?"

"Dad's in the hospital," he answers without fanfare. "He was at a fire. There were some kids trapped on the second storey…the building gave way just as he was getting out. Some of the roof and siding caught him on his way down."

"*What?!*" I cry in disbelief. "Did you just say a building fell on him?"

That same numbness that I felt when Daisy died takes a hold of me. Today, that's a good thing because I have Vicky to look after. I can't fall apart. Not while she's in my care.

"It wasn't a whole building," Jack says, as though that makes a difference. "He's alive and conscious. They're treating him for a minor concussion."

"Where is he?"

"Robina," he answers. "It was the closest."

I nod. "Okay. I'll be there soon. I'll…" I look down at Vicky. "I'll ask Sarah to take Vicky and I'll be there as soon as I can."

"Okay. Good. I'll meet you at Emergency, just text when you get there. I've gotta call Wes."

We exchange quick goodbyes and I sit back for a moment, still numb. On some level, it says something that Jack would call me before his twin, and I'll be emotional about that later, but right now I'm waiting for the panic to kick in. If I lose Will now, I'm almost certain it will kill me, too.

I know I have Vicky to focus on, but I only have her half the time now. I don't have my sister, I don't have my dad, and my mum lives overseas. Will has been my rock since Daisy died and I can't imagine a life without him.

I pull my phone from my pocket and dial the only other number I know from memory, not bothering to scroll through my contacts. Henry picks up on the third ring.

"Con?" The caution in his voice proves to be the tipping point for me. The numbness leeches away and the first of what threatens to be many sobs escapes me.

"Hen."

His concern is immediate. I can picture his frown and the way he would have straightened his spine. "What's wrong?"

With a tremble in my voice, I reiterate Jack's call, and Hen swears. I hear the jangle of keys, the sound of papers shuffling and zips working. "I'm on my way to your place," he says. "I know you said he's fine, but I'd rather you didn't drive like this anyway. I'll take you to Robina, and I'll take the Vickster home with me."

I'm dimly aware that I don't deserve this from him. Not when I've spent the last few weeks ignoring him, unfairly blaming him for not fighting harder to keep Vicky with us. I want to apologise for that, but the words don't come. Instead, I thank him and hang up, and busy myself with packing Vicky a bag and getting her changed.

When Henry arrives, he pulls me into a tight hug. Guilt at how I've been treating him roils my belly.

"I'm sorry," I tell him, finally understanding that my pettiness wasn't helpful. "I've been such a dick."

"Stop it," he demands. He pulls back and physically holds me at arm's length to pin me with the weight of his forceful stare. "Con, in the past few years, you've gone through hell and you've held it together better than I ever could have. You're allowed to break. You're allowed to be irrational. You're allowed to hurt and you're allowed to feel like you have to blame someone."

I swallow roughly and shake my head. "You're my brother, Hen. Of all people to lash out at…"

He shrugs, his handsome face pulling into a smirk. "We've never really had a sibling fight before. It's a rite of passage, isn't it? And, as the older, more attractive brother, I understand."

I don't deserve him, but I take his forgiveness and run with it. "Thanks, Hen," I say softly, not even biting at his 'more attractive' jibe.

He nods, then claps his hands together. "Okay, let's get going. You have a boyfriend to dote over."

"Fiancé," I correct him shyly.

Henry's dark eyes widen, and his face breaks into a wide, beaming grin. "Well, congratulations. We're throwing you an engagement party once he's out of hospital." He reaches out and squeezes my hand. "You said mild concussion, right? That's nothing."

Wordlessly, I nod. I'm afraid that if I say anything, I'll actually break down. Yes, Will is going to be okay, but what if it had been worse? What if he'd been seriously injured? What if I lost him?

Henry scoops Vicky up, and she squeals and babbles delightedly when she recognises him. He talks to her as we make our way down to his car, an Audi sedan he bought to replace the penis extension he'd been driving before Max was born. As he's buckling her into the car seat, he tells her that Max is looking forward to seeing her, and I am almost certain she repeats Max's name.

Okay, so she says 'Ma' and not 'Max', but more and more recently, I'm convinced that she's trying to say real words instead of just babbling.

It provides enough of a distraction from my spiralling thoughts that Henry and I both praise her and encourage her to repeat it. She does.

Hen and I look to each other and cheer.

"This will be the best story to tell when they're older," he says as he walks around the car. I drop into the passenger seat at the same time as he slides into the driver's seat. "He was her first word. How cool is that?"

I love that there's absolutely nothing toxic or competitive in the way we support each other's kids. With them born so closely together, we could have done the passive aggressive 'my kid is doing this thing already' humble bragging, but we never have. Henry and Sarah dote on Vicky like she's their own, and Will and I treat Max the same way when he's with us. They really are growing up like siblings, and Henry's excitement just now drives that all home for me.

Of course, that realisation brings back a wave of guilt. How could I even try to believe that he wasn't trying his best to keep Vicky with us?

"Stop spiralling," he says, proving that he knows me well. "Whatever it is you're thinking, just stop."

There's no sense arguing with him, so I try to let it go. I have Will to worry about anyway.

"He's going to be fine, Con."

"I know."

I just don't know what I would do if he wasn't.

* * *

I hug Jack tightly as soon as I step into the Emergency

240

Department's waiting room. He's not dressed for work, which means he was either not working, or not on shift yet. I don't know why that's a relief, but it is.

After checking that Vicky's in good hands, he leads me down various corridors and hallways until we get to a separate waiting area – smaller and more private than the big room where people come in and wait to be triaged. This space is for people waiting on family members who have been admitted, or for people who have stepped out of the quiet rooms for a breather. Currently, it's just me and Jack occupying the space, and I can't help but have flashbacks to the night Daisy died.

"So, they've taken him to run some scans," Jack says, unaware of where my thoughts have gone.

"Scans?" I echo, bringing myself back to the present. Frowning, I ask, "Was it worse than they thought? Will he need surgery? Will he have brain damage? What about the smoke inhalation?"

"He was in full gear, including SCBA, so smoke won't have gotten him," Jack assures me. Then he shrugs and sighs. "As for the rest? Gotta wait for the doctors."

I remember the waiting. The waiting sucks. I start to pace, trying not to think of the worst-case scenario. I can't lose another person to a freak accident within a year. I can't. Especially not Will. Especially not when Jack said he was *fine.*

Jack sits in one of the uncomfortable plastic chairs and kicks his legs out in front of him. He seems ridiculously calm for someone whose dad might be critically injured, but he's also a firefighter himself. He knows the risks of the job better than I do, and he's probably got a better understanding of the limits of their PPE. And, if he's not stressing out, maybe I shouldn't be.

I eventually sit a few seats away from him, pulling out my phone just for something to do. I scroll mindlessly through emails, then Facebook, but nothing really computes. It's just keeping my hands busy, and my mind distracted enough that I don't fidget or demand answers that aren't yet available.

Wes is led into the room after an hour or so passes, and he and Jack hug just as tightly as Jack and I did. Then I stand and hug him as well.

"How's Vicky?" he asks me after Jack brings him up to date on everything we know so far (a whole lot of nothing, as far as I'm concerned).

"She's good," I answer honestly, "Oh, and I think she's starting to talk."

Both men give me their full attention, matching blue eyes lighting up in the same way. It's uncanny. "Yeah?" they ask in voices that sound like echoes of each other.

I nod. "Yeah. Tonight, I'm pretty sure she tried to say Max."

Jack knows Henry well, considering Hen joined the indoor soccer team with me all those months ago, and he's met Max a few times now. Wes has only met Henry at a handful of gatherings, but even he grins knowingly.

"They'll be two peas in a pod, won't they?" Wes says.

"Yeah," I agree. "Just like Hen and me."

I've wanted that for Vicky from the start. To have a friend her own age, someone she can grow up with, who gets her in ways her parents never will. A partner in childish crime, a shoulder to cry on when Will and I are inevitably *awful* and *cruel* in that way kids often dramatize their parents to be.

If anyone understands what it's like to have that, it's the twins in front of me. Despite the way they bicker and banter, they each had a built-in best friend and sidekick growing up. It's a bond I made with Henry when we met so young. Yes, siblings are different, but the foundations are pretty much the same.

We talk about the kids for a little while, and I'm almost able to pretend that we're just catching up as friends and family do. That is, until a nurse in scrubs walks into the room and we all straighten and turn to look at her.

"Family of William Bradford?" she asks.

We all nod.

She smiles warmly. "He's just been brought back up to the ward. It doesn't look like he's going to need surgery. His helmet did its job and protected him from the worst of the collapse. He was lucky: there's no major swelling or anything to indicate internal bleeding, either."

I want to weep with relief. "Can we see him?"

The pretty blonde woman smiles warmly, nodding. She's short and curvy, with warm green eyes and olive skin that I would kill for. "We've moved him into a private room and you can visit with him now. Be mindful that he's a bit battered and bruised and that we've got him on the good drugs now." She winks.

She doesn't put a limit on how many of us can visit at once, and I'm grateful for that.

"Your dad's a strong guy," she says over her shoulder as she walks us towards his room.

I falter at the words. "Oh. Uh. I'm not…" I clear my throat. "I'm his partner."

I can't see her face, but I can see the flush that travels up the back of her neck before she turns back with the most chagrined, apologetic expression I've seen in a while. "I am so sorry," she says, her cheeks red. "I shouldn't have just assumed. It's just...they told me that his sons would be waiting and I just..."

Jack and Wes are snickering on either side of me, which isn't helping. I glare up at them both, Wes first, then Jack. "You both suck," I say. Then I smile back at the nurse. "It's fine," I wave her off. "Just maybe don't mention it to Will."

It has taken a while to get the chip about our age gap off his shoulders. I don't want to put it back there.

Jack laughs quietly at my request as we turn another corner. He nudges my shoulder with his bicep. "Dad's still sensitive about the age gap?"

"Nah," I shrug. "Not really. Most of the time I think he forgets. But every so often, it comes up and he gets squirrelly about it." I snort. "It's not like I'm expecting either of you two to call me Dad once we're married or anything."

Wes stumbles at my side. "Married?! Not," he rushes to add, presumably just in case I might think he's not okay with the concept, "that that's a bad thing. But..." he looks over the top of my head, exchanging a glance with his brother, "well, we never thought we'd see him get hitched."

"It's, um, it's a new development. I proposed. He said yes. That's as far as we've gotten." I'm not concerned that Will hasn't mentioned it to his boys. I hadn't told Henry until tonight, either. We were both enjoying keeping it as our own little secret: something that only we shared between us.

We've stopped outside the door to a private room, and Jack claps me on the back. "Congrats," he says with feeling. "You're good for him. He's happy with you, Con. And having Vicky in his life..." He and Wes exchange another look. I can't read it. Jack turns his attention back to me. His tone is soft when he speaks again, "Obviously, he loves me and Wes, but he was so young when we were little. I think some part of him felt like he was a kid raising kids, even though he wasn't. But he gets to have the full white-picket-fence life with you and Vicky, and it's awesome to see him loving it, I guess."

There is a lot to unravel there, and I make a mental note to do that later. For the moment, though, all I do is hug Jack again and thank him over the lump in my throat. He squeezes me back just as tightly.

Then I lead the way into Will's hospital room, relieved to find him sitting up in bed, wearing a hospital gown and a very sheepish expression.

Chapter Twenty-Two — Will

~~~
❦
~~~

Since the doctors gave me painkillers, the throbbing in my head has faded following the near miss at the fire. It's not my first concussion, however mild it might be, so I know I'm in for dizziness and nausea once the shock of it all fades. Honestly? I'm more concerned about the severe bruising to my back and ribs, because I caught some more debris as the building and I came down earlier tonight.

Seeing Connor walk into my hospital room ahead of my boys makes that pain fade away, though. I instantly feel bad for having scared him. The matching scowls of frustration laced with worry on my boys' faces only make the guilt stronger.

"Hi," I greet them awkwardly.

Con releases a breath that's somewhere between a chuckle and a sob before he launches himself in my direction. For all of his obvious relief, though, he's careful when he wraps his arms around me, bestowing the softest of kisses to my lips.

"Don't you *dare* do something like this again," he demands.

Pressing my forehead to his, I agree readily. "I won't. I

promise."

Wes steps up beside Jack. "You were insanely lucky," he tells me. He sounds weary. More upset than angry, though, but that's always been one of the things that set him and Jack apart. "Nothing's broken, no internal bleeding, minimal head trauma – well, minus the obvious concussion, they don't think you've damaged your brain. I don't know how you managed it, Dad, but you're basically walking away unscathed. A bit battered and bruised, but otherwise fine."

"Pretty sure you're gonna get your ass handed to you at work, though." Jack adds. His frown is deeper than Wes's, proving me right. He's pissed. I suppose I would be, too, if he had done what I did. If our roles were reversed, I'd be giving him one hell of a talking to.

"You were reckless and stupid," Connor's voice is shrill when I fail to respond to Jack's comment. His hand clutches mine tightly. "Damn it, Will, why would you…" he trails off, his voice hitching. "I almost lost you. *We* almost lost you."

I don't need to ask who 'we' is. It's all three of the men in the room with me. It's Vicky. It's my friends and colleagues.

"I…"

"And don't you dare apologise," he continues. "Two kids are alive because of what you did, so I can't even say it would have been better if you'd followed proper procedures."

A smile twitches the corner of my lips upwards. Even while he's upset and pissed off, he's still a sweetheart. Plus, hearing that the kids are safe justifies the risks I took.

"I'm sorry I worried you," I tell him after a moment's consideration. "But you're right: I wouldn't change what I did. Not even if I knew what would happen."

Connor releases a heavy sigh. His hand grips mine tightly

again. "I know. And I love you for it, even if I'm still mad at you for putting yourself in harm's way like that." There's another moment of silence before he quietly adds, "I never really thought about how dangerous your job is, you know? Like, logically I know it's high risk, but until tonight, I hadn't put two and two together that *you* would be in high-risk situations." A rueful laugh follows. "Denial is more than just a river in Egypt, or whatever they say."

"Sweetheart…" I don't quite know how to respond to him.

"No, I know," he says, assuming whatever it is he thinks I might have said, "it's probably better that I haven't been thinking about all the dangerous things you could be getting up to."

He's so strong. With everything else that has been going on, it would have been perfectly understandable if this had pushed him over the edge, even if I wasn't seriously injured. It might well have broken me if our roles were reversed and I had to worry about him being reckless on top of everything else.

"It's gonna take more than a building falling on me to keep me from you," I tell him, matching his slightly forced humour with my own.

"*Dad*," Wes groans, "too soon."

I crack a more genuine grin at that, at least. But then I sober, thinking about it from my kids' perspective.

With the adrenaline from tonight's events well and truly out of my system, I look at Jack. "The boys really are okay? One of them was named Jack. I couldn't leave them there." My thoughts come out a little scattered, and I frown. "I mean…"

My son scrubs a hand over his bearded face and sighs heavily, nodding. "I get it, Dad." The look he shoots me next is knowing. "And you had no idea the kid's name was Jack before you ran into that warehouse, so don't go trying to use that as any kind of excuse. You're a bleeding heart."

I shrug, and the movement pulls at the bruising to my back, making me wince. "Guilty as charged, I'm afraid. I didn't even know they were kids. Just that I couldn't let someone die in there." I scowl. "Who the fuck declared the place empty anyhow?"

"Pete's already looking into that," Jack assures me. At least he's softening, his frustration finally giving way to concern. I hate it when we're at odds, especially when we both know that he probably would have done the same thing I did. "But, yeah, the boys are okay. Little Jack's got a bit of hero worship going on for you." Finally, a grin pulls at his lips, revealing his white, slightly crooked teeth. "He said you told him you had a son with the same name, and he was very excited to meet me."

"Oh, of course we're making this about you now," Wes complains, pulling over one of the guest chairs. He rolls his eyes. "Dad saves the kid's life, but he's excited to meet you? Spare me."

"He was," Jack insists, his grin widening now that he's riling his brother up. "And when I told him I was also a firefighter, you'd have thought I hung the moon."

Wes makes a gagging sound. Connor snorts.

And, even though I'm in a little bit of pain, everything feels right in the world after all.

* * *

Because of the injuries to my back, the hospital keeps me in for observation and treatment for a few more days. Connor brings Vicky around when the pounding in my skull turns into a dull ache, and seeing her lodges a knot of sadness in my gut which I just can't shake.

The doctors did mention that irritability, anxiety and sadness are all common side effects from a concussion, but knowing that doesn't make it any easier to power through. Especially when Connor arrives to pick me up with puffy red eyes on the day I'm discharged.

It's Saturday again, only the second time we've had to hand Vicky over to her biological father, and I wasn't there to say goodbye. I wasn't there to hold Connor's hand or share his pain. That just makes me feel guilty which intensifies my low mood, not to mention facing another week without my little girl.

However, before we leave, I ask the nurses to direct me to the boys I helped out of the building. I know they're both still here, being attended to for various untreated ailments exacerbated by their homelessness, as well as the smoke inhalation.

They look so small in the hospital beds they've been allocated, set up side-by-side with the curtain that separates them drawn back so they can see and talk to each other. They've been bathed, and their hair is a matching dirty blond, though Mason's has been shaved on one side, a fresh gauze patch covering the scar for whatever issue the doctors had found and fixed.

When I saw them in that building, I had estimated them to be in their early teens, but they look much younger now that they've been cleaned up. It makes something inside me twist unpleasantly to think that these poor, young kids were in such a position to begin with.

Jack's eyes widen when he sees me, and he quickly tells

Mason "This is the fireman who saved us."

There's hero worship in his tone just like my Jack had said there would be and, despite my low mood, it warms me. I give my head a very tiny shake. Movement still sets off dizziness, so I have to be careful. "I was just doing my job."

I vividly recall talking to Jack, keeping him calm and assuring him that he and his brother would get out safe. I'm glad that I was able to keep that promise, because I have to acknowledge that my actions were reckless.

Jack, reminding me of my son, rolls his eyes. "You saved us, Mister. The other fireman…the one who said you're his dad? He said you weren't supposed to come and help us. That it was too dangerous."

"No," I deny, and then sit down on the edge of Jack's mattress. "That's not true. We would have worked to help you a different way. I didn't follow procedure is all." Pete has been to see me and he drove that point home with more gentleness than I would have expected, all things considered. I'm pretty sure he'll tear me a new one when I'm back on the clock, though.

Jack picks at a thread on his hospital issued blanket. "Well, you still saved us. You saved Mason and I couldn't. So thank you."

My heart aches for him. From what little I've gleaned from my Jack's digging (read: flirting with the nurses), these kids ran away from their respective foster homes because they'd been separated. The brothers have had a hard life. At twelve and ten years of age, they've still got a while to go in the system.

I want so desperately to be able to do *something* for them. However, with everything happening with Vicky, and my own recovery necessary, any lofty ideas I might have entertained about fostering them myself are smothered.

Nevertheless, I make a mental note to talk to some of the guys at the station. Surely someone might know a family willing to take in both kids, troubled though they might be.

From the other bed, Mason pipes up and thanks me as well. "Turns out I needed a doctor for other things," he says, not elaborating on what those things are. "I never woulda' gone, so…you saved me that way, too."

Yeah, I decide, *even if I can't help these boys myself, I'm going to ask around until I find someone who can.*

I introduce them properly to Connor, then, and we all sit and talk about less triggering topics for a while. As we're walking out of the room, Connor sends a text off to some friends of his who will get these kids some new clothes and essentials, something I hadn't even thought about. I also tell him that I'd like to buy them something frivolous, like an iPad or a Nintendo Switch. Something to brighten their lives and spoil them a bit. Connor squeezes me close and tells me I'm a good man, but when we reach the car and I spy the empty car seat, the mood falls again.

The drive home is quiet. It's not tense, but it's not comfortable either. Awkward, maybe? Either way, when we finally step through the door to the apartment, I'm feeling off-kilter and exhausted.

I'm going to be at home until I get medically cleared to go back to work, where I know I'll face disciplinary action for ignoring Pete's commands.

I flop onto the couch, making a sound that is somewhere between a groan and a sigh. My bruised back protests the sudden movement, but even the pain from that is finally starting to fade. Patting the space beside me, I look towards Connor. "Come cuddle?"

He toes his shoes off at the door and walks around the couch to drop down by my side. He snuggles in against me as I wrap my arm around his shoulders, and we just hold each other like that.

Tension seeps out of my body as I close my eyes, breathing in the comforting scent of home. It's a mixture of Connor's cologne and the light, but sweet frangipani and vanilla reed diffusers he has placed strategically on shelves around the apartment.

Before I know it, I'm asleep, comforted by the familiar scents and the warmth and weight of Connor at my side.

* * *

Close to two weeks later, I'm still not at work. I'm still suffering from random attacks of dizziness and vertigo, though thankfully they're no longer as frequent. My moods seem to have stabilized, and being home has been nice. I'm only turning fifty on my next birthday, but retirement –or even semi-retirement– is beginning to sound more and more enticing.

The week spent with Vicky back at home has been wonderful. Playing with her, taking her for walks, reading to her, listening to her babble out sounds that are much closer to words than ever before…it has been incredible.

Just this morning, I watched her push up awkwardly onto her hands and almost her knees, accomplishing a commando crawl across the living room until she tired of it and cried to be picked up.

I don't want to miss these moments any more than I have to on the weeks where she's not here with us.

Chapter Twenty-Three - Connor

❧

"Would you hate it if I became a house husband?" Will asks me, seemingly apropos of nothing.

I look up from my laptop, where I'm trying to craft an email to a potential client, and blink. "A house husband?"

Images of my sexy silver fox wearing nothing but an apron and a smile assault me, and I can't keep the goofy smile from my face.

"Well, you're smiling, so I'm guessing that's a no," he says, bringing my thoughts back to the conversation.

Closing the lid of my laptop with a quiet *snick*, I place it on the coffee table before I lean forward to give my man my full attention. "It's definitely a no," I assure him, cocking my head to the side. "But what brought this on? I thought you loved your job."

"I do. But it's been thirty years," Will sighs and rubs the back of his neck, casting his gaze over Vicky who is attempting to repeat her crawling performance with very little success.

The pride I'd felt when she managed to move herself across the floor astounded me. Who knew something so small could inspire such huge emotions?

Will seems to be feeling something quite similar because he continues, "I don't want to miss these moments with her, you know? Or with you."

"You don't need to justify it," I feel the need to tell him.

I recall all too well how hard I had to fight for my right to leave my law career to pursue starting my events coordination business. Ant was never on board. I don't ever want Will to feel like I don't support him, especially when it comes to the big, important, life-changing stuff.

I offer him a warm smile. "You just surprised me is all." Shuffling over to join him on the mat with our daughter, I nuzzle that sexy, bearded jaw of his. "I'll support whatever you want to do." After a moment of hesitation, I add, "I mean, I can afford it."

Will still owns his apartment, holding it in trust for his sons, and gets a steady stream of passive income from leasing it out. I'm doing the same with Daisy's apartment, even though I still haven't seen it in person since before her accident. In addition to that, my apartment is owned outright, and the amount I inherited from Dad and Daisy's combined life insurances is more than comfortable. Because of the way I came into these funds, I'm still uncomfortable discussing them.

"I've got a nest egg, too, sweetheart," Will tells me softly, then he smirks, his eyes glimmering with mirth. "I'm not asking you to be my sugar daddy."

"I'll have you know, I would make an excellent sugar daddy," I tease him in return, relieved that this is something we can be playful about. Ant was always weird about my financial security being more impressive than his, even though I would have traded it all to have my dad back.

"Hmm, well, maybe I'll let you take me out on fancy dates, then," Will agrees before kissing the corner of my lips.

"Oh, you'll let me, huh?"

I love these moments when he's just as silly and playful as I am.

Oh, who am I kidding? I love all the moments with him.

He nods, affecting a serious expression. "I will. I'll let you wine and dine me, and," he tucks his chin down and looks at me from beneath his eyelashes, "if you play your cards right, you might even get lucky."

Vicky squawks indignantly before I can go along with the sultry tease, and we crack up while Will grabs her and tickles her belly. "Were we ignoring you for too long, princess?" he asks her, making me melt like I always do when he switches into daddy mode.

She reaches for her stuffed Batman toy, which has gotten stuck underneath the couch, and I snort, retrieving it for her. "Nah," I answer on her behalf, "Batman was in mortal peril."

She babbles at the toy once its in her grasp. I'm almost sure she says 'Man-man', but it's lost within the baby speak.

It would be just my luck that she says 'Batman' before she says 'Daddy'. She's Daisy's kid all over.

That thought is nowhere near as painful as it used to be, but I still feel a pang of loss in my chest as it hits me. Desperate to redirect my thoughts before I can be swept up by melancholy, I turn the conversation back to the topic Will raised.

"So, retirement?" I ask him.

After setting Vicky back down on the mat with her toy, he leans back against the base of the couch and licks his lips apprehensively. "You'd really be okay with that?"

Taking his hand in mine, I give it a squeeze. "Why wouldn't I be? We can afford for you to not work, and it'll save us money on daycare. And if you decide that being a stay at home dad isn't for you, that's okay, too."

Tension seems to unwind from his shoulders, and he squeezes my hand back. "I want to stay home with her," he tells me, his gaze drifting back over Vicky. "I worked crazy long shifts through most of the boys' childhoods. I don't want to miss out on hers, too."

Oh, my heart.

"You provided for your family," I tell him firmly. "Jack and Wes have nothing but good things to say about you as a dad. You were there when it counted, and they have wonderful memories because of the sacrifices you made. But…" I look down at our little girl, feeling a whirlwind of emotions when I think about how our time has already been limited and how it must be even harder for Will when he has to work on the weeks when she's home with us, "I get it."

Our hands are still clasped. Will lifts them up and brushes his lips over the back of my knuckles. "I knew you would," his voice is soft, filled with both love and appreciation, "thank you."

Nevertheless, I shake my head. "You never have to thank me for loving you."

I know that there are still tough times ahead. We're reaching the end of another week with Vicky, which means facing down another week without her. But, at moments like these, I'm filled with the certainty that we're going to make it through okay.

* * *

Sure enough, it's getting easier to hand our daughter over to her biological father every custody cycle. It still hurts me to do it, but it's going to hurt Vicky more if I'm always so distressed, so I start to make peace with our arrangement as best I can.

Will and I get into new routines during the weeks without her. We go out on grown up dates, have child-free dinners with friends and with his adult kids, fuck like bunnies at any given opportunity, and effectively keep ourselves distracted in all the best possible ways.

At first I felt guilty for enjoying myself and our relationship without her there, but Sarah insisted that it's healthy and normal to like being a couple without one's children. It doesn't mean we love Vicky any less, or that we don't acknowledge that we would be just as happy to have her with us. But we're making the best out of the situation at hand, and we're proving that we are more to each other than just people who agreed to raise a kid together. We love each other outside the bonds of co-parenting.

I love Will for his sense of humour, which is as daggy as my own at times. I love him for his sharp mind and calming presence. I love him for his desire to explore the things that interest me, and his genuine enthusiasm to spend time with me. I love that we just work together and balance each other out. I love that, even without Vicky as a buffer, we never run out of things to talk about.

Would I prefer to have our girl with us all the time? Yes. But is it the end of the world that her biological father also wants to love her? Probably not.

Case in point: Brandon and I are getting along better. I

wouldn't say we're ever going to be friends, but I'm no longer tempted to take Mum up on her (joke) offer of finding a hit man, and our custody hand-offs are much more civilised than they once were.

The week Will goes back to work coincides with another custody exchange. This time, I surprise both Brandon and myself when I invite the man into my apartment and offer him a coffee.

"It's not a trick to draw out my time with her," I tell him with a weak smile. "I just think it's better for Vicky's sake if she sees us getting along."

He seems to vibrate with anxious energy, but he nods and gives me a tiny, brief smile of his own, tucking his hands into his pockets. "Yeah, okay."

Conversation is strained as we sit at my dining table. He wraps his hands around his mug and looks at Vicky on her play mat, probably to avoid looking at me. I take the opportunity to study him, seeing elements of my daughter in the set of his jaw and the dark shade of his hair. Daisy's hair was a similar colour, so I'm unable to say who Vicky's inherited it from.

"So," I clear my throat, reminding myself that I'm doing this to make Vicky's life easier, "how's Bec?" That was his girlfriend's name, right? I think it was.

A pang of guilt hits me when I can't be sure. I really should know the names of the people looking after my daughter every second week.

Brandon winces a little and rubs the back of his neck, gaze still firmly locked on the little girl we both call our daughter. "She's okay," he says slowly. "She, uh, she spends these weeks with her sister, so…" He shrugs.

"Oh." Even though I had so happily stirred the pot during

our mediation sessions, I can't help but feel a bit guiltier when I hear those words. I didn't actually want to break up a relationship. I'd just wanted him to rethink taking a baby on. "I'm sorry to hear that. So," I shift uncomfortably, "it's just you and Vicky, then?"

Brandon gives me a sharp, assessing look. "That's not going to impact custody negotiations," he snaps, and I hold my hands up in surrender.

"*Easy*," I try to soothe the gaffe. "No, that's not what I was trying to…I was just…" I sigh and scrub my hand over my face. "Look, you've already pretty much won fifty-percent custody. Vicky's coming home to Will and me healthy and happy every other week. So, whatever you're doing, you're not doing a bad job."

It pains me to make those admissions, but I also know how hard it was having sole custody of a baby, and I had a support network at hand. I don't know what Brandon has, but I don't want to be the enemy anymore. Our little girl is more important than that.

A look I can't interpret passes over Brandon's face, but he bobs his head. "Thanks." Pushing his half-drained mug forward, he slides his seat backwards. "I'm just going to take her and go, okay?"

The words make my heart ache, but I nod. We're making slow progress, but Rome wasn't built in a day.

I cover Vicky in kisses, remind Brandon that he's got both Will's and my numbers if he needs us for any reason, and then sigh heavily into the silence of my apartment when they're gone.

Things are getting better, but it doesn't mean I have to like them.

Then Will comes home and holds me close, and I'm once again reminded that we're making it through this together.

"I gave notice of my retirement today," my handsome soon-to-be former fireman says over dinner.

The corners of my mouth lift up as excitement flutters in my belly. Just the idea of him being around more makes me giddy. "How'd they take it?"

We're down in the new Burleigh arcade, at Will's favourite Mexican restaurant. This has become a big part of our new routine, the two of us agreeing that being out of the house for the first night apart from Vicky helps ease us into the rest of the week without her.

The colours around us are bright and uplifting, and the staff here all know Will by name. He banters with Sophie, the server, regularly, and I can't help but picture him having a similar relationship with Vicky when she's a teenager. He's definitely going to be the fun parent, while I'll play bad cop more often than not.

It's a good thing that seeing him in sweet dad mode turns me on like nothing else.

"I think they saw it coming, to be honest," Will shrugs, cutting into his chicken mole and mopping the breast meat through the dark sauce, "or Jack forewarned them. Either way," his fork hovers at his mouth, "they were good about it."

"Aww," I tease, "no tears from Pete?"

Will snorts. "Nope. Chase grumbled about having to find a replacement, but he's happy for me."

"As they all should be," I tell him, reaching under the table to squeeze his thigh. "You're making the right choice for you, and you have to put yourself first."

He nods and his smile turns indulgent beneath that sexy

as fuck beard of his. "Your support means much more to me than theirs."

His words warm me up from the inside and I want to rush through the rest of our meal so I can take him home and show him just how much they affect me. He chuckles when I tell him so; the deep, delicious sound only making me want him more.

"I'm so lucky to have you in my life, Con," he tells me, his eyes misting over. The sentiment dampens my need for him, but makes my heart beat faster.

I stand up and lean over the table, kissing his lips softly. I taste the rich sauce from his meal on them, but I keep this moment gentle and chaste. "The feeling's mutual, Will."

And it is.

No matter what is coming our way next, we're going to get through it together.

Making love to him in our bed later on, that feeling only solidifies.

God, I love him.

Chapter Twenty-Four - Will

etirement was the best choice I could have made for myself and for my family. It was hard to say goodbye to the guys at the station, but they threw me an epic party and reminded me that we'd still hang out socially. Suddenly, my weeks opened up, and being in control of my own schedule was disorienting at first, but oh so liberating. Not to mention how joyful it has been spending time with Vicky without a clock ticking over my head. Well, other than the limits of our temporary custody arrangement with Brandon.

Even that is getting easier to deal with, though it still pains both me and Connor to let our baby go every other week.

In the month since I retired, Connor has also taken advantage of my new role as a stay at home dad, happily leaving Vicky with me so he can fully resume his duties and get his business up and running again.

Today, Connor is out meeting with a new function venue he hopes to work with on a regular basis, and I'm teaching Vicky about colours. I'm pretty sure she's just enjoying smashing the plastic blocks together, but I'm enjoying myself as I say things like "This one is red, sweetheart. Can you say red?" or "That block is blue. Does the blue taste good?" as she gums at it.

When there's a knock at the door, I just assume Jack or Wes are visiting unannounced. Both of my sons have been a bit clingier since the accident, and I can't say I'm not secretly enjoying their additional attention. Leaving Vicky to play on the mat, I push myself to my bare feet and open the door with a ready grin. However, my greeting dies on my lips to find Brandon on the other side of the threshold, his lawyer at his side.

Panic seizes me and I prepare to slam the door in his face.

"It's only Thursday," I growl out, planting my feet. If it was Brandon on his own, my response might be different, but the added presence of the man in the suit has my hackles raised.

The lawyer's eyebrows arch up, but Brandon holds up his hands in the universal sign of surrender.

"I'm not here to take her," his tone is placating, "I promise." He lowers his hands and shuffles his feet. "Can we come in?"

I want to deny him, but I can't say I'm not curious about what's going on. So, despite my misgivings, I step aside and allow the pair to enter.

I gesture for them to take a seat on the couch and I hustle by them to protectively swoop Vicky up into my arms. Then I pull out my phone and Facetime Henry and Connor both.

Unfortunately, Connor doesn't pick up. Thankfully, Henry does.

"What's up?" he asks, then makes faces at Vicky, who squeals something that sounds like 'Nen' while she makes grabby hands for the phone.

I press the button on the screen to switch the camera view, and Henry frowns. "What's going on?" he demands, suddenly our solicitor instead of our friend. "This is an unscheduled visitation, unnotified and-"

"I'm dropping the paternity suit," Brandon cuts him off before he can launch too far into his tirade.

My mouth falls open and I collapse back into the armchair behind me. "What?"

This has 'trap' written all over it. It's too easy.

With colour rising on his cheeks, the younger man looks to his lawyer, who shrugs. Brandon sighs and looks back at me. "I'm dropping the custody claim. I…she's a lot, you know? And I…I'm not ready to be her dad. Not even part time. I thought I was, but…" he trails off and shakes his head, looking down at his fidgeting fingers. "I tried. I did. But it's not working."

Connor told me about his suspicions that Brandon's been struggling, and that his relationship with his girlfriend has suffered with the addition of the baby. But still, this is completely unexpected.

Silence descends.

My heart and brain explode with warring emotions.

Selfishly, I am ecstatic. Connor and I will get our baby back full time, and life will go back to normal. But the other part of me is angry on Vicky's behalf. How dare this man walk into her life, upset everything for months, and then reject her so quickly and easily?

I know that she's not going to remember any of this, but she will ask about her bio dad one day. Instead of telling her that he was never in the picture, Con and I will have to explain this shit-storm instead. We will have to tell her that he turned up, fought for her, then gave up because she was too much work. That it seemed like he valued his girlfriend more than his daughter.

"We're getting this agreement in writing," Henry's voice insists into the silence, and Brandon's lawyer nods, producing a manilla envelope.

"It's all in here," he says in a bored tone that has my hackles raising even higher. "Mister Waters withdraws his petition for custody, as well as his motion against Mister Stark's adoption. All he asks is that he be allowed to maintain cursory contact with his daughter."

I growl again. "I don't think he has the right to call her that," I complain bitterly, unable to stop myself.

"*Will,*" Henry warns, and I sigh.

"Sorry."

"Obviously, we need to discuss this with Connor," Henry continues, "but I'm comfortable tentatively accepting those terms on his behalf. We will read over your documents and I'll be in touch if we have any questions or concerns. If we don't, we'll sign our agreement and will forward them back to you later today. I take it this new arrangement is effective immediately?"

Brandon nods, though I'm oddly moved by the mournful look he gives Vicky.

"This wasn't an easy decision," he tells me quietly. "She's… she's awesome. But I'm not…" He's choked up and his eyes are wet. "I can't give her what you and Connor obviously can, and I don't want to resent her, and I don't want her resenting me, either."

Well. Shit.

Some of my ire deflates. Brandon sounds completely

genuine. His remorse and pain are almost palpable. He obviously loves Vicky in his own way, and he's giving up custody for her benefit, not his own.

I can't judge him for that. I also can't say that he's rejecting her, because he still wants to be involved.

"That won't happen," I assure him, hoping that Connor understands. He's a compassionate man, and I think he will appreciate that Brandon is putting our girl first. "We'll find a way to make this work."

Relief washes over his face, and I know in my gut that I've said the right thing.

And, for the first time in a long time, it feels like I can really breathe properly again.

* * *

I manage to convince Henry not to call Connor. Instead, after Brandon and his lawyer leave, I rush through the motions of getting Vicky changed, pack a diaper bag full of essentials for my afternoon plans, and then get us both settled in my car.

I drive to the new function venue in Broadbeach, hoping that Connor will still be there. Spying his car in the parking lot, I pull up in a spare space a few spots away and kill the engine, leaving the battery running to power the soft music coming through my speakers. Vicky's napping in her car seat, and I'm content to sit and wait for my man. By my calculations, he shouldn't be too much longer inside.

Sure enough, I'm only waiting for fifteen minutes before his familiar form catches my eye. He meanders towards his car, fiddling with his phone. I get a text notification just before he reaches his vehicle, but I don't read it. Instead, I open my car door and step out, calling out over the roof of my car to get his attention.

"Hey, sexy!"

He stops and then turns to look my way, confusion drawing his eyebrows down beneath the line of the dark sunglasses he's wearing. Then recognition must register, because his lips pull upwards and he jogs the few car spaces that separate us.

"Hey," he says, pushing his sunglasses up onto his head. "Everything okay? I saw that you called. I was in a meeting. I-"

Having left the driver's side door of my car open, I walk around it and capture Con's lips with my own before he can finish speaking. It's not a chaste kiss. I'm too happy and excited for that. It's long and deep, and he sinks into it happily.

"Not that I'm complaining," he murmurs as we part, "but... what's going on?" His eyes search mine. His shoulders are relaxed, no doubt because my happiness is more than obvious. If I was here to give him bad news, I wouldn't be acting like this and he knows it.

"Brandon's giving up his suit for paternal rights," I tell him, unable to keep the news in any longer. Connor practically staggers forward in shock, and he grabs my forearms.

"*What?!*" He asks me, bewildered. His eyes are wide, and he looks just like I felt when Brandon dropped the bomb earlier. "But...*why?*"

I don't want to drag the conversation out, especially not while standing in the middle of this parking lot, so I summarise the unexpected turn of events as best I can. I explain that Brandon's lawyer emailed Henry a copy of the papers, but I have the originals sitting on the passenger seat now. Then I tell him I couldn't wait until he got home, and that we're going out this afternoon to celebrate as a family.

"Can we leave your car here and come back for it later?" I ask him. "Will they mind?"

Still seeming somewhat stunned, Connor shakes his head. "No, it should be fine. I'll just call and let them know…"

I nod. It would suck to come back to find the vehicle towed away, after all. "You can do that while I drive. Come on."

I wander back around my open car door and he slides into the passenger seat a few moments after I've slid into mine. Vicky's still asleep in the back, but he turns around to smile down at her anyway.

Once his seatbelt is engaged, I start the car and drive us back towards Burleigh Heads, following along the esplanade. Connor laughs when I pull into a free spot on the beach side of the highway. He turns his head to face me.

"We could have walked down after I got home," he says, and I shrug.

"I couldn't wait," I justify. "Plus, the little princess always naps better in the car."

"And you keep indulging her, which isn't going to help that." Even though his words are exasperated, they're laced with fondness. He spent the drive along the coastline reading the documents Brandon's lawyer prepared, and his eyes are bright and sparkling with joy as he looks at me now.

It's like a weight has been lifted from him. Even though he's been working hard to make the best of the situation, his upset has been more than obvious. As has my own, I suppose. But now, with these papers in hand, the remaining stress, fear, and resentment all seem to have evaporated from both of us.

"All right," I urge, "let's get out and head onto the sand, hmm?"

"While I'm dressed like this?" Connor gestures down at his business attire. "I don't think so."

I snicker and reach behind my seat, grabbing the beach bag I'd hastily packed before running out of the apartment. "Bathrooms are over there," I gesture to the public toilet block constructed out of dark red brick. He crinkles his nose and I roll my eyes. "We'll have your clothes dry cleaned later, you big baby. Go on."

I'm already wearing board shorts and a t-shirt, and I kick off my sneakers, swapping for the flip-flops I'd tossed onto the backseat earlier. Then I wander around the car to pull Vicky from her seat, smiling when she blinks awake and then grins at me.

"We're going to the beach, princess," I tell her, pitching my voice high with excitement. I temper it a little when a couple jogging past share a giggle at my expense. "Let's try not to eat the sand this time."

Using the driver's side back seat of the car as a makeshift changing table, I get Vicky changed into a swim nappy and the frilly yellow two piece swimsuit Connor's mom bought her, slather her with sunscreen and wrestle her white, wide brimmed hat on top of her dark, wavy hair.

She's got a lot of hair for a kid her age, and I dread learning how to style it. I used to just shave the boys' heads when their hair became too unruly, but I don't think that's going to fly with Connor if I suggest it for Vicky.

Speaking of Connor, he saunters over in his own board shorts and t-shirt combination, looking good enough to eat. I toss him the sunscreen, knowing that he burns easily, and he covers all of his exposed skin, explaining the process to Vicky as he goes.

270

With our supplies slung over one arm and Vicky propped on my hip, I lead the way across the grass, over the sidewalk, and down onto the gleaming white sand of Burleigh beach. I kick my flip flops off, finding it easier to trudge over the soft sand without them, and Connor picks them up along with his own.

A minute or so later and we're at the water's edge, where the sand is hardened and much cooler to walk on. I sit my ass down and put Vicky beside me. I drop our bag on the dry sand just behind us, not bothering to pull out her spade and bucket just yet.

The little girl squeals and starts patting the cool, damp sand with her pudgy little fingers, just as a wave crashes to shore and trickles up towards us. It barely gets her tiny feet wet, but she kicks, shrieks, and babbles as she reaches towards the water, which is already receding back again.

Connor sits on my other side and leans his head on my shoulder.

"This is perfect," he says a moment later, just after another wave has thoroughly entertained our girl. "Thank you."

I take in our surroundings: the flawless blue sky, the rocky headland outcrop to our right, which protects this part of the beach from winds and rougher surf, the large Norfolk pine trees that stretch along the grassy area where sand meets scraggly grass and sidewalk. I can't deny that it's picturesque.

However, what makes it perfect is the company I'm keeping. I'm so lucky to have found this. I never would have thought that I'd have more kids, that I would settle down with someone so much younger than me, or that I would be planning to marry him, but I wouldn't have it any other way.

Well, actually...

"I'd like to adopt Vicky, too," I tell Connor. "I don't know how to go about that when you've still got to finalise your adoption, but I don't ever want to go through anything like what we just have. Never again."

Connor beams back at me, his eyes glistening with tears. He grips my hand and nods. "We're going to make that happen. Whatever it takes. You're my family, Will. You're *our* family."

I never would have thought that there were three little words I'd enjoy hearing more than 'I love you', but there they are.

Choked up, I press a soft, chaste kiss to his lips. "And you are mine."

With everything that we've weathered so far, and whatever the future brings, I know that that will never change.

Epilogue — Connor

"Where do you want the cake set up?"
"What about the gift table?"
"Is there a wishing well?"
"I've got the balloons; how do you want them arranged?"
"Is that the marquee?"

The barrage of questions coming from my friends and family almost has me regretting opting to organise this event myself. Almost.

Honestly, there's nobody else I would have trusted to manage today's events. Even though it's stressful, I'm glad to be the one in charge. Besides, it's not like it's my wedding or anything. I'm not that crazy.

No, today is Vicky's first birthday party. We've paid the Gold Coast City Council for the right to set up a little marquee in one of the pretty ocean front parks down the highway from Burleigh, and I've called in favours with my friends in the functions world to put on a party to end all parties.

Yes, I am that OTT first time dad. So sue me.

There's a grazing table set up under the white marquee, with rugs and cushions for guests to sit and stare out over the ocean front. Because we're in a public park, we're not *technically* allowed to have alcohol out and about, but the esky of sparkling white wine and beer (as well as non-alcoholic options for those not drinking) is hiding under the table anyway.

Vicky's not going to remember any of today, of course, but this party isn't really for her. It's for me, and for Will. It's to celebrate her coming into our lives and bringing us together. It's to celebrate Daisy's life, because Vicky's birthday will always remind me of the day we lost my sister and there's no getting around that. It's to thank our friends and family for their support over the past twelve months. It's to welcome the new friends we've made through taking Vicky to events like story time at the local library, or Gymboree, or playgroup.

The day itself is beautiful. Even though it's summer again, it's not too hot with the ocean breeze drifting over our little set up. The marquee provides shade, too. I'm still slathered in sunscreen, and so is Vicky, but we're also both wearing matching linen outfits to cover our sensitive skin. Hers is a tan linen jacket over a white singlet and tan coloured leggings. I'm wearing long, loose beige coloured linen trousers and a long-sleeved white linen shirt, unbuttoned at the collar. Will refused to wear his matching outfit, even though he took about a thousand photos of me and Vicky on his phone.

The past few months have been nothing short of perfection. I've often had to pinch myself to be sure I'm not dreaming. After Brandon revoked his paternity claim, he also submitted his support towards my adoption proceedings, and included his support for Will to also adopt Vicky as my partner.

274

After that, I couldn't continue to hate the guy, so Will and I have made an effort to keep up our side of the agreement, allowing Brandon time to come and visit with Vicky and get to know us properly. He's even apologised for his original homophobia, citing ignorance and his own stupidity at the cause. While that's no excuse, it was a relief to receive the apology. Especially if he's going to remain a part of Vicky's life.

I don't think we'll ever be close friends, but we're good with each other now.

Having directed the cake and the balloons, and having answered all the other random questions, I finally heave a sigh of relief. The set up is perfect.

"We could have gotten married today," Will murmurs into my ear as his strong arms wrap around my waist from behind. "It looks good enough for a wedding. Definitely too fancy for a one-year-old's birthday party."

I laugh and turn around in his arms, nuzzling my face into his still sexy AF silver beard. "Trust me, babe, our wedding's going to be fancier than this."

He groans, but the sound of complaint is ruined by the smirk on his face. "This is what I get for falling in love with an events guy, isn't it?"

"Events guy," I repeat, rolling my eyes as I sling my arms around his neck. "I'm so sorry that we can't all be retired heroes."

Will's retirement is going to save on babysitting or daycare, even if he finds a part-time job to prevent himself from going too stir crazy. Still, I support him in whatever he wants to do, just as he supports me (banter about my occupation aside) and he's been enjoying his past few months as a full-time dad.

That, by the way, is still a fucking turn on.

"You know I love that you're doing something you're passionate about, right?" he asks me, staring into my eyes. "And I'm proud of how successful you are."

It's sweet that he still feels the need to correct his teasing sometimes, too, but it's completely unnecessary.

Will's banter is never malicious. He's never snide or condescending. He never makes me feel like I need to work harder to be worthy of him. I'm not just a trophy for Will. I'm his equal. His partner. Soon, I'll be his husband.

"I know, babe," I assure him, finally giving in to temptation and kissing his lips gently. "And I love that. I love you."

"*Ugh*," Henry's voice cuts in playfully. "Get married already. I promise, once you do, the sappy shit stops after a while. *Ow*!" I turn in Will's embrace to catch my best friend rubbing the back of his head and pouting at his wife.

Sarah looks completely unrepentant. "Language," she scolds him, then wanders off to the other side of the marquee to corral our unruly infants, who have abandoned their stash of toys and are crawling in opposite directions to cause untold mischief.

"I should go help her," I say, wincing as Vicky screams her displeasure at being grabbed before she could tug at the tablecloth for the grazing table.

Will pulls me a little tighter against him. "Mmm, not yet. I wanna show you something."

"If it's what I think it is, you could get arrested for showing it to me in public," I tease. "There are children present."

"Get your mind out of the gutter," he laughs, then releases his hold on me to pull out his phone. He brings up his emails. "Henry sent this through earlier."

I glance over at Henry and then back at Will before taking the phone from him. I scan the email quickly, my eyes filling with happy tears. "Really?" I ask, turning to my best friend.

He nods. "It's one hundred percent official as of close of business yesterday."

The adoption has been finalised and Henry's looking into the process for Will to also adopt her as my soon-to-be husband. Hen's already told us that stepparent adoption isn't possible until she's five, but he's still investigating our options.

Anyway, even though I was already Vicky's dad, this makes it completely, utterly legally binding.

I throw my arms around my best friend and sob happy tears into his shoulder, thanking him profusely for everything he's done to get us here.

"I thought it was fitting to tell you today," he says as he pats my back. "I felt like it was a sign from Daze, or whatever. Her approval? I dunno. Somethin' like that."

I nod and laugh, wiping my eyes as I pull away and find myself wrapped back up in Will's arms. "Yeah," I agree, and look out over towards the ocean. Today, the colour is a deep, sparkling blue that reminds me of Daisy's eyes. Vicky's eyes. "I think you're right."

* * *

The party kicks off not long after our emotional moment, with guests arriving and bringing a pile of gifts that leave my little girl thoroughly spoiled, not that she realises it. Along with the friends we've made at playgroup, some of Will's friends from the station arrive, those with children bringing them along to play on the playground a few meters away from the marquee, as does Will's friend, Toby. I learned about their failed *Grindr* date months ago when we were first introduced, and I find the other man charming and funny. Some part of me wants to attempt to hook him up with one of my single friends, but I know better than to play matchmaker. Wes and Vanna arrive as well, and she and I immediately launch into wedding planning talk, much to Wes's chagrin.

However, Jack's nowhere to be found – a fact that doesn't evade Will's notice.

Will lifts his head with a frown every time someone walks past our little celebration, clearly expecting to see his other son. We've both also been checking our phones, but there hasn't been a peep from him.

An hour or so into the event, it's obvious Will and Wes are beginning to get concerned. If I'm honest, so am I. For all his laissez faire attitude, Jack is a pretty punctual person. He also adores his sister (as strange as it is for me to think of her as such) and wouldn't just forget her birthday party.

"I'm gonna call him," Wes eventually declares when the couple walking a dalmatian past us turn out to clearly *not* be Jack joining the party. He pulls his phone from his pocket, swipes at the screen and then brings the device to his ear.

Clustered off to the side of the marquee, we all wait and watch Wes. His shoulders sag with relief when Jack answers the call. "Where are you?" he demands of his twin, not bothering with pleasantries. He pulls the phone from his ear and sets it to speaker so we can all hear the response.

"…thing's come up," Jack answers, sounding flustered. "It's… I-" There's a wail of some kind on the other end of the line, cutting Jack off.

Our little group exchanges concerned glances.

278

"Was that…" Vanna starts, confused.

"…a baby?" Will finishes.

"Not, uh, not *a baby*, no…" Jack answers, then, "Shit, no, don't touch-" There's a crashing sound, and then distinct crying. "Damn it."

My eyebrows are at my hairline, and one glance at the others in our little powwow shows my expression mirrored on their faces.

"Jack," Will's tone is that authoritative dad voice that usually does things to me. Even now, distracted, a shiver of pleasure runs up my spine. "What's going on?"

The crying in the background of the call continues while Jack sighs heavily down the line. "I think I'm going to need some help."

Will looks across at me, and I nod. Whatever it is, we're a family. That includes his kids, who have become my close friends as well. With all the support they've shown me over the past year, I'm happy to be able to return the love in kind.

I reach out and grab his hand, squeezing.

"I love you," I mouth to him. "We've got this. Together."

THE END

Thank you for reading *Where There's A Will*. This was something different for me, but a passion project I've been thinking about for a long time. I genuinely hope that you enjoyed it as much as I enjoyed writing it.

If you would like to read more about Will & Connor, the link below will take you to sign up for my MM Romance Newsletter, which does often include talk of the kinkier/taboo MM romance I read and write as well. However, signing up will get you a free steamy extended epilogue for *Where There's A Will*.

Sign up here:
https://annasparrows.com/newsletter-subscription/

Similarly, I live for feedback, so please also consider leaving a review or even just a rating on your retailer of choice. Reviews and ratings drive the visibility of our books online, too, which also helps.

And, as a special gift from me to you, keep turning pages for a sneak peek of Book 2: *You Don't Know Jack*.

Sneak Peek: You Don't Know Jack

Prologue - Jack

"I had a lot of fun last night," Steph says as I try to usher her out through the front door of my studio apartment. She's angling for more, her smile equal parts sweet and sultry, but I made my position perfectly clear when we started chatting on *RedHotPie*. Even my profile is very clear about what I'm looking for.

Sex.

That's it.

One-night stands, no commitment, just a bit of fun and done, *thanks*.

Steph's profile had said she was after the same thing. So we spent a couple of days messaging back and forth and eventually arranged to meet in person at a pub a few blocks away from my apartment. We had a couple of drinks, just enough to feel buzzed and comfortable, and it was clear that the chemistry we'd shared via our online chat was also present in person, so I invited her back to my place.

Obviously, she spent the night.

Steph's an attractive woman. With brown hair a shade or two lighter than my own, big brown eyes, and full pouty lips, she's definitely my type. But I'm not the dating or settling down type. Hell, I'm not the type to bring the same woman home more than once. Maybe twice if the sex was off the charts.

And, while Steph and I certainly had fun last night, I can't say it was anything mind blowing.

Yeah, okay, I'm a bit of a dick. But I want it on record that I never led this woman on, okay? My profile clearly states I am not interested in anything more than sexual release. I don't even want anything casual and ongoing.

Wham, bam, thank you ma'am. The end.

My life is great just the way it is. At twenty-seven, I love my job, I have close friends and family, I get to play and watch a lot of sport, and I live in paradise. Literally. My apartment, tiny and run down as it might be, is in the middle of Surfer's Paradise on Australia's Gold Coast.

When my brother and I moved half-way around the world with our dad as teenagers, I was just excited to have the chance to see more of the world. I never imagined that I'd feel at home in a country so far from the one I grew up in, but this is a beautiful place to live.

Yes, the wildlife here can be a little daunting, but there were rattlers and scorpions back home, so I can't say there's that much of a difference. In the time that I've lived here, I haven't come across many venomous snakes or spiders, and most of the encounters that I've had have happened while I was at work. Snakes, like most creatures, don't like fires destroying their habitats. Go figure.

Anyway, more to the point: the weather in Queensland is subtropical, the winters short and not exactly what I would call freezing. The summers are hot and humid, but I live so close to the beach that the weather is a blessing rather than a curse.

Oh, and my accent gets me a lot of attention from the ladies here, too.

So…paradise.

It would be a lot more like utopia if I didn't have to let this poor woman down gently, though.

"I had a lot of fun, too," I tell her, because I'm not a complete asshole.

Nevertheless, her smile falters at the 'but' I'm sure she can sense coming. Still, I'll give her props for shrugging it off and shooting her shot anyway when she cocks her head, walks her fingers up my bare chest and asks, "Wanna go for round two sometime this week?"

My hand closes over hers between my pecs, over the inked in artwork she trailed with her tongue last night. My smile is rueful as I shake my head. "I don't do ongoing flings," I remind her gently, giving her hand a soft squeeze. "I'm not into commitment. And," I add before she can tell me that she's totally just interested in being *casual*, "I don't want to risk things going from fun to serious right under my nose."

That's happening to my twin brother right now. Wes started dating his girlfriend on a casual basis, and now he's talking about moving in with her.

Ugh. No thank you.

283

Wes and I might have been born identical, but we've taken vastly different paths since our early teens. He's a nerd and I'm a jock. He's bookish and I, after years spent in the gym and playing sport, am broad and, dare I say it, *beefy*. We're the same height, and our faces are fundamentally the same (I like to think mine has filled out a little alongside my body, and I tend to wear a beard where he is usually clean shaven), but we are otherwise chalk and cheese. Even in sex and romance, he's all about monogamy and settling down and I…well, I am very much *not*.

Steph sighs and pulls her hand out from underneath mine. "Fine," she bites out, and I try not to wince at the sharpness in her tone. "I'll lose your number, then."

There's no point in reminding her that we both agreed to a one-nighter from the beginning. I get that feelings can change and that people can get attached unexpectedly. I do. But I haven't. I can't help that.

So, instead of trying to placate her or protesting, I just nod. "That's probably for the best."

She growls at the back of her throat, stomps to the door and wrenches it open with obvious irritation. I'm not a complete idiot: I know a lot of that is probably coming from her hurt pride and embarrassment, and isn't an indication of how invested she was in the idea of being with me.

I don't know if that makes my mild feelings of guilt worse or not.

"Don't worry," she spits at me as she crosses the threshold into the dim hallway, her heels dangling from the index and middle fingers of her left hand by their straps, "you won't hear from me again, Jack."

Those parting words are designed to hurt me, but they're

secretly a relief.

Until four and a half years pass, and those words turn out to be a lie.

Anna Sparrows
Romance Author
Littles, Lace & Love

About the Author

I've been writing* for as long as I can remember. I started with silly short stories as a kid, moved on to fanfiction in my teens (and still write it now), and am also a published MF romance author under a second pen name.

I have been an avid reader of MM romance my whole life. (Ask me about my beginnings with *Buffy* fanfic, haha.) I wrote a sweet and kinky MM romance novel in 2021 and the reader response changed my life. From there, I knew I had found my niche.

And thus Anna Sparrows was born.

*All of my writing is 100% my own. No part of it is generated by Artificial Intelligence (AI) software of any kind. Yes, that means that it's sometimes flawed, but I'm okay with that.

You can connect with me on:

🌐 https://annasparrows.com

📘 https://facebook.com/annasparrowsauthor

Subscribe to my newsletter:

✉ https://annasparrows.com/newsletter-subscription

Also by Anna Sparrows

I write ridiculously sweet & steamy MM romance with guaranteed HEAs...and sometimes with a side of kink.

Littles & Lace Series
The Littles & Lace series is an MM Age Play series, following a group of like minded friends in the BDSM community. You'll find mild ABDL, light Pet Play, Femme Play and more here.

Book 1: Asher's Answer

Book 2: Matteo's Mettle

Book 3: Ted's Temerity

Book 4: Spencer's Satisfaction

Book 5: Chance's Choice

Book 6: Josh's Jackpot